TWISTED DESIRES SERIES

S.D. PAINE

Dueling Obsessions by S. D. Paine –– Copyright © 2026

All rights reserved.

No part of this publication may be reproduced, stored or transmitted in any form or by any electronic, mechanical, photocopying, recording, scanning means, including the information storage and retrieval systems, without written permission from the author. It is illegal to copy this book, post it to a website, or distribute it by any other means without permission, except for the use of brief quotations in a book review.

This novel is entirely a work of fiction. The names, characters, and incidents portrayed in it are the work of the author's imagination. Any similarity to real persons, living or dead, events, or localities is entirely coincidental.

No AI Training: Without in any way citing the author's exclusive rights under copyright, any use of this publication to train generative artificial intelligence (AI) technologies to generate text is expressly prohibited. The author reserves all right to the licensed use of this work for generative AI training and development of machine learning language models.

No artificial intelligence (AI) was used in the creation of this publication.

ISBN ebook: B0CY895BZP
ISBN Paperback: 979-8-9997972-3-0

Cover Design: skullxbonedesign
Editor: Andrea at Halland Publishing
Formatting: Nicole Kincaid at Naughty Nook PR

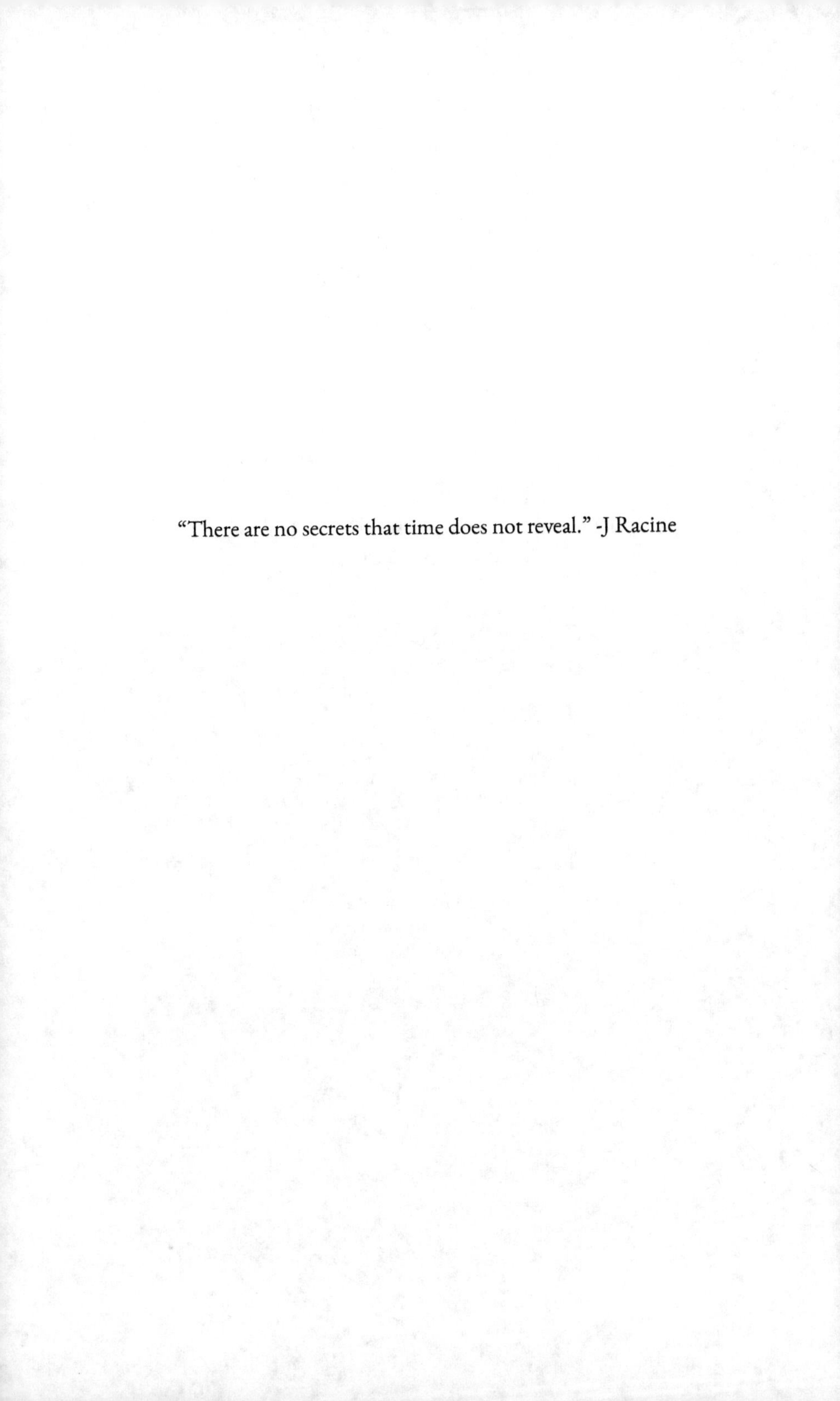

"There are no secrets that time does not reveal." -J Racine

To all the true crime lovers who take one look at the
bad guy and say "the mask stays on."

Author's Note

This book contains very dark themes and the characters often make morally questionable decisions. Tropes and triggers include graphic violence (including sexual violence), self-harm, torture, and physical and mental assault. These characters are NOT role models and all of their behaviors are generally bad.

If you or someone you know is struggling with self-harm, there are people and organizations available to help. 988LIFELINE is available for calls, texts and chats.

For more information about this book and future books in the series, visit my website and sign up for my newsletter!

You can also stay connected with me on my socials (@everafterauthor):

Instagram

Threads

Facebook

TikTok

Playlist

Find me on Spotify to listen to this Dueling Obsessions Playlist!

Southbound by Artemas
Dimples by Rob the Sun
Heart on Fire by Lauren Martinez
After Midnight by Dorothy
Best Version of Yourself by Lenzpot
Messy by ROSÉ
Watch Me Burn by Michele Morrone
Fade to Blue by Roniit
Desire by Meg Myers
I sacrifice by Armut & Ayparia
Tear Me to Pieces by Meg Myers
Over Me by Camylio
Beg by gonedark
Stained by Brittany Broski
Dark Do Wop by MS MR
If I had a Heart by Fever Ray

Into Hell by I Prevail

All the Things You Said by Tatu

Pretty Distraction by SkyDxddy

Touch Ne Like a Gangster by Jessie Murph

Always Been You by Jessie Murph

Secrets by Omido, Ordell & Rick Jansen

The Sun by Brittany Broski

Sex & Candy by Marcy's Playground

Stereoqueen by Stela Cole

I Like You Best by Ella Red

S&M by Rihanna

Love Me by Ex Habit

Curiosity by Bryce Savage

Let me fall (slowed) by Ex Habit & Bury

BITTERSUITE by Billie Eilish

Set Me on Fire by Estelle

Limits by Bad Omens

Haunt Me by Bryce Savage

Vigilante Shit by Taylor Swift

Man I Need by Olivia Dean

Ghost of You by Austin Giorgio

Lights Go Out by YZMN

Destroy Myself Just For You by Montell Fish

Something I Can Never Have by NIN

Halo by Izzy T

Wicked Game by The Newton Brothers (feat Daisy)

R U Mine by Artic

Red Room Slowed by Bryce Savage

NFWMB by Hozier

Angel by Massive Attack

Just Like Heaven by The Cure
Figure You Out by VOILÀ
Good Girl (Praise) by National Haven
Damn Your Eyes by Alex Clare
High by Whethan & Dua Lipa

Suspect List

Primrose Eleanora Kingsley - aspiring crime journalist living under the alias Nora King

Declan O'Rourke - a Reaper, hired hitman, son of Harold, younger brother of Ellis

Ellis Bainbridge - a businessman, estranged from his brother Declan and father Harold

Sienna Wilkers - columnist for the *London Times*, friend of Nora and Josephine

Lyra Montclair - cousin of Nora

Dr. Josephine Beck - close friend of Nora

Jameson Moore - fiancé of Primrose

Cecilia Kingsley Roosevelt - mother of Primrose

Felix Theodore Roosevelt - younger brother of Primrose by marriage

Alec Vasiliev - CEO of the *London Times*

Mason Avery - coworker of Sienna and Nora at the *London Times*

Harold O'Rourke - father of Ellis and Declan, leader of the 3M Crew

Benjamin Burkett - bodyguard of Harold

Merrick Thompson - manager and lead bartender at Provocateur

Prologue

Nora

Late morning sun filtered into the room, and my head spun, contemplating too many things. None of the memories of last night were sticking. My head felt foggier than normal. I remembered the whiskey at dinner. My least favorite liquor, but Jamie always ordered for me and insisted I drink it.

We met up with some friends of his, more pompous assholes with plastic housewives on their arms. It was incredibly dull, and I chose to drink instead of speak. Let them think I was a mute or a mouse, but I was honestly just exhausted from playing this role. I wanted out.

Waking up after a night out with Jameson was often distressing. For one, I didn't like him all that much, and the longer we were together, the more anxious I became while spending time with him. And then there was the issue of him being horrible to other people, especially anyone he thought was beneath him, which was almost everyone. I lost count of the number of waitstaff I'd apologized to over the last five years. Getting shitfaced was often the only way to cope with his terrible personality. It was fine if people judged me for spending so many years with someone like him. I judged myself. Too many years groomed into being the world's most perfect, people-pleasing daughter turned me into a doormat who said yes out loud, even when her insides were screaming no.

But the thing that was causing my heart to race and bile to rise up my throat wasn't any of those reasons. Sometimes, more often than I cared to admit, Jamie liked to push boundaries, sexually. He would force me to try things, and sometimes I ended up enjoying them, but most of the time I was just happy when it was over. The part I liked, and I was loath to admit it to anyone else, were the videos. I liked to watch. Which was why I never told him when I found out he was cheating on me. Because of course he was. A manchild like him could never be faithful, not when he was so sure everyone loved him, everyone wanted to fuck him, everyone wanted to be close to him.

There were some who did. The women he fucked were leeches, bimbos looking for a leg up in the political world or just wanting money. Jameson Moore would never admit to paying for sex, since he believed his dick was a gift to all women, but he did. I checked his bank accounts. And I saw the videos. He kept a collection, hidden in a safe he thought I was oblivious to.

Before I was introduced to Jamie, I dreamt of becoming a journalist. I was fascinated with finding out the truth, which I was sure was some kind of trauma response, but therapy wasn't something I was ready for. Obsessively watching episodes of *Law & Order* in high school became into a journalism degree in college and the desire to pursue a career in crime journalism. Of course the career part never happened, because my father introduced me to Jameson at a party, and his family's support was very important to his career. He was on his way to becoming a Supreme Court Judge, and the Moore family had quite a bit of political sway.

Even though my father wasn't all that great, I wanted to please him, so I said yes to a first date, and then a second, and then it was years in, and an obscene diamond strangled my finger, an iceberg, an omen of the cage that would be my future. If only it were big enough to drown me instead.

More pieces of the night came back, and I recalled saying something about ending things with Jamie. As I moved my feet to the edge of the bed, pain, sharp and hot, pressed into my body, my face. My fiancé had hit me. Slapped my cheek hard when I told him. When I cried, he apologized, told me I shouldn't provoke him like that.

We came home, and I vaguely remember trying to sleep in the guestroom, but he wouldn't hear of it. But what happened next? The memories were gone, lost behind a haze of shame and alcohol. Slowly getting to my feet, I noticed a small USB drive on the nightstand next to a scrap of paper.

Something for you to see before you think about leaving me, Primrose. There's more than one copy.

A horrible, terrifying feeling crawled up my spine. The sore muscles and aches in my body were suddenly too strange, and I knew in my gut something awful happened last night. And I was not ready to face it, but I was ready to leave.

Quickly, I packed up as much as I could in a single suitcase and carry-on tote. My phone was nowhere to be found, but I didn't need it. Jameson tracked me with it anyway, and I had a very short window to get the fuck out of here. Some part of me knew this day would come. Roughly six months ago, I got the sudden urge to have an exit plan. I pretended to lose my passport, and Jamie never had me get a new one. Said I didn't need it when we had private planes and connections enough for me to fly without it.

Rushing from the room with my suitcase, I made my way to the kitchen. Jamie spent very little time in here; we had staff to cook our meals, do our shopping, and he couldn't be bothered to care about such things. It wasn't safe to trust even our kind staff with my secret, so I'd planted a container of cookies in the pantry with a false bottom. My one and only friend, Josephine Beck, procured it for me.

Snatching my passport, new ID, and a prepaid credit card with emergency money, I stuffed them into my tote and made for the front door. The house was silent, a mausoleum for a girl that lived here, who lost herself and didn't dare ask for help. She was dead now. Whatever happened last night, even though I still wasn't certain, I knew it had killed a part of me. And if I wanted to escape this prison, I had to go now.

My once home was located in Wicker Park. It wasn't always a sad place; I still recalled how excited I'd been to make it my own when Jameson purchased it after our engagement. He also had a luxurious apartment downtown, but I stopped going there ages ago. It belonged to his side chicks and lecherous business bros.

I hailed a cab and gave the address for Northwestern Memorial. Jo, the only person I trusted, was a neurologist. We met in college, and while we were both fascinated with crime and serial killers, she fell in love with science while I went off to journalism. We stayed close, even when Jameson forced me away from almost everyone, she never gave up. When I finally confided in her the terrible position I was in, she never once berated me or made me feel stupid for staying. She only said, when I needed a way out, she would be there.

The drive wasn't long, and I practically ran into the hospital and made my way to her office. Jo was a beautiful woman, tall and athletic, with black hair she kept short and neat. She had slate-gray eyes and skin even more fair than mine. Jo preferred the company of women and was always ready to talk shit about my fiancé when I needed it. She was absolutely a man-hater, and I was often annoyed that my love for women didn't extend to sexual relationships. Maybe this entire situation I was in would never have occurred.

Jo looked up from her computer the second I opened her door. Her clever gaze noted my heavy breathing, and my luggage. She stood quickly, knocking her chair back. "Time to go?"

I nodded, unable to say the words.

She came around the desk in a hurry and gathered me into her arms. "This is the right move, my friend. A fresh start."

Tears welled at the edge of my eyes, and I willed them away. "I know."

Jo pulled back, holding my face in her hands. "Primrose dies today. You are no longer that girl. You are a new woman. Welcome to the future, Nora King."

Letting her words sink into my skin, I took several deep breaths. Primrose Eleanora Kingsley, the girl who buried her true self, was dead. Today, Nora King was born. I chose Nora because my middle name, Eleanora, came from my grandmother on my father's side, the only family member I ever connected with. She was a fierce woman, taking no shit from anyone, and my new life as Nora would be modeled after her.

"Thank you, Josie," I whispered, calling her by the nickname only I was allowed to use, emotion rising within me. "He will come here first, you know?"

She grinned and winked at me. "I hope to fuck he does. I'll finally get to junk punch the guy."

I wanted to laugh, but anxiety bees filled my insides. "He's dangerous. Don't forget."

Jo nodded and rubbed my arms affectionately. "I won't. But you will. Leave him behind. Start your new life in London and don't look back."

She was right. RIP Primrose of Chicago, hello Nora King, future journalist for the *London Times*.

Nora

The blank screen stared back at me in an accusing manner. "I'm sorry, don't look at me like that," I grumbled.

I had this thing, it was called anthropomorphism, which is a crazy long word to say I gave inanimate objects feelings. When I ran into a table, a mumbled sorry escaped my lips. Or if one of my pillows was getting more attention than the other, I had to switch them so they wouldn't get upset. It was ridiculous. And yet, here I was, worrying that my laptop was upset with me because I still hadn't written a damn word today.

Technically, getting in a new story wasn't required, but staying busy and diving into someone else's problems suited me right now. My boss and Sienna, the only coworker I really spent time with, both called me a workaholic.

It had been almost a full year since I escaped Chicago and landed at Heathrow Airport. Sienna Wilkers had been waiting for me, fully aware of my situation.

She was friends with Jo and offered to assist. She was, for lack of a better term, a knockout. Everyone in the airport was staring at her, and she glowed under that spotlight, unlike myself. Her supermodel body and perfectly styled long auburn hair was beyond intimidating. I wasn't ugly, by most standards, and pretending otherwise was childish. My naturally golden hair and green eyes usually received a fair bit of attention as well. But there was something about Sienna that drew the oglers in, like moths to a flame. The moment our eyes connected, she smiled, and in three long strides, because the girl had legs for days, she pulled me in for a fierce hug.

"Hello, love," she said, her violet eyes bright and inviting. "Welcome to England. It's often raining, the trains are cleaner, the pubs are fun, and the people are the sweetest."

"Well, they've got something on Americans then." I smirked. "We're ass-holes."

Sienna laughed, and the sound was as bright as her smile. "We are indeed. I'm half-American. Mother married a Brit. And she was absolutely the sassy ass in that marriage."

"I take it they're no longer together?" I surmised, following her through the airport.

Sienna shook her head. "No, she died years ago. Got addicted to nasty drugs. I was raised mostly by my father. He and I moved back here after I finished high school."

Sienna spoke with a hint of a British accent and had the commanding presence of a runway model. Her legs were twice as long as mine, and it made me feel like a scurrying mouse trying to keep up with her. We were different in a million ways, but by the time we reached her apartment, I knew she and I were headed for a lifelong friendship. Of course Jo wouldn't send me off to just anyone, and I was continuously grateful to have her looking out for me.

Until I could get on my feet, Sienna let me stay with her. She had a spare bedroom, and while it wasn't massive, it was all I needed. Her apartment was colorfully decorated, with knickknacks she picked up on her travels. Sienna had one of those wandering souls, never satisfied in one place for too long. She worked for the *London Times* as well, writing a weekly column related to said travels. I'd only been in England for ten months, and she'd already whisked me away on two separate trips. Life with her was fascinating, even more so after the first few times we got drunk and she kissed me.

All my life, I'd only been with men. And while she was beautiful, the attraction wasn't there in that way for me. Sienna called herself pansexual. She based her love life on vibes, no matter what the other person defined themselves as. She was currently single, like me. I was not ready to date, and while flirting with a few men at pubs was fun, the idea of bringing anyone back to our place, let alone going to theirs, did not feel good.

My trust in others regarding intimate relationships was essentially shattered. I fell for someone who took my mind, body, and soul and stabbed them over and over until I finally bled out. Well, maybe not completely. There was enough life left within me to leave, and that was something. So many women didn't, and all that was left was a headstone.

"Watcha working on, Nora?" Sienna's perky head appeared over the wall of my cubicle. There wasn't a lot of personal space in this office. At least not for me or Sienna.

Our desks were still in the bullpen. Although Sienna's was at the other end of the hall, just outside Aleksandr Vasiliev's office. After I started my new job, she asked him if she could switch spots with Mason Avery, another writer for the *London Times* who was currently next to me. Our boss refused. Wasn't exactly sure why, until the first time we went out to a pub after work and he showed up. Sienna would deny it, but it was obvious he was into her.

Shoving away from my desk, I stood up and stretched my arms over my head. "Currently not working on shit. I'm bored with the love life column. I need something else."

My eyes drifted over to Mason, merrily typing away. He currently worked for a news outlet and the magazine, and he was rather skilled at digging up criminals and salacious stories. My spidey senses told me there was more to him than the quirky Clark Kent vibe he put out. Was there a Superman bodysuit beneath his endless closet of white button-down shirts and khaki pants?

I was determined to figure him out. And maybe borrow one of his sources to work my own story. Aleksandr Vasiliev gave me a job, but I still had to prove I could do more than manage a dating column.

"Should we find a seedy bar to lurk in and see if any murderers turn up?" Sienna waggled her eyebrows and clicked her tongue at Mason. "Hey, Masey. Where should we go to find dangerous men?"

Mason's cheeks flushed as he cleared his throat. "Uh. Well, I don't actually recommend this, but the Red Clover is unofficially known as a meetup spot for the 3M Crew."

"Are you certain?" I asked, my eyes absolutely bugging out of my head.

Sienna crossed her arms and laughed. "What a lame gang name."

I giggled and rolled my eyes. "Hardly. It stands for three murders. Allegedly, to become a member, you have to murder three people first."

She wrinkled her nose at me. "It's so weird that you know this."

I shrugged. "I'm sure Mason knows as well. The names of prominent clubs and gangs around the world are fairly easy to find. What's proving to be more difficult, is pining down actual members. Actual members would never reveal their status. So if some asshole is loudly bragging about his affiliation, he's probably lying."

Sienna grabbed my arm, pulling me away from my desk. "I'll keep that in mind, you crazy crime junkie. And I'm done working. Let's go to this Clover place."

I snatched my purse just before it was out of reach and let her pull me away. "We should change first. The fashionable corporate office look will stand out like crazy."

"Nope," Sienna said, the P making a pop sound as she did. "We want to stand out. Maybe the sexy office chick vibes will draw these dangerous men right to us."

The thought was terrifying and thrilling all at once. This particular club was on my short list. There weren't just dozens of murders, or hits, connected to them, but whispers of prominent families, political takedowns, and some serious cash flow. If I could get at least one member to spill a few secrets, it could be the story of the year. And I'd finally be able to call myself a real crime journalist.

2

Nora

The Red Clover was located in Southwark, about a fifteen-minute drive from the office in Canary Wharf. London was fairly easy for me to navigate. It reminded me of New York, only cleaner and with all the winding streets, specifically The East and West Villages. Most of Manhattan was an easy grid, but the villages were harder to learn. Growing up in Chicago, I had similar experiences with city living, and I was a city girl at heart. The bustling streets, endless noise, and never knowing what would happen next was thrilling to me. Each day was a new experience.

When Jameson would take me out of the city to one of his family's estates, the claustrophobia set in. You'd think it would be the opposite. All that open space and quiet should have been refreshing. Instead, it made the blood pound in my ears like a tidal wave.

"This place is not as seedy as I expected." Sienna frowned. "Although I've never been here, or even heard people talk about coming here."

I smiled up at her. "Were you picturing dark alleys and men in trench-coats smoking cigars?"

She laughed as we walked toward the entrance. "Something like that."

"If it was, these clubs and gangs would have been demolished by the police decades ago. The seedy underworld had to evolve with the rest of us."

Sienna pivoted in my direction and patted my cheek. "You might be blonde, but you sure aren't dumb."

"Wow, thanks," I deadpanned. "You're buying the first round, bitch."

She grinned and her stormy eyes twinkled with mischief as we walked into the pub. It was dimly lit, with sconces lining the walls and deep mahogany wood everywhere, from the tables, to the bar and the walls. Brassy stools lined the right wall of the bar on the right wall, with high-tops in the middle, and booths with high walls for more intimate groups on the left side. The Red Clover was also bigger than it looked from the street. Sienna led us to the bar and was instantly assisted by a bartender who looked barely old enough to serve drinks. He flirted with her, and she returned the gesture. In a few moments we had martinis, on the house, and wandered to one of the open hightop tables.

"I'll have to buy the next one, since my new bartender bestie gave us these for free," Sienna cooed, sipping her espresso martini.

We toasted, each taking in the clientele around us. The pub was relatively full for a Wednesday evening, but then I wasn't fully hip to the happenings of London. Maybe this was a slow night. Most of the people in the bar were men. There were plenty of boring business suits and slicked-back hairstyles sported by the finance bros. It was all very typical, and I was becoming increasingly disappointed.

"Maybe Mason was wrong about this place," I grumbled into my drink.

Sienna was facing the door, and her eyes widened just as a little gasp escaped her full lips. "Or maybe not. Don't turn around, but shit, this man looks dangerous as hell."

It took every ounce of willpower not to turn around based on her reaction, but I kept my back straight and my body facing her, trying to remain casual. When he walked past our table, I knew instantly this was the man she had seen. He oozed danger. Number one, he was insanely tall. Had to be at least a foot taller than me, and I was around five foot five. He wore black jeans with multiple tears and worn spots, obviously his favorite pair, and a black leather jacket that looked cut just for his lean, muscular build. His boots were also black leather and reminded me of the bulky footwear bikers wore. I'd bet money he arrived on a big, brash motorcycle. His hair was lighter brown, almost a dirty blond, and unkempt. It was long enough to run your fingers through, and a teeny tiny part of me imagined doing just that.

He walked with the grace of a jungle cat, not speaking to anyone, but multiple people acknowledged him in a differential way. This guy was clearly someone, and I needed to find out who that someone was, pronto.

The baby bartender handed the danger guy a beer without having to ask, telling me what I already knew, this was his regular spot.

"Your bartender friend knows him," I whispered, keeping my face neutral and sipping my drink.

Sienna gave me a sly smile before she stood, making my own lips turn up. She was unbelievably charming when she wanted to be. It was something I lacked, and as a journalist, a real detriment to my career choice. Why did I always come off so blunt? I blamed my grandmother. She was the sassmaster of our family and someone I aspired to be like. According to my mother, I succeeded, and this was not a compliment in her mighty opinion.

Mother hated her because Grandmother was my favorite relative and wasn't from her side of the family, but my birth father's. He died when I was young, a car accident. It was sudden, but not nearly as sudden as her new husband's debut. Our relationship soured after that, and I spent as much time away from her and my slimy stepfather as possible.

When I got older, I came to the obvious realization that she married him for money. For power. For status. Her side of the family came from nothing, but she never let anyone know it. Image was everything, and as long as people believed you had wealth, they'd give you more of it.

My stepfather came from a family of bankers, finance asshole types. So of course he loved my asshole of an ex-fiancé.

My mood was souring the longer I sat here, and I prepared to join Sienna at the bar when a shadow fell over the table. His scent was intoxicating. Worn leather, charred embers, and mint. Target acquired.

"Looking for me?" He spoke softly, his voice deeper than I expected. He didn't look much older than me, but something about his eyes spoke of decades of life lived in too many short years. I could see his ghosts just beneath the surface and was eager to pull every skeleton from his closet.

"Who said I'm looking for you?" I kept my voice casual, feigning indifference.

He leaned forward, resting his arms on the table and closing the distance between us. His lips twisted up into a deadly grin, and danger lurked behind wolfish hazel eyes. "You've never been to this bar. I would remember you."

I took a sip of my drink, feigning indifference even though my heart was racing. "So? My friend is from around here."

He didn't even spare Sienna a glance, his eyes lasered in on my face. The man should be a detective for how much attention he was paying me. I could see the assessment of my person from every minuscule movement of his body.

"She's never been here either, otherwise she wouldn't be wasting time on Jace. That fool won't have any information on me."

All right, this guy was way too smart for his own good. I leaned away from him, straightening on my stool and eyeing him with a sharp look. "So there's information out there, then? What wouldn't you want him to know about?"

His smirk remained intact, but his eyes flicked over my head and narrowed slightly before he returned his attention to me. "If there was, I wouldn't be telling you, now would I? You and your friend should find another bar. The men here will make a girl like you blush."

Irritation heated my cheeks, and I scoffed at him. "You have no idea what kinds of things could make me blush."

He stood then, towering over me as he rounded the table. He leaned down, and I froze when his lips just barely brushed against the shell of my ear. "I think I'd enjoy finding out."

Before I could respond, he was gone. My mark had thoroughly blown my entire plan to hell. Sienna returned, frowning at me.

"Well that was a bust," she sighed. "But he did say something about club meetings at the warehouse. There are a couple not far from here, by the river."

I swiveled on my stool in time to see the danger guy leaving with a few others and made a quick decision to follow. Turning back to Sienna, I stood and wrapped my coat around my shoulders. "Stay here."

"Hell no." She stood. "As if I'd let you go following bad guys alone."

"Stay here and make sure no one follows me," I pleaded. "It will look weirder if we both run out. I'll be twenty minutes tops. After that, call the police."

Sienna rolled her eyes. "Fucking hell. Twenty minutes and not one more."

I grinned at her and fled the bar as inconspicuously as possible. Danger guy was gone, but I followed a path behind the bar that led down toward the water. Three warehouses lined the street, and only one was lit from within.

Adrenaline flooded my veins. This was reckless, but it could lead me to a story that changed my career. And I'd be lying if I said danger guy wasn't intriguing as hell. Only one way to find out what he was hiding.

Declan

While the men leading this meeting droned on, my thoughts stayed thoroughly captivated by the green-eyed reporter. I clocked her instantly. Women like her don't just happen upon the Red Clover. It wasn't on the way or near to any of the corporate buildings housing news or even tabloids. She was dressed impeccably well in a pressed blouse and a pencil skirt that did wonders for her ass. The moment I entered the bar, I fantasized about slashing my knife straight up the center to reveal the flesh hidden beneath it. I'd bet she didn't even have tattoos.

Fuck, I wanted to ruin her. That thought alone confused me. It had been ages since I'd fucked a woman. Or a man. I was no longer used for such things. It wasn't always that way. The first twenty or so years of my life, I was owned by the club, by my father. And when his pretty boy son caught the eye of people he needed on his side, well, that was no trouble for him. Even when I begged him to let me go. To let me do anything else.

He refused. Only after a particularly low moment when I slashed open my lip in an attempt to mar my face, did he finally relent. I knew it wasn't because he cared about me; someone else was involved. He wouldn't explain anything, only said it was done and I was free to go.

By then, my life belonged to the club. The underbelly of London was my home, my sanctuary. When I attempted to pledge for another club, they refused me. No one would have me, and I fucking knew that was my father's doing. So after two years of sulking, I returned to him and offered to be something else.

A Reaper. Most gangs and clubs with any legitimate power had a handful of men whose singular job was to eliminate threats. Father had such men, but now he also had me. Always in a mask and silently lurking, I was the shadow that haunted London. When powerful people began to die and his club grew in strength, word spread of a new killer on the payroll. My identity was kept hidden. People feared what they didn't know, and I was the monster lying in wait.

Tonight was an informal meeting with another gang, and while they chatted, I circled the warehouse. They had men posted about, just as we did, but there were always dark corners for assholes to hide in. Or in tonight's case, pretty little reporters.

She was well hidden, unseen by anyone else. But not me. A whiff of amber mixed with jasmine drifted through the air and brought my steps to a halt. I followed the alluring scent to a small control room on the second level. It looked over the open room below where the others were discussing business. She was snapping photos with her phone, bent over the control board with her head low in the event that someone would look up. But the room was dark. They wouldn't see her, and she was much too focused to notice me.

Creeping up behind her, I snapped my arms out and covered her mouth with one hand and her waist with the other.

She screeched, but the sound was muffled by my glove smothering her face. I wore full tactical gear, every inch of skin hidden behind black clothing and a mask to keep my identity a secret.

"If you scream, they'll hear you," I whispered against her ear. She was so small and delicate in my arms, and her ass pressed to my dick was about to be a problem. "And if they hear you, I'll be forced to kill you."

Her chest rose and fell more slowly at my words, and she nodded, understanding. When I released her, she spun around instantly, her eyes widening as she took in my appearance. "Who are you?"

"To most, a nightmare." Even in the darkness I could see her eyes widen at my words. "To you, little dove? A proposition."

My words registered quickly, and she took a step back, pressing her ass into the control panel. "What do you want?"

"You first."

She arched a brow, and a hint of brattiness crossed her face. My dick throbbed, and my hands itched to punish. My body was reacting to her so viscerally, and I didn't know what to make of that.

"I'm working for the *London Times*. A columnist, but I want to be a crime journalist." Her words zipped out of her in a fast whisper. "I got a lead on some big players were in the area. And they might have information on the Reaper of the 3M Crew."

I almost laughed. "You're looking to unmask the most dangerous killer in London? Do you have a death wish, American?"

She wrinkled her nose at me in the most adorable way. "My grandmother is British, thank you very much. I have roots here."

A chuckle escaped my lips, and the sound shocked us both. "Perhaps I can help."

She crossed her arms. "And what do you want in return?"

Things were about to get interesting. "You."

Her mouth dropped open, and I grinned. Of course my reaction was hidden behind the COD-style mask. "I'm not a whore. I won't just fuck a guy for a story."

The vulgar words coming out of her pink lips were making my dick increasingly hard. Fucking hells. "Aren't you feisty?" I stepped toward her. She tried to move, but I trapped her petite frame between my arms. "Who said I wanted to fuck you? I simply want you, in whatever fashion that becomes."

Her breaths quickened, and her green eyes sparkled in the darkness. It was just light enough to make out her expressions, and I was eager to see them all.

"I...need to think about it." She spoke softly. "What do I call you?"

I cocked my head. "How about Bane?"

She smirked. "As in, you're the bane of my existence?"

Her sassy attitude was addicting. I traced one hand up her side. She froze beneath me when I slowly wrapped my hand around her throat. "As in I am the darkness you seek, and the shadow that follows. Think about it, little dove."

She tried to keep her breathing even, but her parted lips and shining eyes told me everything I needed to know. The journalist in her was too curious to resist my offer. She tried to step back, but I refused to let go.

The American rolled her eyes and sighed. "Well, my name is Nora."

"Looking forward to our next meeting, Nora." I released her, stepping away from her intoxicating scent before I did something I likely wouldn't regret. "Now get the fuck out of here."

Nora didn't hesitate. She tiptoed out of the room swiftly, her heels impressively silent. I followed slowly behind her, keeping an eye on the men to make sure she exited safely.

My night quickly went from average to incredibly fruitful. Nora would accept my proposal. The eager flick of her tongue over her lips when I spoke told me what I needed to know. She would be mine.

Nora

The next two weeks of work were a bust. I'd listened to the audio recording from the secret meeting over a hundred times, and there was nothing usable in it. The men spoke in such bland terms, and sometimes they didn't make sense. There was one voice more commanding than the others, and I was certain this was the leader. His voice was gruff, like he'd smoked a pack of cigarettes a day for a few decades. The one sentence from him before the meeting ended, well, before the Grim Reaper asshole interrupted, played on a loop in my brain.

Peter flies at midnight, when the dust settles, the lagoon will be vulnerable.

"What the hell does that even mean?" I whine loudly, slumping over in my chair and resorting to pouting. I'm the worst journalist ever.

Maybe I could find the masked man again and try to get more information out of him? He wasn't stupid enough to just tell me what all the code words meant, but he was definitely interested in me, even if he pretended not to be. I could use sex appeal as a weapon. Well, Sienna could, and I could make her teach me how.

"What are you whining about over there?" Speak of the temptress, and she will appear. Sienna rested her toned arms on my cubicle wall. She wore a short-sleeved maroon sweater and black pencil skirt, paired with sky-high black stilettos. Stunning, as always.

My work outfits were less stylish. Nice slacks, silk blouses, and shorter heels. There was too much walking in London, and I was too lazy to cart around extra shoes to change into. Sienna kept a whole-ass closet full of outfits at work. How our boss allowed this was a mystery. Okay, not a mystery. He was in love with her. It was obvious to everyone except for Sienna and him.

"The recordings I got from the night we went out." I reached for my mouse and hit play on the audio file. "I am apparently too stupid to crack their weird codes."

The older man's voice spoke again on the tape. "...the lagoon will be vulnerable."

Sienna frowned. "Huh."

That was a curious "huh," and my eyebrows rose. "You have an idea over there, secret genius?"

Sienna smiled. "Maybe. It's obviously a *Peter Pan* reference, with the name, the dust, and lagoon. You guessed that much, right?"

I nodded without speaking, because no, I did not. Disney movies were not part of my childhood. I was raised by a nanny with very strict instructions. My mother groomed me to be a housewife from infancy. "Cartoons were not part of my mother's strict curriculum."

Sienna wrinkled her nose in disgust. "Gods, girl. Each new thing I learn about your family makes me want to throat punch them even harder." Sienna pretended to write on an invisible notepad. "Next girls' night will include copious amounts of wine and all the best fairytale movies."

Starved for honest affection and a sense of normalcy, I smiled back at her and nodded eagerly. "Deal. Now, what does it mean?"

Sienna sat on the edge of my desk, long legs swinging. "Well, there's a club called Neverland that's known for some crazy parties. Dust is probably drugs. Peter flies at midnight...maybe the nefarious deal is happening at midnight? And the lagoon bit. I'm not certain, but saying it's vulnerable makes me think—"

"They're taking something. Like the stash is unguarded," I said excitedly, interrupting her.

She grinned and nodded. "Precisely."

I stood up and hugged her. "You're a genius."

"What's going on over here?" The voice of our hot boss sliced through the party mood. For me, at least. I was always professional around him, Sienna, not so much.

"Just celebrating your future top journalist cracking a gang's secret code." She hugged my shoulders proudly.

Alec arched a brow in my direction. "Is that so?"

The blood crept up my neck, and I could feel my cheeks heating. "Sienna helped."

He nodded without giving an actual acknowledgment to Sienna. "Is this related to the murder of Timothy Jones?"

I shook my head. "I don't think so. I know it's insane, but I'm honestly leaning towards a female serial killer for that one."

Alec's eyebrows scrunched together in disbelief. "You'll need a lot more than what you've got to convince me of that. Serial killers are more rare than Hollywood makes them out to be. Female killers even less so."

The dig at my American background was mildly insulting, but I was also new here and determined to prove my theory. "I know. And I'll get it. Back to the story for today, though, I think something big is going to happen this weekend at a club called Neverland."

Alec nodded. "And you plan to go?"

Sienna and I both nodded, and I spoke first before she could say something to irritate the man, as was her MO. "Yes. I think we should be there. Even if we don't see exactly what goes down, I'm hoping to unmask a few members of the gang and see who looks vulnerable."

Alec eyed us both for a few moments before responding. "Very well. I will have a VIP booth reserved for you on Saturday night. There will be two near the booth for protection."

"Thank you, Mr. Vasiliev." I spoke quickly, hoping Sienna would let it go.

But of course, she did no such thing. Sienna scoffed and crossed her arms, standing squarely in front of him. "We don't need guard dogs, Alec."

"It's non-negotiable, Ms. Wilkers," Alec snapped, straightening his shoulders. "I will have a car pick you up as well, and bring you home."

Before she could respond, I grabbed her wrist and squeezed in warning. "Thank you, we appreciate your assistance."

Alec left with a curt nod, and I could practically see the steam bursting from Sienna's ears. "Fuck that guy."

"Chill, friend." I laughed at her. "You're only riled up because you like it when he bosses you around."

Sienna's eyes widened, and she smirked at me. "Fuck off, Nora. Let's go out for a long lunch. That's enough working for today."

I let her drag me out of the office, because I was too pumped to care. Alec would reprimand Sienna for leaving early, but he would never actually fire her, or me, because I was best friends with her. The sexual tension between those too was fit to burst before the end of the year. If I was a betting girl, I'd give it maybe until November. By New Year's, they'd be kissing at midnight at our company party.

5

Nora

Nightclubs in London had a completely different vibe from the hotspots in the US. Of course cities like New York and LA had luxury clubs, but even the feel of this place was foreign. Not in an uneasy way. More like that feeling of butterflies when you go on a rollercoaster for the first time. Sienna had begged me to go to clubs with her the moment I arrived, but I needed cozy nights in, then. After several months of getting my bearings, it was time. Besides, this was more for work.

Neverland required one guest in your party to be a member to gain entry. Alec Vasiliev was ours, and apparently that meant something here. Sienna and I were personally escorted to our VIP table by the manager, with champagne popped and poured upon arrival. Our table was more like a living room, with two small couches, high top tables, and a small bar with an attendant.

The VIP area was located on the upper level and looked out onto the bar and dance floor below through a glass floor. The VIP guests literally danced on a glass floor.

"So, does that mean everyone down there is looking up my dress?" Sienna whisper-shouted to the manager.

He coughed up a laugh before responding. "Of course not, miss. It is mirrored glass, and they only see their own reflections."

Sienna winked at him. "Mmhmm. That's what the cops say as well."

The poor fool stuttered, awestruck as they all were by how stunning she was. And funny. So damn funny. Tonight Sienna wore the tiniest, sparkly gold dress from her closet. The fabric shimmered and hugged her curves like a second skin. Her gold heels had silk straps that wrapped up her toned calves. And her dark hair was pinned up to show off her elegant neckline. Even I struggled not to drool looking at her.

Our escort ushered us into the corded off area. "Welcome to your court. Each esteemed guest has their own court, with bottle service and an attendant to see to your every need." The manager glanced in my direction, his eyes wandering a bit before he finally retreated.

"That man wanted to eat you up," Sienna teased, handing me a glass of champagne.

I laughed. "He was fawning over you. You look like a damn Charlie's Angel."

Sienna clinked her glass to mine. "As do you, friend. I counted as many men and women licking their lips when you sauntered in."

Pleasure zipped through my body at her words. I wasn't ugly, I knew that. But after being with someone who constantly pointed out all the things you did wrong, it was difficult to remember. Tonight Sienna gifted me a new dress. It was emerald green, matching my eyes, and velvety soft. The top half was corseted with a sweetheart neckline, and the skirt hugged my ass perfectly. The dress would absolutely not pass the bend test. Even sitting required a bit of finesse.

I chose sparkly gold heels and jewelry to match. My hair fell down my back in rippling waves, a nod to the 1930s style.

"To us then," I cheered. "And all the secrets we will uncover tonight."

Sienna waggled her eyebrows. "To us. Kick-ass Charlie's Angels."

Ellis

The only reason I was here and not sleeping comfortably in my bed was because of a damn debt I owed to Alec. The man was ruthless, which was probably why I liked him. We'd moved from business acquaintances to friends in the last few years. Alec understood the need to get away from family, toxic family. Family who lie and steal. In a moment of weakness, I got too drunk at a posh bar and found myself chatting with the Russian American. His accent was odd. Born in Russia, but shipped off to the States as a child. His relatives had underworld connections that he wouldn't give too many details on. He spoke multiple languages, including heartbreak. It was its own language, and only those who truly experienced it could understand.

While our souls were crushed for different reasons, we bonded all the same. After a few more evenings swapping stories, we realized we could help each other. Alec became a silent partner for my club. In the beginning, it was little more than a burlesque bar. Now, it was even more exclusive than Neverland.

"Mr. Bainbridge, sir. Good evening," the manager of the club stammered. The idiot even dipped his head in a bow.

I wasn't a member of any royal family, but in posh London circles, I may as well have been. "Evening, Yuri."

"Can I get you anything, sir?" His eyes darted anywhere and everywhere but my face.

"My usual. I'll be in Vasiliev's court," I responded curtly, ignoring the man and making my way to the upper level via a private elevator.

The upper level was reserved for VIPs. Each separated space was called a court. They all had names related to the tale of Peter Pan, but I never remembered them. The entire club was themed that way, bringing fantasy to life. Caged dancers dressed as pixies, the bartenders akin to Lost Boys. And even an extremely private lagoon with sirens ready to make your wildest desires come true. It was well done, I'd give them that.

But it had nothing on Provocateur. We had dancers, hot bartenders, all the usual draws for the young and rich. But it was the second half of my club that brought the elites. We catered to the darker cravings. The fetishes people kept secret, afraid to even name them.

At Provocateur, we celebrated those kinks. Gave people a safe place to fulfill their dark desires, something I could never do myself. But I found purpose in giving others that chance. What I truly desired, it wasn't allowed anywhere.

Shaking off the sullen mood attempting to swallow me up, I forced a smile as the elevator opened and made my way to Alec's court. There were two women dancing near the ropes separating the court from the main floor. The brunette was beautiful, but it was the petite blonde that made my mouth run dry. The emerald-green dress she wore fit her perfectly, caressing her curves and giving every male, and female, for that matter, a teasing glimpse of her perfect body.

Her hair cascaded down her back in waves. My hands curled into fists, instantly wishing they were wrapped up in her golden locks.

They were too entranced with their dancing to notice my approach. I cleared my throat audibly as I came up behind them.

"Shit!" the brunette exclaimed. "You scared the fuck out of me."

The blonde grinned at her friend before turning her attention to me. Her green eyes glowed in the low lights of the club. Her red lips were so fucking inviting I nearly leaned in for a taste. "Who are you?" she asked, arching a sculpted brow.

I bowed my head slightly and took her hand, pressing a kiss to her knuckles. "My name is Ellis. Ellis Bainbridge. I'm a friend of Alec's."

The woman smirked but didn't remove her hand from my grip. "I'm Nora. And that's Sienna. We work for the paper."

I nodded. "I heard."

Sienna scoffed, pulling Nora's arm away. "Alec sent a babysitter? Come on, Nora. Let's go dance."

Nora slipped out of her friend's grasp. "My feet need a break. I'll meet you out there."

Sienna waved and left for the main floor without another word. A man dressed in a bespoke black suit followed, lingering on the edge of the dance floor. One of Alec's, I was certain. And not the only guard dog monitoring a guest on the dance floor. Powerful people came here to relax, but most weren't stupid enough to leave home without protection.

Nora moved to the couch, and a server placed a glass of champagne in front of her. I was feeling brave, so I took the seat next to her. The urge to be close to this beauty was too strong to resist. The server placed my whiskey down as soon as I was seated.

"So, Ellis," she began, sipping her drink with delicate fingers. "What do you do? How do you know Mr. Vasiliev?"

I noted quickly the formal name versus the casual way her friend called him Alec. He mentioned an unruly employee, and a secret smile lifted my lips. That asshole was in love with her. It was obvious.

And it pleased me that Nora stayed professional with him. Probably because I'd have to force them apart if I found out he was interested in Nora. Fucking Christ, Ellis. We'd only just met and I was already jealous.

"We've been friends for some time. Business and pleasure," I responded coolly, hoping she didn't read anything more of my inner turmoil on my face.

Unfortunately, I was failing. I could see in the way she watched me, Nora was far too clever. Alec mentioned she was working on a few stories, one of them being the recent string of murders. Three bodies and counting, different ages and races, but all male. Because of my father and his particular life choices, I also followed stories like these. For years, he kept his seedy business dealing away from me and my club. It was one of my stipulations when I left him and that life behind.

My father wasn't the kind of man to accept someone disobeying, let alone leaving him completely. But I did. I realized quickly if I wanted any kind of normalcy, I had to leave the club life behind. No more dirty money deals, no more threatening people just for being late on a payment, and no more guns.

I didn't miss any of it; that was never the life for me. The part of my life I did miss, I refused to think about. At least, not actively.

"So, what kind of business do you do, Ellis?" Nora asked, pulling me away from the darker line of thoughts I was spiraling toward. Her smile was soft, green eyes wide and inviting. Her body faced mine, our knees brushing against the other's.

With her attention so focused on me now, it was impossible to think of anything else.

"Many things over the years, I'm a bit older than you," I teased her. Nora was likely in her twenties, with so much life ahead of her, and not someone I should want. And yet... "I own a club."

Her mouth opened in surprise. "A nightclub, like this one?"

A smirk crossed my lips. "Not exactly." I leaned in, inhaling her sultry amber perfume and bringing my lips to her ear. "It is a place where all desires are fulfilled. Where the dark wishes of your heart are brought to life."

Nora's chest began to move faster with her quickened breaths. Her thighs tensed, and blood rushed to my dick at her reaction. Before either of us could speak again, Sienna rushed over, sitting on the couch across from us. Nora pulled away from me.

Sienna flicked her eyes between the two of us. "Nora, let's go to the bathroom."

Nora nodded, and the two girls fled the area, arms linked and Sienna whispering. I watched them go—watched Nora's backside mostly. The song shifted to something slower, the base notes bumping to drown out my dark thoughts. Our server brought me another drink, and I leaned back, waiting for Nora to return.

I knew I shouldn't want her. She was young and full of life, and she didn't need an old man with baggage like mine dragging her down. Nora's soothing scent lingered in the air, and I sighed. Of course I should leave her alone, but I wouldn't.

7

Nora

"Honey, that man is in lust with you." Sienna laughed. "And you were so into it."

She pulled me along, but not toward the bathrooms.

I paused, bringing our quick pace to a halt. "Where are we going? I saw the signs for the bathrooms back that way."

Sienna rolled her eyes. "Hello, it's almost midnight."

My eyes widened and I gasped, realizing I was about to miss my window to find out what was going on with the lagoon clue. "Shit!"

My friend grinned, fanning her hair. "And there's more. On the dance floor, some guy showed up whispering to the guy I was dancing with about heading to the lagoon. But then he said, 'See you below.'"

Scrunching my brows in confusion, I stared at Sienna, waiting for her to continue. She was like a damn puppy, fidgeting with excitement.

"The Lagoon is on this floor, Nora." The words flew out of her mouth rapid fire. "He said below. I bet there is a back access or whatever to the basement from there. Somewhere quiet they can get away from people. And the Lagoon is like a damn orgy room. No one would be paying attention if people were slipping out."

I absorbed her words, becoming more eager with each passing moment. She was right. I grabbed her arms and forced her to listen to me. "Okay. I need you to go keep Ellis company while I check this out."

"No fun," Sienna whined. "I want to play spy. And he's not my type."

Her comment made irrational anger bubble up inside me, as if I had some claim on the man we just met, and the idea of her flirting with him sent me into a rage. "Number one, two girls sneaking around is more suspicious. Number two, don't flirt with him for real, or I might have to kill you."

Sienna grinned, her eyes twinkling. "Oh my. Staking a claim on daddy vibes out there, Nora?"

I shrugged, pretending I didn't just go insane with jealousy. "Whatever. Just be your chatty self and I'll be back soon."

Sienna gave me the rough layout of the club before sauntering back to our court. Part of me itched to go with her and return to Ellis. There was something so inviting about him. He had secrets, that was obvious, but so did I. And his club sounded intriguing. Since moving here and getting away from my ex, I hadn't slept with anyone. Flirted, but not sex. It just didn't feel right. Or maybe I no longer trusted people not to hurt me.

Whatever it was, the way my body reacted to Ellis was new. *A little white lie, Nora*, the voice in my head teased, and I knew exactly why. Only one other man had brought that kind of visceral reaction out of me. The man in the mask.

The music thumping loudly in the club faded the further away I got from the dance floor. The Lagoon was located beyond a set of fancy suites for men and women to change their clothes. There was a walk-in closet full of clothing within each. I browsed the room for the women. Bikinis, robes, and an assortment of pasties. Guests could show as much or as little as they wanted.

This was not part of my original plan, but if I walked into the Lagoon in my dress and heels, I'd likely stand out even more. I plucked a simple black bikini and a silk robe to match from the closet and dressed quickly in a changing room.

An attendant placed my clothes in another closet with a number attached. She also passed me a pair of black kitten heels to wear. Neverland really pulled out all the stops, and it was obvious why the richest of the rich frequented the nightclub. Everything was meticulously designed and catered for ultimate comfort.

A dozen or so people occupied the Lagoon. There were mini pools throughout the space surrounded by rocks, moss, and even a waterfall to make the patrons believe they had been whisked away to some magical mermaid lagoon. And there were mermaids. Women with the most beautiful, realistic-looking tails lounged in several of the pools. There were even water tanks with mermaids swimming and performing tricks along one of the walls. Their bodies were flawless. It was impossible not to stare, and even harder to turn my attention away from the people in the room to scan the walls for a nondescript door.

Softer music drifted through speakers, barely concealing soft moans of pleasure coming from several of the pools. Blood rushed through my body, and the voyeur in me desperately wanted to stay and play. I'd never been able to explore that particular kink, not in a safe, happy way. My ex saw to that.

I stopped suddenly when a small silver handle on a door blending into the dark wood caught my eye. Without looking back, I went through the door and hoped there weren't a bunch of dangerous gang members waiting on the other side.

Luckily for me, it was a stairwell, lowly lit with sconces on the walls. I followed the stairs to a landing that looked over another floor. There was a section of laundry, a wall of closets with various equipment labels on them. And a group of very scary looking men. Slowly, I inched backward on the landing until my back bumped up against something rough, but it wasn't the wall.

It was him.

8

Nora

"We have to stop meeting like this," he whispered against my neck, one hand covering my mouth. "Do you get lost in dangerous places often, little dove?"

I grabbed his wrist, tugging hard to pull his hand away from my face, and he let me. Of course, if he didn't want to, he was strong enough to stop me. He was twice my size, and I could feel his strength from the other arm still tightly wrapped around my waist.

"Or maybe I'm exactly where I need to be." My words came out far more confident than I felt.

He chuckled, the mask covering his face rough against my cheek. "A thrill seeker, eh? Do you have a death wish?"

Struggling against his hold, I grabbed his arm to release me, but he wouldn't budge. "I don't have a death wish, but I do have a job to accomplish."

From our position, I couldn't hear what was being said below. The masked man had pulled us into a shadowed alcove on the landing, safely away from any wandering eyes that happened to look up. I needed to get down there, or get him to tell me what was going on down there.

"Maybe if you can answer a question or two, I can just leave you and this little secret meeting?" I asked, keeping my voice as steady as possible.

His arm tightened around my waist, and the other hand inched down my chest beneath my robe. The scratchy fabric of his gloves sent chills down my spine. "And what do I get for answering your questions?"

This was the moment where I had to offer him something, but I had nothing. Except for my body. I hated the idea of trading information for sexual favors. At least, the sane part of me hated it. The horny part of my brain was already raging with lust each time his hands moved against my skin. So far, he wasn't groping me or touching anything sensitive, more like a slow exploration that was driving me mad with need.

"What do you want?" I asked him this before, and he'd said, simply, he wanted me. Would his answer be the same?

He chuckled softly. "I'm not going to fuck you, Nora King."

I gasped when he used my full name, my body going completely rigid. I didn't recall giving him my last name. He knew who I was. Which meant I was the opposite of safe in his arms. Before I could speak, he continued.

"When I fuck you," he growled into my ear. "I want everyone to hear your screams. When I fill your pretty mouth with my cock, I want to see the tears in your eyes."

My pussy throbbed at his words even as my heart raced in fear that he knew who I was.

The man continued, his hand around my waist now slowly opening my robe. "For now, I want your pleasure. Just one sweet release, the evidence of your arousal soaking my glove. Can you do that for me, little dove?"

He could take whatever he wanted from me. I was beyond vulnerable, completely at this devil's mercy, and yet waited.

"Yes." The moment I said the word, his left hand returned to my mouth, smothering any sounds I might make, and the other ripped off my bikini, top and bottoms. My nipples ached at the sudden onslaught of cool air. His fingers slipped between my legs, the gloves causing friction against my clit instantaneously.

My legs wobbled, and I moaned, leaning against him to keep myself upright. He chuckled again, the sound filled with lust. "That's it, love. Roll those hips and fuck my hand. I can already feel how soaked you are for me."

Another whimper escaped my lips as his middle finger pushed slowly inside me. The hand clamped down over my mouth tightened, nearly enough to bruise, and the pinch of pain only heightened the pleasure he gave me with the other.

His mask brushed against my neck, lips and teeth hidden behind the fabric. "Someday soon I'm going to taste your flesh for myself. What a tease you are, always finding me when I'm covered up."

I wanted to respond, to find out his identity now that he knew mine, but I was too far gone in the blissful crescendo his fingers were quickly bringing me to the edge of. His thumb rubbed circles over my swollen clit as he filled my pussy with a second finger, stretching me wide. The moan that came out of me was purely animalistic, muffled fully by his hand.

"I can feel you tightening around my fingers, little dove," he murmured gruffly. "Your body is so desperate for me. Let it out. Come for me, Nora."

The command broke the dam within me, and pleasure flooded my body with the next few movements of his fingers. My legs shook as the orgasm lingered from his continued touches. I tried to escape, but he held me tight. The hard length pressing into my ass told me he was enjoying this just as much as I was.

"Good fucking girl," he purred. My masked man continued to toy with my body, forcing every ounce of pleasure from me as he spoke. "This meeting is about the murders. Someone is killing gang members. Ours, and others'. Tensions are building between different clubs, and many are pointing fingers. It won't be long now until the city's underbelly implodes."

I bit at his finger to get him to release my mouth, and he did. "Do you know who is doing this?"

He finally pulled his hand from between my legs and brought the soaked glove to my lips. The man rubbed his fingers over my mouth, forcing me to taste. "Perhaps."

Rolling my eyes, I stepped out of his arms and snatched up my bikini, quickly pulling it on while staying hidden in the shadows.

The door I'd entered through opened suddenly, letting in light from the hallway, enough for me to make out his general visage and the tattoos crawling up his neck. This man was not a member of the club meeting below, but another. And he was holding a gun.

Two things happened almost instantly. A gun was pointed at my face, and a knife stuck out of the man's throat.

My masked man shoved me into the alcove seconds before the gun went off. The intruder coughed and sputtered, blood leeching out of his body from the wound and his mouth. My masked man ripped the blade out and slashed it across the other man's throat, officially silencing him.

"What the fuck is going on up there?" someone shouted from below.

"Caught us a spy," the masked man spoke calmly. "He's dead now."

Several men cursed and shouted. My masked man stood in front of me and pulled me toward the door, keeping my body behind his. He shoved me into the hall and shut the door without another word.

Turning quickly, I walked as fast as I could back to the Lagoon. My body hummed with adrenaline, but it wasn't from fear. There was the smallest moment of fear when I saw the gun, but the sight of how efficiently the masked men took him out was dominating my thoughts. He moved with lethal force, steady and calm and quick all at once. He went from giving me euphoric pleasure to offering death within a matter of minutes. This masked man was more than just another club member. He was death, a Reaper.

There were rumors of such people in the clubs. And if those were true, this masked man was absolutely one of them. And I was quickly becoming obsessed with him.

Nora

The Lagoon no longer captivated my attention as I made my way back to the club. I'd changed quickly and made sure my hair and makeup still looked normal. Both were in slight disarray, but a quick touch-up had everything back in place. The taste of my own arousal lingered on my lips, and the feeling of my masked man's hands was imprinted on my skin.

The moment I reappeared in our court, Ellis stood, his dark blue eyes filled with concern. "Where did you run off to?" He fidgeted with his suit, attempting to seem merely curious.

I smiled at him, a genuine smile, because it was impossible not to when he looked at me the way he did. "Some girls in the bathroom talked about the Lagoon, and I had to see it for myself."

He arched a dark brow, something I couldn't name passing over his face. "Without me?"

Sienna laughed. "Nora's a wild one, Ellis. And she can't turn those investigative powers of hers off for anything."

A blush crept up my neck at her teasing. "Plus they were just...copulating. Out there in the open."

Ellis adjusted his suit jacket as he walked towards me. "Did you enjoy that?" His navy eyes scrutinized my face.

There was no point in lying, and for whatever reason, I didn't want to lie to him. "Perhaps. I like to watch."

Ellis reached for me, his hand squeezing my waist as he stepped in close enough for our bodies to brush against each other. My heartbeat ramped up to a thousand beats per minute having this man's full attention. He was not only physically built like a god, but his presence was shadowed and alluring. I was desperate to know his secrets.

"Aren't you a curious little thing," he purred, his voice like velvet. "And what about being watched? Do you enjoy that too, Nora?"

Hearing my name on his lips, his voice so low and inviting, was enough to send shivers straight to my lower belly. Words escaped me, so I simply offered a quick nod.

Ellis grinned, a laugh playing about his very kissable lips. "The Lagoon is cleverly done, but it has nothing on my club. I'd love for you to come see it." He brushed his hand over my wrist, his thumb pressing gently against my pulse. "As my personal guest."

I stared up at him. He wasn't quite as tall as the masked man, but still several inches taller than me and my three-inch heels. How I could possibly be interested in him when I just had another man's fingers inside me was a mystery. But it was true all the same. Ellis Bainbridge intrigued me.

"I'd love to," I responded with a smile.

"Um, hello," Sienna cut in. "I'm coming too."

Ellis smiled at her, something softer and less inviting than what he offered me. "Of course. Monday evening? I'll put you both on the list."

A server entered the court and passed each of us fresh drinks. I sipped the champagne, a giddy feeling settling over me. I'd learned more than enough to pursue the murders as a top headline for the paper. And managed to catch the eyes of two men.

"Looking forward to it." I clinked my glass to his.

Sienna joined in, never to be ignored. "To new kinks."

Ellis smirked, his eyes locked on my face. "To uncovering our truest desires." His gaze never left my own as we sipped our drinks, and my face flushed at the laser focus. The strands of silver in his hair glinted in the shining lights of the club.

He couldn't be that many years older than me, based on how young his face still looked, but I'd find all that out easily enough. Tomorrow, Sienna and I would be having a good, old-fashioned girl party with junk food and wifi to find out exactly who these men were. The masks were coming off.

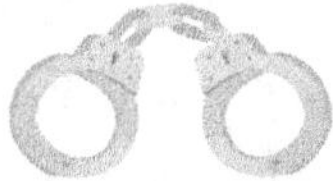

Our girls' day started with a pilates class and brunch with mimosas as a reward. Sienna was more of a runner and weights type, but she took classes with me occasionally. I hated cardio, and the movements in my pilates class were more my style. The mind and body workout blend was soothing to my busy brain. Busier than usual, after my third attempt this week to reach my cousin failed. Other than my grandmother, she was one of the only family I liked. And the only one who I kept in touch with after leaving. I knew I shouldn't, because doing so could put her in danger, but it was impossible. She was like a sister to me. And as easy as it looked in the movies, cutting ties with everyone in reality was much more difficult.

After brunch we retreated to our apartment oasis and changed into comfy clothes. Sienna believed in taking quiet days without work, set plans, or stress.

So at least once a month, we took a day to do all the things we enjoyed, ending it with takeout and movies. It was also her rule that no computers or phones were allowed during girl time, which was a fair rule considering I had a problem shutting out work when any devices were nearby.

"One hour," she warned. "Timer is set."

Due to the fact that I was increasingly worried for my cousin, Sienna made an allowance so I could peruse the tabloid news for any signs of my ex. It wasn't hard to find him either. Apparently he was making a point of appearing in public, and in the last week, always with Lyra nearby. Jameson, of course, wanted me to know what he was doing, and who he was doing it with.

Anxiety flooded my system the more I swiped through the photos. But how in the world could I get to her without giving up my new life? Her phone would of course be tapped. I could use a minute phone, but that would still give him my general location. Sienna could try to reach her, but that would be suspicious too.

If only I could trust my family to help me, to hear my truth and believe that Jameson was the monster I knew him to be. He was just so fucking good at hiding it. Disguised his rage with charm and soft touches. The way he manipulated everyone around him until somehow, they ended up owing him allegiance. Jameson collected secrets and used them as weapons. That thought reminded me of the USB drive. I still hadn't found the strength to watch whatever was on there. It would be devastating, of course. But now that I was free, safe, could I handle it, or would whatever secret he held over me on that drive send me back to the girl I was before? The one too afraid to leave.

"Times up," Sienna chirped in my ear, plopping down on the couch with a bowl of buttery popcorn. "What movie should we watch?"

Stuffing my tablet into the drawer of the side table, I curled up next to her and snatched a handful of popcorn. "Something with bad bitches reclaiming their power."

Sienna dipped her head in understanding. "Hell yes. How about *Columbiana*? Let's watch Zoe Zeldaña kick some ass."

45

Declan

Last night was fucking hell. My father was in a rage about the intruder. Blaming everyone and anyone for giving up our meeting location. Funny thing about that, though. I gave up the location. To three very specific people.

When my father ruined all chances I could ever have at a normal life, I vowed to make his life as miserable as my own. The only way to destroy him was from the inside. It wouldn't be killing those closest to him, no. Donovan O'Rourke loved no one. After my mother died years ago, he never remarried. He slept with women, mostly the kind you paid for. His personality wasn't nearly as charming as mine. Going after his club was the way to upend his life. And once the club was dismantled, maybe then I could sail off somewhere, live quietly. Finally be alone.

Only now, that sailboat wasn't quite so empty. A stunning blonde with eyes greener than the Wicklow Mountains in summer sat beside me. Ireland was the furthest I'd been able to travel under my father's ever-present shadow. And even that was difficult. Several years ago we spent a weekend in Belfast, meeting up with the Irish to discuss a new arms deal. My father drank more than usual. For a handful of seconds, he looked almost wistful. He mentioned my mother.

It confused me, because our mother wasn't Irish. She died when I was born, but my older brother spoke of her often. He was never the same after she died. But she was British, and I said as much to my father. He mumbled something incoherent about her cousins. It never came up again, and I honestly hadn't thought of it since. Strange that it would work its way back into the front of my mind now.

Perhaps it was the scenery. Nora King lived in an apartment with her roommate, Sienna. Belgravia was posh as hell, and not a part of London I frequented. It was close to a handful of parks and green spaces, all of which still bloomed in the late summer.

Unfortunately someone like myself stood out in places like this. I borrowed a car for this particular night of surveillance. Pulling the glove out of my pocket, I brought it to my nose and inhaled like some kind of crackhead. The scent of her soaked cunt still lingered on the fabric. It was maddening in the most exquisite way. The muffled sounds she made and the way her body responded to my touch was driving me mad. Not even twenty-four hours had passed and I was staked outside her place.

Nora didn't have a car, but her roommate did, so I planted a tracker on it. They bopped about the city all day, pilates, mimosas, and now seemingly staying in for the night. Tomorrow while they were at work I'd have a camera installed inside. Complete violation of privacy, but I couldn't give a fuck about that. This siren had lured me in, a predator lurking in the dark, and there was no chance of me losing sight of her now.

Opening my laptop, I quickly signed in and hacked Sienna's computer. Her firewalls weren't quite as strong as Nora's. Growing up with no friends, I became an expert in two categories, killing and computers. Learning coding and hacking was honestly easier than killing. Murder was messy, and almost everyone who tried to cover their tracks missed a step. Which was why my own skills were in such high demand. Also why my father charged exorbitant sums of money when loaning me out.

Sienna's computer didn't have much to intrigue me, but there was an unusual number of times she looked up American tabloids and entertainment news related to one specific name. Jameson Moore. Curiosity won out and I looked the man up. He was a piece of shit rich boy, that was obvious. Powerful family, strong political connections. I was close to losing interest when a story from several years past popped up and a familiar–but not–face appeared on my screen. Squinting at the caption, I read it aloud. "Jameson Moore and girlfriend, Primrose Eleanora Kingsley, attended the Elegance for Animals Ball at Carnegie Hall in New York last weekend."

Nora was now the most riveting woman I'd met. Not only was she hiding her past with her new pseudonym, it seemed she was running from it too. *Good riddance.* It pleased me she left this one behind. Otherwise I'd have to kill him. Curious that Sienna would be keeping tabs on the man. Was he a threat? Was that why she changed her name? Nora King didn't exist until less than a year ago. Had she run from this asshole?

These were all questions I needed answers to, and one way or another, she would give them to me. For now, I'd feign ignorance. If I spooked her by letting her know I knew her secret, she might very well disappear, and that would not be happening.

After another two hours of surveillance, the lights went out in their apartment and I quietly made my way to their garden in the back. I slipped on a simple mask to hide my face. Not from security cameras, because they had none. Fucking irritating. She was meant to be in hiding and didn't even live somewhere with security cameras. The mask was only to keep my identity hidden if she woke up.

There were not enough secure locks on their building, something I would remedy soon enough. It was entirely too easy to enter the building and slip into their apartment. An average thief could achieve as much as I had, and that wouldn't do. No one would be stalking Nora King besides myself.

Their apartment was cozy but tidy, a small square footage, with bedrooms on opposite ends of the living space. My siren's perfume lingered in the air, and I followed the scent to her room. Slowly pushing open the door, I held my breath, remaining silent as a jungle cat on the hunt. Nora was sleeping soundly, lying on her back, covers askew to reveal her silky camisole riding up over her flat stomach. Her nipples were visible through the thin fabric, her perfect tits rising and falling with even breaths. Her sun-kissed blonde hair was splayed out around her head like a halo. Nora was indeed an innocent, and I was the devil come to corrupt her soul.

A jewel glinted in her navel from her piercing. So my little dove could handle some pain. Licking my lips, I zeroed in once more on her peaked nipples, imagining how they would look with pretty gold bars through them. Gold was definitely her color. She was an angel sent to tempt me to heaven, when I knew full well hell was the only path for me.

Nora murmured softly in her sleep, one hand slipping below the covers. She moaned softly, and the sound instantly caught my dick's attention. Her hand was moving, and I desperately needed to see her. Slowly, I pulled her blankets down the bed, revealing her perfect body. Her hand was inside her tiny silk shorts, between her legs. The scent of her arousal hit my nose, and a feral need crawled up my spine. As quietly as I could, I straddled her thighs.

My body weight would wake her, of course, but my hand was already covering her mouth. Her eyes widened in horror.

"Hush, little dove," I murmured, leaning close. "What were you dreaming of just now?" With my legs locked around her thighs, her hand was firmly trapped between her legs. "Were you dreaming of us? When I fucked your sweet cunt with my hand?"

Her body relaxed beneath me, and that pleased me more than anything. Nora might have been weary of me, but she also didn't want me to go, that much was obvious from her actions. I removed my hand from her plump lips.

"How the hell did you get in here?" she demanded.

I tsked at her. "You have a filthy mouth, Nora. Perhaps I should fill it?" Her heartbeat quickened at my words, and I chuckled. "I was only planning to watch you, but then you started touching yourself, and I grew jealous. The mess you made on my glove has been driving me insane. I need to taste you."

Her lips parted, heaving breaths drawing my attention back to her chest. With a bit of a struggle, she pulled her hand from her shorts and brought her fingers to her lips, licking them. "Then taste me."

Nora

Only moments before I felt the weight of a body on top of mine, I was dreaming of my masked man. But it wasn't just him. Ellis was there too. These two men, so completely different but equally stealing my mind, body, and soul. And now one of them was here, straddling me in bed, still wearing a mask, but not full tactical gear. He was dressed in black jeans and a leather jacket with a simple ski mask. It was too dark to see his eyes, but I could feel them gliding over my body.

He said he wanted to taste me. And after the dream he woke me from, I was feeling particularly brave.

"Then taste me." The words were seductive and confident when they left my lips. My body was alight with desire, and adrenaline fueled my decision to taunt my masked man.

It was addicting, having this dangerous man so focused on me. He wasn't dangerous like the ones from my past. Even now, he didn't force himself on me, but waited for permission. And in that moment, I felt more powerful than ever.

He groaned at my words, sliding off the bed and ripping my silk shorts off as he went. The cool air against my skin brought goosebumps to the surface. His hands weren't gloved this time, and he dragged the rough pads of his fingers up my thighs, digging into my flesh and pulling my legs wide.

"Your scent is intoxicating, little dove," he murmured. "You smell of wild-flowers and spiced honey. And your pretty cunt...smells like the most forbidden fruit."

He didn't wait for my response. My masked man's mouth latched onto my swollen clit and sucked hard. I cried out, slapping my own hand over my mouth to hide the sounds I was making. His tongue felt divine, lapping up the arousal dripping between my thighs. His fingers dug into my flesh enough to bruise as he devoured me. Pleasure danced up my spine and tingled all over my body. I squirmed beneath him, close to oblivion, but he held me down. One of his hands moved slowly up my belly and circled my throat, squeezing just enough to take away my breath. I moaned again, the sound more animal than human, my hips ratcheting up to get more of his mouth.

He chuckled, his lips leaving mine momentarily, and I whimpered. "The sounds you make for me, love. I'm becoming addicted to them. Soon I'll have you scream for me. But for now, come on my face, siren."

My masked man dove between my legs, his tongue thrusting inside me before two fingers shoved in without warning. His thumb circled my clit, and with his other hand, he squeezed my throat until black spots began to appear at the edges of my vision. Pleasure rocketed through my body, a wave of ecstasy I could hardly stand rushing through me. He held me down as I shuddered beneath him, prolonging my orgasm until my body went completely limp beneath him.

He lingered between my legs, lapping up the mess I made for him for several minutes while I caught my breath. My hand moved over his head, covered by the mask. I wanted desperately to feel him, to run my fingers through his hair. He wasn't bald, that much I could feel, but what did he look like? Why did he hide from me, even now?

"What is your name?" I asked between shallow breaths. "I've got to have something to call you other than my masked man."

He laughed softly, crawling up my body and pressing his own flush against mine. His dick was thick and hard, digging into my thigh through his jeans. "*Your* masked man? I rather like the sound of that."

My cheeks flushed at his response and the emphasis on the word "your" was clearly noted. "I still want a name."

He paused for a moment. "I'll tell you mine, when you tell me yours." Before I could respond, he moved off of me with the dexterity of a jungle cat. His words barely registered in my pleasure-addled mind. "Sleep sweet, little dove."

Nora

Tonight Sienna and I were going to Ellis's club. Provocateur was indeed everything he described it to be. Of course I looked it up, digging around for any scandalous stories related to its patrons, but there was nothing. This place was pristine, at least as far as its financials and historical data. Ellis Bainbridge had similar files. There were few things about him on the internet, which was a major red flag. Everyone was on the internet. It was the twenty-first century for crying out loud. But he had nothing. No Facebook photo albums from his college days, no old Instagram accounts, not a damn thing.

Despite being new to London, I made sure to find friends in places that would become beneficial to my famed journalist aspirations.

Marge Malloy was a middle-aged woman with an Irish accent and an inability to keep a secret. The last bit, not exactly a quality the National Crime Agency would welcome. But Marge was a legacy employee. Her family were longstanding employees of the NCA, Britain's somewhat equivalent of the FBI. Marge was given a menial administrative position, which was plenty good enough to access information I needed.

"Happy Monday, Miss Marge," I greeted her over the phone. "How are you?"

Her voice was boisterous as ever. "Oh just fine, lovely girl. Spent the weekend in my garden."

A smile played across my lips. Her positive energy was infectious. "Sounds relaxing."

"Indeed it was." She laughed. "And you, dear? Tell me you met a man. I need to live dangerously through you and that wild roommate of yours."

I giggled at her, rolling my eyes, even though she couldn't see me. "Perhaps. But this man is more of a work connection."

Marge scoffed. "Oh let's have his name then."

Success. "Ellis Bainbridge. Owns a club of sorts."

Her nails clacked against the keys of her computer, and I waited for the juicy details she could find. "Curious. His digital footprint is relatively small. A birth certificate lists parents, mother deceased. A father who he emancipated from as a teen. And that man I've heard of. Allegedly murdered a handful of people. And has ties to several dangerous groups on the Interpol shortlist. Mr. Bainbridge does not seem to be connected to those groups anywhere that I can see. I'll send you what I can, dear."

I sighed. "Thanks so much, Miss Marge. You're my favorite."

She laughed. "You're too sweet. Be careful, now, dear."

"I will. Bye for now."

Marge sent over what she could without raising any red flags, and I perused the email for anything worth noting. Ellis was almost squeaky clean. But his father was not. The most exciting bit was his photo. This man was at both meetings I snuck into recently. He was more than just affiliated. He had the persona of a leader. Keen eyes and a sharp tongue. I supposed it was a green flag that Ellis wanted nothing to do with such a monster. There was another who did, though. My masked man.

Just the thought of him made my damn thighs clench. Never in my life had I experienced something like him. The way his touch set my body on fire and turned my logical mind to melted Jell-o. In my early college years, I fooled around, attended parties, and had a few moments of passion, but nothing like that.

The man was a killer. He literally killed someone in front of me, and I was sitting here drooling about the idea of seeing him again.

He likely wouldn't answer any of my questions about Harold O'Rourke, known criminal mastermind and someone who would definitely have the answers I needed. A stray thought crossed my mind, an image of the sexy man at the Red Clover. Perhaps he was connected to the leader. When I followed him to that warehouse, I didn't actually see him at the meeting, but my masked man showed up fairly quickly. And he wasn't at the second meeting either. Then again, my masked man quickly stole all of my attention then too.

Perhaps another visit to the Red Clover was in order. Sienna could flirt with that bartender again. Who knows, he could be more involved than we were initially led to believe.

"Knock knock," Mason called out as he walked into my cubicle. He held out a thick envelope to me. "Mail for you."

I smiled up at him from my seat. "Thanks, Mason."

He smiled back, staring a little too long. "What did you get?"

Turning slightly away, I adjusted my blouse and placed the package on my desk. "Just a few newspapers and tabloids. You never know when some salacious news will pop up."

Mason chuckled, his eyes shifting as if he didn't want to look directly at me. "Sure, sure. Say, Nora. Do you have plans later? I was thinking—"

"She has plans," Sienna cut in, stepping into my cubicle with her hands on her hips and a look of irritation on her face. "Bye, Mason."

For a moment, so swift I almost missed it, his eyes narrowed in irritation. But then his forced smile returned quickly, and Mason begged off. "Right, then. Bye."

Sienna waited until he rounded the corner at the end of the hall. "Gods, he gives me the creeps." She faked a shiver.

She wasn't wrong, though. He always tried to be pleasant, but there was something about him that had my alarm bells ringing. After everything I'd been through, I was learning to trust those more than ever. Opening the package, I pulled out the literature. I subscribed to a handful of American magazines and the *Chicago Times*. Despite my desire to leave my past firmly in the rear view, I felt the urge to stay informed. My ex was an affluent member of society, as was his family and my own. If any of those assholes were up to something, the trash magazines would print it.

Luckily for me, things had been quiet since my quick departure. No one was even talking about my lack of appearance, which could only mean my family and Jameson's connections paid them to focus their paparazzi on someone else. That wasn't unusual though. We had enough connections to keep them out of our bushes and printing only what we wanted them to see.

If Ellis happened to give my name a look, he'd find a background just as redacted as his own. I supposed I was a red flag too.

But mine was hidden for safety. The one friend I had back in the US, I communicated with her via alias emails, and she told me Jameson had stopped harassing her for information about two months ago. I wasn't entirely sure what to make of that, so I set up regular subscriptions to keep an eye on things back in Chicago. As I flipped through the first magazine, nothing notable caught my eye. The second, however, had blood rushing through my veins in a most unpleasant way. Jameson stared at me from the photo. A fancy gathering of wealthy people pretending to care about a charity. He was dressed impeccably, an inviting smile lighting up his stupid face. But the danger bells blaring in my head weren't because of his photo, they were for the girl wrapped up in his arms. My cousin, Lyra Montclair.

Sienna leaned over my shoulder. "Who is the girl?"

She knew who my ex was. Sienna was the only person in London who knew him. Mr. Vasiliev knew that my name was changed, and that I preferred not to talk about my past, but not why. I had to give him something when I was hired. A smart business owner doesn't just accept a strange woman's word without some kind of proof of her credibility. Sienna likely told him a little more, but it didn't bother me. Alec Vasiliev had only been kind, and I trusted him for now, because Sienna trusted him. Even if she pretended to hate him.

"My cousin," I finally answered her. "Fuck. What is she doing with him?"

Sienna sighed. "Dating, apparently, as of this week. If this article is accurate."

This was meant for me, I was sure of it. Jameson would never let me walk away from him. There was no investigation into my sudden disappearance. Our families would never allow that. But they were looking. Even if I didn't have proof of that. Parading my cousin on his arm at a party was a warning.

Lyra and I were close friends, only three years apart. I didn't have any real siblings, and Felix, my sort-of brother, barely counted as one. Ly was the little sister I always wanted. And I would die before I saw her hurting because of me. Maybe no one else could see it, but her eyes already looked haunted.

"He's taunting me," I whispered angrily, crinkling the pages of the magazine. "This is a warning, Sienna. If I don't go back, he will hurt her. I know he will. He may have already."

Sienna swiveled my chair away from the magazine on my desk to face her instead. "No. You don't know that." I shook my head, but she persisted. "If she were harmed, after being with him publicly, he'd be the prime suspect."

I shook my head again. "He wouldn't. You don't understand how connected he is. Our families, they have ties all the way up the chain politically. His father is a fixer. And he's got dirt on everyone. He could kill her, and no one would know the truth."

Sienna frowned, crossing her arms. Her curves were accentuated in the brilliant blue bodycon dress. She looked fierce as hell. "Then we'll get her here. Or get someone to tip her off to stay away. You're not going back there, Nora."

I slumped over in my chair. "I don't want to go back there. But if I can't reach her, I will. Until I have the proof to ruin him, I'll do what I need to do to keep her safe."

Sienna didn't argue; she could see my resolve was sound. "Fine. But no secrets. If you go, I go."

13

Ellis

This was the longest work day of my fucking life. Nora was coming to my club tonight, and apparently my insides were reverting to teenage male behavior. I was a fucking mess. Since meeting her at Neverland, I'd fucked my hand no less than three times. I couldn't get her out of my mind.

She was not only stunning, with golden hair and peridot green eyes that glittered with mischief, but clever. Even in the brief conversation we had, she was witty and discerning. Her guard was up the entire night, only slipping slightly when she danced with Sienna. It was obvious she didn't trust easily. And for whatever reason, I was desperate to earn her trust.

Mondays at Provocateur were generally busy. Every night of the week had a theme, and tonight brought out the members of our voyeur and exhibitionist community. The rooms were arranged for optimal play, and the main room nearest to the bar and lounge became an intimate theater. While some enjoyed being watched by only their partner, others craved the spotlight. Members could choose to play in rooms with cameras connected to the theater, or privately with their own chosen partners. The theater was arranged with intimate table settings and private booths. The energy from that room was electric and filled me with pride.

It took several years to build a collective of individuals who trusted Provocateur to be a credible, safe place for the BDSM community. There were too many unlearned outsiders opening bars with BDSM themes only to completely ignore the boundaries, the trust, the truth of it all. Not only did ignorance cause harm to the community, but physical and emotional damage were rampant within these uneducated groups.

After my own experiences helped my desires manifest, I knew opening a place like this was my path. I didn't have a family to judge me, or any friends, really, to tell me it was a poor business move. And thankfully, my own determination was enough to see it through.

"Merrick," I knocked on the oak wood of the bar, getting his attention. "We all set for tonight?"

He nodded, eyes scanning the crowd. "Of course, boss."

My bar manager, Merrick Thompson, was a cheeky fuck but excellent at his job. I only hired the best, and he was one of them. Alec helped me with hiring, being a member of the BDSM community himself and someone I trusted.

Merrick set a glass of scotch in front of me, and I nodded in thanks, taking a sip.

Nora, I deduced, was not someone with experience in this world. Curious and open-minded, but not a player. Her soft admission of interest was enough to make my dick hard, and I took another sip of liquor to quell the desire coursing through my veins at the memory. I was beyond curious to know what she would feel when she arrived. Hopefully not disgust, but that was only my insecurities threatening to take over.

Patrons began filling the rooms, and I wandered among them, greeting those I recognized. I knew all of my VIP members by face and name, and did my best to learn the names of new members as well. My club also boasted three house managers, and each of them were experts in specific kinks. Every employee of mine had been vetted and took the time to get to know our members.

By 8 p.m., my nerves were becoming unsettled. Nora and Sienna were due to arrive soon. I retreated to my office, if only to stare at the security cameras in peace instead of the front entrance like a damn pup. My office included a small apartment over the club. I didn't live here permanently, but built it out into a studio apartment for nights when it was too late to drive home.

The moment she entered the lounge area, all the blood in my body rushed south. She was a fucking work of art. A priceless creation that I wanted all for myself. Nora wore a black silk halter dress that dipped to her waist, a glittering jewel dangling from her navel. The curve of her breasts on display was enough to make my mouth water. The dress was tea-length, with a high slit, and she wore black stilettos to match. Her golden hair was piled high on her head, a mess of curls my hands were desperate to sink into. Sienna looked lovely on her arm, but my eyes were glued to every inch of Nora King. The two women were ushered to the bar, taking a seat and immediately being served drinks. Gulping down my own, I adjusted my suit, fidgeted with my watch, and headed downstairs.

While Sienna flirted with another patron, Merrick was chatting heavily with Nora. Jealousy snaked its way through my veins at the sound of her laughing at something he said. Quietly, I took the seat to her left. Nora's body angled towards me immediately, her lips parting in a smile that made my stomach flutter like a damn teenager's.

"Good evening, Nora." I took her hand, kissing her knuckles like I did at our last meeting. I wasn't a gentleman, I just needed to kiss her. If her hand was all I could touch, it was enough. For now. "Welcome to Provocateur."

She smiled, her green eyes glittering. "This place is amazing, Ellis. I didn't know what to expect, but whatever it was, this is better."

Her praise was a shot of ecstasy to my pride. "Thank you. Would you like a proper tour?" Before she could respond, a man walked up behind Sienna, and I grinned. "Evening, Alec."

Sienna's eyes narrowed, and Nora smiled like the Cheshire Cat. It was Sienna who responded first. "What the hell are you doing here?"

Alex adjusted his suit coat. "A little bird told me this was the place to be tonight." He nodded to me. "Ellis."

I winked at Nora before responding to him. "I was just offering the ladies a tour, but since you know your way around, would you mind showing Sienna?"

"Hell no," Sienna whined. "I'm going to the kinky movie lounge. Come find me when you finish your private tour, Nora." She emphasized the word private with a wink at her friend and stalked off. Alec muttered irritably and followed her, his longer legs making it easy for him to catch up.

Nora giggled, and the sound was indescribably pleasant to my ears. "Those two are an explosion waiting to happen. And it will happen. I'd bet money on it."

I smirked down at her. "I'd wager one of them is on their knees tonight."

She arched a brow at me, her red lips parting. "Oh really? That would be interesting. I'll take that bet. I say two weeks at least, until she caves."

My grin widened. "And what do I get when I win?" I walked away from the bar, and she stayed at my side, arm linked through mine.

Nora scoffed. "Why are you so confident?"

Ushering her through a velvet curtain down a wide hallway, I leaned in close to her ear, breathing in her soft jasmine perfume. "Kinks are my specialty, Nora. I've made a business of uncovering desires in others."

She hummed to herself, taking in the new space. The hall was more like an atrium, with dimly lit chandeliers, plush couches, and attendants at each door. There was a small bar at the far end with a handful of high top tables where guests congregated. There were ten rooms around the atrium, each designed with different types of play in mind. There were also extras that could be added to enhance particular kinks—toys, cameras, clothing, and more. Provocateur was meticulously outfitted to meet every need.

"And what about your desires?" Nora asked. "You said others."

She was entirely too clever, and it was one of the qualities I enjoyed most about her. "I forget how carefully I need to choose my words around a journalist," I teased her and was rewarded with a blush. "I find ways to satisfy my own needs, but it gives me greater pleasure to satiate yours."

Nora

Ellis led me through a solid wooden door, deftly typing in a passcode on the keypad. Each door had a keypad, and I assumed codes were changed regularly to give guests access. I was beyond curious to know which room he had chosen. When we met at Neverland, I'd mentioned a little of my interests, but not enough to create a full profile, and yet, this room looked as if it was designed for me.

There was a massive bed with a canopy of golden silk and chiffon fabrics. The bedframe and other furniture in the room created an atmosphere I could only describe as princess locked in a tower theme. All of the toys were made of gold. Golden chains rested against the far wall, leather cuffs at the end of them. A massive floor-length mirror rested against the opposite wall. There was a plush chaise made of green velvet and a bar cart with champagne and chocolate covered strawberries.

Ellis moved to the cart, pouring two glasses of champagne while I made my tour about the room, taking in the beauty of it. The details were insane and so cleverly done. The moment he shut the door, I truly felt like I was transported to a faraway land, a lonely princess hidden away from the world. How could he know I spent days with such a fantasy in my mind?

Turning back to him, I meant to say as much, but gasped instead when a large picture frame shimmered to life. It previously looked like a painting, but it was a television in disguise. And now the screen showed a room that I could only describe as a dungeon.

In said dungeon, a woman was strapped to one of the crosses with her arms and legs splayed out wide. She was completely naked. Her body had small welts from obvious play. Another woman in a full-body leather outfit came into view, holding a riding crop. She teased the leather slowly over the restrained woman's nipples before giving them each a few slaps. I was wholly mesmerized.

When Ellis's arm brushed against mine, I nearly jumped out of my skin, and he chuckled at my expense. "Beautiful, aren't they? Tasha is the one on the St. Andrew's Cross. She works for me. The other is a player."

That surprised me. "I would've assumed it was the other way around."

Ellis nodded, less surprised. "Yes. Most assume new players come to submit, but we have all types here. Tasha is a switch and enjoys playing with new people. She is also exceptionally empathetic. It works in her favor with members who are new to the scene and need guidance."

I was mildly jealous of all the praise he was giving the woman, but held that ugly feeling in because I couldn't pretend she wasn't turning me on with this whole display either. "She's beautiful."

Ellis smiled, turning his gaze to me. "In her own way, yes. Not my type, though." He handed me a glass of champagne. "This room allows the players to watch others, not just the dungeon room. There are also cameras in this room, so others can watch. They are currently turned off. All rooms are designed for the players to choose what they want to do or share with others."

The idea that we could be watched on a TV just like this one by others was, in fact, a kink of mine. "I...like that a lot. I don't know that I am fully ready to be watched, but the idea is hot as hell, to put it plainly."

Ellis smirked, his eyes dilating slightly. "I also enjoy the voyeur and exhibitionist scenes."

His statement sounded unfinished. "But?" I prompted.

He took one step closer, bringing his chest flush with mine, and cupped my chin in one massive hand. "But I don't entirely like the idea of letting anyone else see your pleasure. I'm feeling a bit greedy about keeping you to myself."

My thighs clenched at his possessiveness, and I licked my lips, needing moisture in my mouth now that it had all flooded south. "I don't...I mean, I want..." Words failed me in that moment with this impressive man's full attention directed my way.

"Tell me what you want, Nora." He murmured the command.

Yep, I was a goner. "I want to watch others fucking, while you...do things to me." Keeping my voice steady while saying those words was nearly impossible. But Ellis didn't laugh. Didn't judge me or say anything condescending. He simply bowed low and kissed my hand.

Ellis shifted my palm up and kissed that, too, then my wrist. His lips were soft, and I wanted desperately for him to kiss me. When he straightened, he stared into my eyes with so much desire it made me gasp. "You are a divine creature. That you would let me offer your pleasure is a gift. I won't waste such a thing."

"What will you do?" I asked, already breathless.

Ellis circled me like a predator sizing up his next meal. He flipped the channel on the television to another room. This one was plush like ours, only less castle vibes and more modern. Two men were working in tandem to make the girl scream so loud she'd pass out. How in the hell could he know I'd enjoy watching multiplay? This man was going to be dangerous to my health.

Ellis wrapped his hands around my waist, pulling me close to him. The woman on the screen was on her knees, the two men moaning as she sucked their dicks. For some reason, a shudder went through my body, and not the good kind. Ellis noticed immediately and spun me around to face him.

"What's wrong?" His navy eyes were full of concern. I tried to turn away from him, but he forced my chin back until our eyes met. "Don't hide. Don't be ashamed to express your needs and your boundaries."

His soothing tone forced the breath I was holding from my body. "I don't know, really. Had an odd reaction to seeing that woman performing oral like that."

Ellis cupped my face with his bearpaw-sized hands. "Then that is a boundary we won't cross. And just so you know, the plans I had for you tonight didn't include my dick." He leaned in close to my face until our lips brushed against each other. "I'm desperate to taste you, Nora. Allow me?"

A rush of pleasure engulfed my entire body at his words. "Yes, please."

He smiled, eyes twinkling with delight. "I do quite enjoy that word on your lips directed at me."

Ellis stepped back and shrugged out of his suit jacket, expertly hanging it on a hook and rolling up his shirt sleeves in a matter of moments. He looked fine as hell. What was it about the rolled up sleeves that made my knees weak?

He returned to me, guiding me with a hand to my back to the chaise. "Let's get you out of this dress. Wouldn't want to ruin it."

I giggled. "You just want to see me naked."

Ellis emitted what could only be described as a growl. "You're not wrong, love. I've been dreaming of it since the moment I saw you."

His admission pleased me, and I licked my lips in anticipation of what he would do next. Ellis placed his hands on my waist once more and whirled me around, so the chaise was in front of me and I had a direct view of the television. His rough fingers quickly unclasped the gown from around my neck, and the silk shift dropped to the floor. My nipples hardened at the sudden open air, and only a slip of lace covered my nether parts. The thong was soaked through already.

"On your hands and knees, love," Ellis commanded, giving my ass a swat. "Watch the players fucking like rabbits while I make you come on my tongue."

A whimper escaped my lips at his words, and I followed his commands instantly. His hands were all over my body, massaging my thighs, my shoulders; he was everywhere at once. The girl on the screen moaned when the first man began fucking her from below. Ellis teased my nipples in time with the man on the screen doing the same to her. We moaned in unison.

"How wet are you, Nora?" Ellis murmured. "I think it's time to find out."

He didn't wait for a response this time, ripping my thong down my legs and spreading my ass to give himself full access. The lights in the room were dim, but not so much that he couldn't see every inch of me.

"Fucking soaked," Ellis groaned. "And so fucking beautiful." His finger slid between my legs, teasing my pussy with steady strokes. My hips rocked of their own accord. "That's it, love. See how your body craves my touch already?"

"More, please," I begged, unable to keep the needy sounds from coming out of me.

"Tell me what you need, Nora." Ellis delivered another command, the dominant tone driving me mad with desire. "When you want something from me, you ask for it."

"I want your mouth on my pussy, Ellis. I need it." My body shuddered, angling in his direction as if it had a will of its own.

I could practically feel the smirk in his next words. "That's a good girl." He swatted my ass harder, his fingers tapping against my bare pussy and eliciting another whimper from my lips. Finally, blessedly, his mouth was on me. His tongue licked from my clit to my ass and back.

Ellis moaned loudly. "Fuck, I knew it. I knew the taste of your pretty cunt was going to be my next addiction. Now scream for me, Nora. I want to hear my name on your lips when you come."

He dove in again, teeth nipping at my flesh, tongue and fingers expertly bringing me wave after wave of pleasure. The sounds I was making with his every movement were positively sinful. The girl on the screen began to scream, and I wanted to come with her, follow her into oblivion. Ellis slipped a third finger inside me, his thumb circling my clit and tongue teasing my ass. With his other hand, he twisted my hardened nipples, the pressure too much to bear.

"There you go, love," Ellis praised. "Now say my fucking name."

And I did, I fucking screamed his name when the orgasm surged through my body. My legs shook as his hands continued toying with my flesh, dragging out the pleasure coursing through me.

My arms shook, and he gracefully pulled me into his lap, hugging me close. Ellis gripped my chin and crushed his lips to mine, dominating and devouring all at once. I melted into his kiss, tangling my tongue with his and tasting my arousal.

Ellis pulled away first. "Exquisite."

Nora

It was completely impossible to focus on work when visions of two blissful scenes filled my head. This was shameful, honestly. Two men brought my body to ruin in the last seventy-two hours. Sienna only knew about one of them, and I was still undecided about telling her about the other. When Ellis walked back into the lounge, the bartender said Sienna had left with Mr. Vasiliev. We didn't have time to chat, as she was asleep when I returned and out the door this morning before I could check in with her. The behavior was strange. All day she stayed at her desk, head down and engrossed in her work.

Something definitely happened with our boss, and I was worried it wasn't good. Mr. Vasiliev didn't show up at the office today, and his calendar was updated to out of office for the week. An email pinged in my inbox and pulled me away from the worry I was feeling over my friend. Marge sent me more details on Harold O'Rourke. I scrolled through it absentmindedly, sipping my coffee, and then nearly spat all over the computer screen when a photo appeared. The hot guy from Red Clover stood in the background with a group of men, but he was impossible to miss. There was a caption below listing all the names of the men, one of them being Declan O'Rourke. Harold must have another son, and a tingling feeling in my gut told me it was that guy. Ellis had a brother, and it looked like his brother took after his father in the business of being shady.

This was big. I had to go back to the Red Clover and find him. He could be the connection I needed to discover who was behind the now seven unsolved murders in London. The victims were all men, ages ranging from twenty to forty-five. The trouble the police were having, though, was these men were all affiliated with different gangs, but not just members, they were all known Reapers. Specialized assassins from different gangs were being eliminated. Some kind of turf war was brewing. It made sense to kill the ones who posed the biggest threat. My masked man was without doubt a Reaper, and that meant his life was in danger. The thought sent panic rushing through my veins. Should I warn him?

He was a bad man, a monster, a killer. I should stay out of it, leave him to his fate. He chose that life, after all. And yet, I knew that I couldn't. Decision made, I sent one final email, asking Marge for information on Declan O'Rourke, and packed up my things to run home and change. Blending in at the Red Clover was easy enough, but not so much in office attire. Popping over to Sienna's desk, I tapped her shoulder.

"Hey," I said softly. "I'm following a lead for my story, heading back to the Red Clover. Do you want to come with? We can chat afterwards, maybe with junk food?"

She sighed, her face less than enthusiastic when she swiveled around in her chair. "Not feeling the bar scene tonight. But I'll go, you shouldn't go alone."

I shook my head in protest, giving her arm a reassuring squeeze. "No, you go home and get comfy. I'll meet you there and we can take tomorrow to veg out."

Sienna frowned, clearly torn. "I don't want you going to a sketchy bar alone, Nora."

Mason suddenly appeared at my side, tapping my shoulder in greeting as if we didn't notice his arrival. "I can go with you, Nora. If that helps."

My friend narrowed her eyes at him, immediately suspicious. "And why would you do that?"

He shrugged, keeping his eyes averted. The guy wasn't exactly small, but he gave off such weak vibes. I doubt he'd be much help if I was in danger. And yet, women alone at night were always targeted, even someone weaker like him would still be a deterrent for predators. Strength in numbers, and all that.

With a sigh, I nodded in acceptance of his offer. "Better to go with a guy, I suppose."

Mason grinned a little too eagerly. "I'll go get my things and meet you in the lobby."

Sienna watched him walk away, her frown deepening. "I know he seems harmless, but I am not a fan of this plan." She swirled in her chair and pulled a phone from her drawer, shoving it in my direction. "Take the phone."

When I escaped from my ex, one of the many ways I stayed off the grid was my no phone rule. But Sienna added a second line to her plan for emergencies, which she decided this was. Not wanting her to worry, I shoved the phone in my purse.

"Text when you get there, and when you are heading home," she demanded.

I grabbed her hands and squeezed. "I promise."

We arrived at the Red Clover rather quickly, Mason having driven to work today and offering his car as transport. I decided not to stop by the apartment for a change of clothes, considering it was in the opposite direction. And less time in the car with him was preferred. The ride was mostly silent. His Mini Cooper was impeccably clean and smelled new, almost like it was a rental car. Not really caring, I didn't ask. Mason Avery was from London, his family a long line of police officers. Of course I looked into him the second he came into my orbit. Nothing much came back, other than a few arrests of his troubled cousin. Petty crimes, mostly. Sienna's unease was noted though. I learned to trust my gut, and Sienna's too, which is why I also had pepper spray in my purse, just in case his chill demeanor morphed into something sinister.

Once inside, Mason grabbed us a table in the corner and a couple of draft beers. The place was packed.

"What now?" he asked, sipping his red ale. "Is this some kind of stakeout?"

I shrugged, scanning the crowded bar. "Sort of. Someone I saw here once before might have answers I need for my story."

Mason cocked his head to the side. "Which story, for your column?"

"No." I shook my head. "I'm working on something else. Trying to move away from the entertainment news and into crime journalism."

He raised his brows in surprise. "Wow, that's great, Nora."

I smiled and clinked my glass to his. "Hopefully it works out. Thanks for the assist."

Mason dipped his head. "Anytime. I'll be sure to call on ya when I need a favor."

His words were innocent enough, but that nagging feeling crept up my spine. Shoving it down, I sipped my beer again. The golden liquid cooled my throat, and I could already feel my body relaxing. Normally it took a few drinks to feel this way, but then I couldn't remember if I ate lunch. Probably not. The woozy feeling increased, and I nearly slipped from my chair.

Mason caught my forearm. "You all right?"

No, I was most definitely not alright. This feeling was suddenly all too familiar. More than once after a night out, I'd woke up with very few memories of how the night actually ended. And at least twice I recalled feeling just like I did now. This was not natural.

"I need...help." The words slurred out of my mouth, and fear surged through my veins. The adrenaline attempted to burn the dizzy feeling from my head, but it wasn't enough.

"I've got you," Mason spoke, too close to my face. He wrapped an arm around my waist, holding me close. "Time to go, I think."

Declan

The club had an early meeting tonight, which only meant one thing, drinks at the Red Clover and then a long night of stalking my new obsession, Nora King. I honestly would have preferred going straight to her apartment, but the guys insisted on a beer. We were nearly at the entrance when a man and woman burst through. She hung on his arm, head lolling as if she were drunk. The guys laughed, teasing the man for letting his woman get hammered.

A breeze lifted her hair, and just as I recognized her scent, I saw her face. Rage flooded my system, but I couldn't move. The men ignored the couple, entering the bar and leaving me standing there, staring after them. The shock finally wore off, and I moved swiftly into action, trailing the man with his hands all over my fucking woman. He was a dead man. If he had anything to do with the state she was in, he would be a heavily tortured dead man.

The fucker dragged her to a car and began stuffing her into the passenger seat. As soon as he shut the door, I grabbed him from behind, wrapping my arm around his neck and squeezing. He flailed in my arms but wasn't nearly strong enough to escape my hold.

"How you answer my questions will decide your fate," I snarled, and the piece of shit stopped fighting me. "Was this your idea, or someone else's?"

He didn't respond, so I gave him a swift punch in the side. He gasped, ribs likely bruised. "He'll kill me."

I chuckled menacingly in his ear. "I'm sure he will. But when I get started, you'll be begging for death. Let's go somewhere a little more private." A quick punch to the head, and the fool was knocked out. I stuffed him into his trunk and got into the driver's seat. The car was too fucking small for me, but I'd manage.

Nora was nearly passed out in her seat, mumbling incoherently. I pressed my hand to her cheek. "It's all right, little dove. I've got you."

The drive to my apartment was quick. I rented the space above a tattoo parlor, the owner of the shop being a friend. It was a two-bedroom apartment with a simple eat-in kitchen and living room. The second bedroom was unfurnished, and covered with plastic. This asshole was not the first I needed to torture information out of. And it was just easier to have a little room of horrors in my place than dragging people around the city to one of the club's warehouses. Besides, this one was personal.

I carried Nora up to my bedroom first, doing a quick check of her vitals. She didn't appear to be injured, and I surmised she was likely drugged, not drunk. She wore another tempting pencil skirt and blouse. A part of me was tempted to tie her up and punish her for last night. Nora and Sienna visited Provocateur. A place I avoided at all costs because of him, my older brother, Ellis Bainbridge.

He took Bainbridge when he emancipated himself. It was a family name on our mother's side. I knew very little about the family, considering she died giving birth to me. Ellis knew her for a time, seeing as he was about five years older than me. When he left me behind, our father said it was because of her. Ellis resented me for killing her.

Hal's words never sat right with me, but Ellis never gave me the chance to ask him about it. Until I was fifteen years old, we were inseparable, him and I. We shared a bond akin to twins, always knowing exactly what the other was thinking or feeling. By the time I hit puberty, I was half in love with him. Ellis was broad where I was lean, and his muscles filled out quickly. Even though we both spent hours in the gym, his body changed faster than mine.

I knew it was wrong to want him like that, and did everything I could to bury those forbidden thoughts. It became awkward, seeing him half-dressed. But something inside me wanted him, more than I'd wanted anything, and my soul fucking knew he felt the same way. After months of tormenting myself, I finally acted on it. For several blissful minutes, Ellis and I crossed a line without a single care about what it would mean.

Until Father walked in on us. Ellis left the following day. And my tutelage as Father's most skilled killer truly began. I hated my brother for leaving me behind, and hated him for running away. And I hated myself even more for feeling what I felt for him. I was fucked in the head.

Nora murmured in her sleep, bringing my mind out of the dark spiral into the past. Brushing her hair from her face, I watched her for a few more minutes before returning to my task, torturing her abductor. And possibly spanking Nora's ass raw until she told me why the fuck she was at my brother's club.

Nora

My entire body ached the moment I woke, and my head throbbed as if I'd drunk an entire keg by myself. Keeping my eyes closed, I mentally checked my body for broken bones and bad vibes. I was laid out on a plush bed, and I could feel all my clothes still on and fully intact. Good news so far.

I remembered going to the Red Clover and drinking a beer, waiting for the Declan guy to show up. And then things got very fuzzy. Drugged, I was fucking drugged. Shards of memories filtered through my head. Getting into a car, but there was someone else there. He was there. My masked men. He called me little dove. But it wasn't him, he wasn't wearing a mask.

"Holy shit." I sat up quickly and immediately regretted the movement. Swinging my legs off the bed, I barely registered the room and focused on the door.

If my memory was accurate, the masked man and Declan O'Rourke were one and the same. Which meant I was likely having a nap in a fucking serial killer's house. I needed to get the fuck out of here fast. Tiptoeing as quietly as I could, I slipped out of the room and down a hall, passing a bathroom and another closed door. There were strange sounds, and someone was speaking softly. He was in there, the Reaper. Declan O'Rourke. The masked man who had now given me insane orgasms on two separate occasions. Spotting my purse on a coffee table in the living room area, I snatched it and was nearly to the door when a voice I recognized all too well spoke behind me.

"The door is locked, little dove." He chuckled.

I shifted around slowly, pressing my back to the wood. He strode forward, looking every bit the killer he was. Declan wore black jeans and a white T-shirt with very obvious blood stains on it. His hair was a disheveled, sandy brown mop, strands falling across his hazel eyes. Despite the scary blood splatters on his clothes, my stomach fluttered when he came closer.

"Can't leave until I say so." Declan loomed over me, one hand on the door above my head. "Do you know who I am?"

Nodding slowly, I decided honesty was best here. "I remembered you called me little dove. You're him. The masked man. Declan O'Rourke, a Reaper."

He hummed in response, a smirk on his lips. "Nice to finally hear you say my name. Shall I give you yours?" His words confused me, and I waited for him to continue. "Primrose Eleanora Kingsley."

The blood drained from my face with each syllable he uttered. "How do you know that?" I whispered, fear laced within my words.

Declan stepped back, shoving his hands in my pockets. "I know a lot of things. And when something catches my eye, I make a point to find out every little thing about it."

Trying not to panic, I shoved off the door and pushed my shoulders back in false confidence. "So what? Lots of people use different names. You do the same."

Declan arched a brow at me with a smile. "Did I say it was a problem?"

I huffed in response. He was infuriating. This man gave away even less than I did, and I had become an expert on hiding my emotions. The fact that he was hotter than hellfire didn't help either. My head began to pound, the effects of whatever drug I was given still wearing off. Wincing, I rubbed my temples.

"Are you in pain?" he asked quietly, stepping closer to me.

His presence was a balm, and one long inhale of his woodsy scent relaxed my nerves. "Some. Where is Mason?"

"In there." Declan spat the words out like bad medicine.

"Alive?" I asked, because I honestly wasn't sure, given the blood on his shirt.

Declan shrugged. "For now. I questioned his motives, but thought you might want to do the same."

"You thought right." I squared my shoulders and pushed past the giant tree of a man.

Declan followed closely behind me, my own personal dark cloud. But not the kind of cloud you're sad to see. More like when the thunder rumbles and the air feels electric with the coming storm, and the clouds blot out the sky in a menacingly beautiful way.

My logical brain was prepared to see a man who'd been tortured, but not at all well enough for the scene before me. The room was completely tarped over, the windows blacked out with heavy curtains, and only ugly fluorescent lighting lit up the space. A chest of tools, bloodied but organized, was to my right, and beyond the chest a shell of a man was tied to a chair. Both of his eyes were swollen, one unable to open. Blood dried around the edges of his mouth and nose. His shirt was gone, and cuts of varying depths coated his pale flesh. His shoes were also removed, his feet resting in a bucket of water. I had a million questions for the killer hovering behind me, but right now, I needed answers from Mason.

"Do you know who I am?" I demanded, getting straight to the point.

He twitched in his chair, but remained silent.

Declan sauntered toward the man, tapping his shoulder with some kind of baton. "When she asks a question, you answer immediately." Without warning, he smacked the baton across Mason's back. The man yelped in pain, followed by a whimper.

"Only recently. I have a few connections with private investigators. Your ex is looking for you, and willing to pay." His voice was hoarse, and every word sent a bolt of fear straight through my chest.

My breaths quickened, and black spots blurred my vision. "No. How? It's too soon." I staggered back, shame smothering my brain at how quickly my body reverted to this weakened state.

Declan was at my side in seconds. In one quick motion, he pulled out a gun and shot Mason in the head, killing him instantly. The sound was dulled by a silencer, but it still rocked through me. This was now the second time this man had killed someone in front of me. Did he think I wouldn't go to the police? He was a murderer, and I was a witness to his crimes.

And yet, both times the fear threatening to choke the life out of me had nothing to do with him. Declan scooped me up in his arms, and I let him, too lost in my thoughts to protest.

"Come on, little dove." His tone was gentle. "I've got you."

One moment he was committing murder, and the next he was holding my body gently against his own and speaking quietly as if I were a frightened rabbit on the verge of running. Not entirely an incorrect assumption, either. He carried me back to his living room and lowered himself to the center of the couch, still holding me in his arms. It was incredibly comfortable, and I was grateful for his stability while my mind pieced itself back together.

Was I shocked that Jameson used every connection he had to find me? No, but I had hoped he would just move on. What was so damn special about me? There were plenty of wealthy families with idiot daughters he could marry instead.

"I need to leave," I whispered.

Declan's fingers brushed absently against my arm, and his wolfish eyes gazed into mine intently. "Where would you like to go?"

I sighed. "I don't know yet, but it's not safe for me to stay if someone like Mason found me already. What an asshat he turned out to be. Sienna's creep-o-meter was correct."

"Seems your ex-fiancé is quite desperate to get you back," Declan mused. "That won't be happening. And if you think I'll just let you walk out of here on your own, you're quite mistaken, Nora."

His words were confident and final. But he wasn't my keeper, and I made my own choices now. Attempting, and failing, to extract my body from his hold, I glared at him. "No one will tell me what to do, I make my own decisions. And I will never be a man's prisoner again."

Declan's face remained impassive, which was annoying as hell, but there was no malice behind his eyes. It wasn't the look Jameson had when he wanted something, this was something else. "You will never be anyone's prisoner, including mine. Until I know how many people Mason told about you, however, it's not safe for you on your own."

I rolled my eyes. "I've managed it on my own so far."

He arched a brow at me with a less than amused look on his scruffy face. "If getting drugged and kidnapped by a toad like Mason managing, then sure, you're doing fine."

Smacking his chest, I attempted to look fierce. "Whatever. What time is it, by the way? Sienna has probably already called the cops."

"She knows you're safe." He leaned back, his arms still clasped around my waist to keep me on his lap. "Now, before I get you home, how the fuck do you know Ellis?"

Declan

My dick was struggling to stay uninterested with Nora squirming in my lap, but I also refused to let her go. After interrogating that piece of shit for a couple hours, he was useless. I planned to let her have a go, but when Nora spiraled after hearing her ex was hunting her, he had to die. Well, her ex had to die, but Mason was closer. She seemed generally unphased by the fact that I killed two people in her presence. But the blush creeping up her neck and tinting her cheeks at the mention of my brother had my blood boiling.

I snatched her face when she tried to turn away from me. "Answer the question, Nora."

The little shit rolled her eyes at me again. If it happened a third time, a punishment would be in order. "From my boss, Alec Vasiliev. They're friends. He was at Neverland that night..."

Her words trailed off, the blush blooming in her cheeks once more, and I smirked. "The night you came all over my fingers like a needy slut?"

Nora's eyes widened in shock at my words, but her body belied her feelings. Her thighs clenched, and she attempted to free herself again. Nora was maybe a handful of inches over five feet, and her petite frame was no match for me at six feet six inches tall. Not only did I spend most of my teen years developing an addiction to the gym, but I had a fondness for swimming. My body was near to zero fat, with muscle making up the bulk of my weight. Not quite as broad as my older brother, but I could still kick his ass, probably.

Abandoning her feeble attempts to escape me, she rolled her eyes for a third time. "And what if I said he also had a taste?"

Well, that was it then. Without warning, I stood up, bounding to my room in four long strides with the wiggling brat in my arms. "And what exactly did he taste, little dove? I think I made it pretty clear from our first encounter. You're mine."

Before she could respond, I tossed her onto my bed. She yelped, but again, I moved too quickly for her to escape me. There were restraints tied to the four legs of my bed, and using her momentum against her, I tied her ankles and wrists tightly, so she was starfished lying on her stomach.

"What the fuck are you doing?" Nora shrieked, but her voice sounded more curious than afraid.

My dick liked that a little too much, and I adjusted myself through my jeans. "That was the third eye roll, and the last." I growled the words at her, flicking open my pocket knife. Ever since she walked into the Red Clover, I dreamt of tearing these damnable tight skirts right off, so I did.

"Declan!" She shouted my name as soon as my knife sliced through the fabric, revealing her perfectly round ass. She wore a black lace thong, leaving little to the imagination. Her exclamation became a whimper when my fingers gripped her pussy through the fabric.

"Don't pretend you're not enjoying this, little dove," I purred, my dick leaking in my pants like a damn teenager's. "Your slutty cunt is dripping for me already." Pulling away from her just long enough to grab my leather crop, I tapped her ass with the smooth side. "Three sharp slaps for three eye rolls. Understood?"

She shifted her head to the side and glared at me, but her emerald eyes were filled with lust. Biting her lip, Nora nodded her head.

I shook my own, bringing the edge of the crop under her chin. "No. Use your words, Nora. Ask for your punishment."

Blood rushed to her cheeks, and I was tempted to lean down and lick her face like a starved animal. "Fine. Three slaps because I rolled my eyes three times, please. Asshole."

She muttered the last word under her breath, and I couldn't help the grin on my face. "Name calling? Maybe I should plug you up, too? That should keep you quiet."

Walking over to my dresser, I snatched a silk bag and pulled out a gold metal butt plug with a green jewel. The stone matched her eyes perfectly, almost as if the toy was meant for her. I bought it on a whim a few months ago, but never used it, until now.

Stalking to the edge of the bed, I used my knife to slice through the lace thong and ripped it away. Both times I teased and tasted her, it had been completely dark. Seeing her pretty pussy on display now was enough to drive a good man insane, and I was far from good.

"Fuck, that's the prettiest cunt I've ever seen," I praised, and she tried to clench her legs, but my restraints held them open. Leaning over her, I teased her pussy with the plug, coating it in her juices. She was fucking drenched, and my dick demanded attention. With my other hand, I unbuttoned my jeans, and my dick bobbed, fully hard and desperate for this woman.

Stroking roughly with one hand, I teased her ass with the tip of the plug with the other. "Ever had a man inside this tight hole, Nora?"

She moaned when I shoved the plug in further. "Yes, but I didn't want to."

Her response made me pause, anger dousing the mood instantly. "What?"

"Don't stop," she replied quickly. "Please."

Her needy tone was enough for me to continue, but we would be revisiting that comment later. With a gentle nudge, the plug slipped in her ass, the heart-shaped jewel glinting between her cheeks like the most tempting stolen treasure.

Picking the crop up from the bed, I slid the end of it between her legs, toying with her pussy while I stroked my dick. She moaned into the blankets as I teased her with the crop. "You're a fucking sight, little dove. If you could see how perfectly your ass took my plug, you'd come for me on the spot."

Before she could respond, I ripped the crop away and slapped her left asscheek hard. Nora yelped, a red welt appearing almost instantly. Pre-cum leaked out of the head of my dick, and I knew I wouldn't last long. I smacked her left asscheek a second time. Her hips pushed up, giving me an even better view of her soaked pussy.

"Look at you, Nora," I groaned. "Your body is begging for my attention."

"Please make me come," she whined, wiggling her ass at me. "I need it."

The way she begged for me was impossible to resist. Nora might have been the one tied up, but this fucking woman had me by the balls. I brought the crop down on her ass a third time, the mark turning bright red. Tossing the crop aside, I slid two fingers inside her needy pussy and groaned. "So fucking tight, so fucking wet. Good fucking girl, Nora."

I tugged and twisted my dick faster, feeling the pressure building and knowing I couldn't last much longer. "Come for me, love. Squeeze my fingers like a little slut. That's it."

Her moan grew into a scream as her hips rocked against my hand. Keeping my eyes firmly on the goddess before me, I groaned her name as hot spurts of come jetted from my dick. I aimed for her ass, coating her reddened flesh with my seed.

"Remember who marked you and made you beg for it next time you see my brother." I snarled the words, but even she would be able to hear there was no malice in them.

If anything, there was jealousy. Ellis had been my best friend once. My everything. And for one very brief moment, I was his too.

Nora

For a third time, I invited a killer to not only touch me, but to wring another delicious orgasm from my body. Not even with his dick. Three times now this devil ruined me with only his mouth and fingers. I was almost scared to think what would happen when we finally fucked. And not if, when. Because I could lie about a lot of things, but my growing obsession with this psychopath was not one of those things.

After cleaning up the mess we made, Declan gave me a pair of his sweatpants and a hoodie to wear home. He'd ruined my clothes, and also refused to let me shower, and my ass was still tender and sticky from his punishment. I absently wondered what Ellis would think if I told him. Would he get all growly like Declan? Or would he back off? Ellis Bainbridge seemed like the type to have rules, and maybe if he knew of the things I did with his brother, he'd hate me, or shame me.

No, not shame. He was too good of a man for that. After seeing how thoughtful he was with his club and making people feel safe, he wouldn't shame me. But he might be disappointed, and that I didn't want to see.

The car ride home was relatively quick and mostly silent. Declan had to get rid of the dead body in his apartment, which didn't seem to bother him much. And it didn't bother me much either, which meant I should probably find a therapist immediately. He surprised me when we arrived at my apartment. First, because I didn't give him directions. And second, when he insisted on walking me up.

Sienna's eyes bugged all the way out of her head, seven thousand questions on the tip of her tongue. Declan tugged me against his chest, wrapped a possessive hand around my throat, and ravaged my mouth with his own. No words were spoken. Only that fiery kiss filled the silence. My body melted into liquid fire, and I all but submitted my soul to the monster. He shoved me away, uttering only one menacing sentence before he left. "See you soon, Nora."

With the click of the door, Sienna launched into crazy mode. "What in the absolute fuck was that? That was the guy from Red Clover, wasn't it? How, HOW, did this happen?"

I filled her in on everything, including the first two times I met him and what we got up to in dark corners. She was only mad for about sixty seconds.

"So. He can get into our apartment? Not sure that's a green flag, Nora." Sienna crossed her arms. She was dressed in leggings and a cropped sweatshirt, cozied up on our couch across from me.

I still wore Declan's clothes. They were entirely too big, but they smelled like him, and the scent was oddly relaxing while I told her about Mason and almost being kidnapped.

"I fucking knew he sucked." Sienna leaned in, grabbing my hands while tears pooled in her eyes. "I'm so fucking sorry I didn't go with you. I should've been there."

But I wouldn't hear any of that. I squeezed her hands affectionately. "No. This is not on you, and don't even think about feeling guilty over the actions of a shitty man. We're done with that behavior, remember?"

She sighed, nodding. "I know. I just got so wrapped up in my own feels."

Something clearly happened with our boss. "Did Alec hurt you?"

She laughed, eyes downcast. "No. He just made me want him even more then ran away. It was one of the hottest nights of my life, Nora. Then he freaked, drove me home, and said never again. Now he's back in Russia visiting family for a few weeks. Bullshit."

As much as I liked our boss, that pissed me off. "Sienna, you don't deserve that. As much as I like him, and can see he likes you, don't settle for that kind of behavior. When he's ready to treat you like a queen, make him beg for it."

She smiled, wiping a tear from her bright-blue eyes. "You're right, of course."

I smiled back at her. "I usually am. Since neither of us are working today, let's veg out together. Movies and junk food."

Her smile disappeared, and Sienna pulled away from me. "Okay. Don't be mad. I just needed to know you were okay before telling you."

The shift in her demeanor had my hackles rising. "What are you talking about?"

Sienna grabbed her laptop from the coffee table and opened it slowly, pushing the screen in my direction. "Well, from your story, obviously your ex is hunting you. But he definitely knows you're here. I got an email."

My body started to vibrate with anxiety when his name appeared on the screen, an email sent directly to Sienna.

Hello, Sienna,

I believe you to be a friend of my future wife. I can't seem to get in touch with her directly. Perhaps you can pass along a message? Josephine Beck had an accident at work. Didn't survive, I'm afraid. And Lyra, sweet young thing, is even more delicate. And disposable. You seem of heartier stock. Let Primrose know her friends are in danger, would you?

Jameson

At the end of the email there were two photos. A news article about a freak accident at the hospital with an unstable patient. Dr. Josephine Beck was killed. Tears blurred my vision as I scrolled to the second photo. It was of Lyra. Her face looked terrified as she held up her shirt to reveal a nasty bruise.

I jumped off the couch, but Sienna gripped my wrist hard. "Nora. He wants you to go there. You can't."

"He will kill her! He had Josie killed," I shouted the words at her. "I will not let anyone else die because of me.

Sienna refused to let go of my arm. "What did you just tell me? We don't bow to bad behavior. To bad men. Think, Nora. Because if you go there, I'm going with you."

"Absolutely not," I snapped. Grief tore through me at the murder of one of my only real friends. Grief and rage. We knew there was a chance he would ask her about me. But I suppressed the thought that he would go to such lengths. Which was stupid of me. Jameson was a vile monster. Josie's death was my fault, and nothing Sienna said could convince me otherwise. Especially now that he threatened her and Lyra.

Sienna squeezed my arm. "I was friends with her, too, Nora." Her voice was soft and filled with pain. "And I know that right now, the last thing she would want is for you to go running back to him."

She was right, of course. Josie hated men, and Jameson was at the top of her hit list. But she was gone, and he was still a threat to the people I loved. Of course he knew that would be the only way to get me back. What he didn't know was that I was no longer willing to hide my bruises and pretend to be a happy housewife. He could bully me all he wanted, but if he hurt another person I cared for, his secrets were going public too.

I would return to Chicago. But it wasn't just Sienna I had to sneak out on. Declan was watching me. You'd think that would scare me, but for whatever insane reason, his attention didn't fill me with dread. I relished it. The idea that he was watching me, even when I didn't know it, made my soul light up with desire.

He would never allow me to go back to Jameson alone, not with what he knew, now. A plan formed in my mind, and I had the shortest window of time to accomplish it.

Ellis

Work continued to be a struggle today, and most days since Nora walked into my life. No, not walked. She sauntered in with those shining green eyes, impossible to look away from. I couldn't stop thinking about them, about her laugh, and the moans she made when I had her bent over in my club.

I made certain every camera in that room was shut down before we began. Not a fucking soul was going to see Nora's perfect body besides myself. Which meant I had no video to replay of our time together, only the memory of it, which wasn't enough.

Nora didn't have a phone, which was strange, but considering there was next to nothing on a Nora King, I assumed she was hiding from someone. There were a few men and women in the police force who frequented my club, and it would be easy enough to ask about her, but I refrained. When she trusted me enough, she'd tell me. God knew I was keeping secrets from her.

Instead I messaged her roommate and coworker, Sienna, asking her to give Nora a message. I wanted to take her on a proper date. While I waited for her reply, I scanned the cameras in the club from my laptop. I'd had enough mingling for one night and retreated to my apartment above the club for a bit of quiet. The night of relaxation I had planned came to a screeching halt when Sienna responded to my text.

Sienna

What are you talking about?

Ellis

Sorry?

Sienna

She left here like two hours ago saying she was heading to meet you for lunch.

Confusion rippled through me. I checked the cameras, but Nora was not in the lounge, nor had she reached out to me. After triple-checking every device, I replied as much.

Sienna

Fuck. She's gone back to Chicago.

Ellis

For what? What's going on?

My phone vibrated, and I answered Sienna's call before the first ring finished. "What's happening, Sienna?"

The woman snarled into the phone. "Don't be sassy with me right now. My favorite human is in danger. She's gone back to her ex who will probably kill her, and now she has a two hour head start!"

My unease exploded into fear at Sienna's words. "We'll find her. I know enough people to figure out what flight she's on."

Sienna made a strangled sound. "Ellis, he's not just an abusive ex, he's already killed—"

I cut her off, fear sizzling in my veins. "Tell me exactly what she's walking into, Sienna." My left thigh throbbed, and I resisted the urge to take out my blade.

Sienna spoke in a flurry of words, vomiting them out on a single breath. "She fled from a psychopath, and now he's found her again and one of her friends in Chicago is dead, probably by his hand. She's going back before he hurts anyone else, like her cousin, Lyra. She's a damn martyr, and he's going to kill her."

Fear transformed into rage, and I pinched my thigh, needing the pain to keep my head from exploding. Without thinking, I slipped a razor between my fingers and down my joggers, pressing the sharp edge to my skin. Relief oozed into my veins as soon as I felt the skin split.

Shame clouded my head, Sienna's voice fading away as I succumbed to the dopamine invading my system. It had been seventy-three days since my last relapse. The fresh cuts had healed, and the scars were ignored. Until now.

"Ellis? Are you there? NORA NEEDS HELP!" Sienna shouted into my ear and the haze drifted away the moment she said her name. Nora. Nora was in trouble.

"I'm here, fuck. I'll find her." My voice shook with too much emotion.

Sienna was silent for a moment before continuing in a softer tone. "Um. I don't know if this is weird but...Nora has had a couple run-ins with Declan O'Rourke." She said his name instead of the words "your brother," but it was obvious she knew exactly who Declan was. "I'm quite certain he would assist if you asked."

As if the devil was listening, my phone beeped, an unknown number calling on the other line. "I'll call you as soon as I know more." I hung up before Sienna could respond and clicked over to the other line. "Declan."

"Do you have the jet ready or what?" he snapped, wasting no time with pleasantries. "And don't even try to talk me out of coming with you. I've tasted her, too, brother."

He sneered the final word like a slur, and pitch-black jealousy slithered up my spine. The razor in my hand stabbed into my thigh once more, the pain of it more enticing than acknowledging his words or the hurt hidden behind his own fury.

"Meet me at the airport." I hung up the phone and ripped the razor from my flesh. Blood trickled down my leg, and I cursed at my own weakness. Snatching a cloth and bandage, I wrapped it all up and quickly rushed through my loft to pack a bag. Texting Alec, I made sure the jet was ready to go.

Alec

It's gassed up and ready. What's going on?

Ellis

Nora's in trouble. Sounds like Nora's friends are also getting caught up in whatever this is. Maybe keep an eye on Sienna.

Alec

Done.

Our conversations were generally brief. Alec wasn't much of a sharer. A black car waited out front for me, Merrick having called it while I furiously barked out orders. Hopefully this entire thing wouldn't take more than a day, but I also wouldn't underestimate my opponent. If this man had truly already murdered one of her friends with no repercussions, he may very well be formidable.

I had a private hangar roughly forty minutes outside of London with two planes, a luxury jet and a two-seater plane. Finding things to occupy my time and avoid dangerous thoughts meant a few trades learned, including my pilot's license. But I most definitely was not flying today. My nerves were shot, and with Declan joining me after years of no contact, flying and not crashing would be impossible.

Speaking of the devil, Declan waited calmly in the hangar, two security guards flanking him. As if they would be able to restrain my younger brother. He was a trained killer, likely able to bleed them out before they even had a chance to grab their weapons.

"Sir," the first guard spoke. "This man says he's with you."

My eyes locked with Declan's. His face was a mask of indifference, and only boredom looked back at me. That hurt, but I refused to let him see it. It was my choice to leave, after all.

The memory of the last time we were together surged forward against my will.

Declan's hands brushed over my thighs as he knelt between them. This was so fucking wrong, and yet I didn't have the strength to say no.

"Tell me you don't want this, Ellie, and I'll stop," Dec pleaded. He licked his lips, sandy blond hair in his face. A bead of sweat dripped down his temple, and I reached out to thread my fingers in his hair. I loved him more than anything. More than anyone.

Years only brought us closer together. Father hated it, said we were flirting with danger, with the forbidden.

As much as I wanted to tell him to stop, I couldn't. My silence urged him on, and in seconds, he ripped my shorts down and licked the head of my cock.

My hands tightened in his hair, and I groaned, shoving his head down. He gagged, taking me in to the back of his throat.

The door slammed open, and Father appeared. "What the fuck are you doing to him, Ellis?!"

My throat was dryer than a damn desert, making it impossible to speak, so I only nodded then swiftly left my brother behind to follow me onto the plane. The fresh cuts on my leg throbbed, and it took all of my willpower not to pull the blade out again. I should've left it at home, but I wasn't strong enough to do so. I was weak, always fucking weak.

"Spending a bit of time at the gym, Ellis?" Declan smirked. "You look like a damned gorilla. Steroids?"

I shot a glare at him, and he grinned, but the smile didn't touch his eyes. "Of course not. Jealous, Dec? You look all right. Could never fill out quite like me, though."

"Not everything is about thick thighs and gorilla arms," he retorted. "Father made sure of that."

I didn't respond, but neither of us needed to. Of course I knew what he'd become. Despite my father kicking me out and threatening to send me to prison for assaulting my younger brother, I had ways of keeping tabs on him. Our father was not the good kind. Even before I left, we grew up learning how to lie, cheat, and steal. How to play others' weaknesses against each other. How to read the smallest change in body language. Being stealthy required not only bodily strength, but mental fortitude.

And yet I was too weak to stand up to our father, the biggest cheat of all, and I hurt the one person I loved most. The shame of what I'd done ate me alive until that first slice of my skin brought relief. For years that pain kept my failures locked up in some dark recess of my mind. I started searching for Dec, only to find out what our father forced him to become. A cold-blooded killer.

Declan

Being alone with Ellis was not on my bucket list this year. Well, that wasn't entirely true. He still featured heavily in my dreams. I knew now how wrong it was, what we did when we were teenagers, but my secret desires were impossible to avoid in my dreams. Seeing him now, dark sweatpants and fitted shirt tight enough to count his abs, well, this was going to be difficult.

Did he still remember that night? It was the best and worst of my life. The way he moaned for me, the way he tasted. Until Father came and kicked him out. He whipped me that night. The lashes left scars on my back. A reminder of what we'd done. I thought I was the only one to receive Father's wrath, for years, until my computer skills improved enough for me to hack into any system. I found Ellis easily enough. And the payments he made regularly to our father.

I assumed he did those under duress, likely being blackmailed or threatened with jail time for assaulting his younger brother. But I never thought of it that way. I had initiated it. It was my fault. Unfortunately our father could sense my weakness, and after a few hundred days of physical and mental torture, most feelings that normal people had were gone. And all that was left was a killer.

Until she showed up. Nora would be chained to my bed for weeks when we got her back for pulling a stunt like this. I tracked her to Provocateur, assuming she was meeting Ellis. In the short window of time I wasn't stalking his security cameras, she must have slipped out.

"Merrick saw her, you know," I mused aloud. "She did go to your club. Said something to him and left."

Ellis frowned. "What are you on about? She didn't come see me. And how the fuck would you know that?"

"Your firewalls suck, big brother. Hacked into your cameras ages ago." I smirked. "Wonder why he didn't tell you she popped by."

Ellis frowned. "Merrick has been a loyal manager for years. So whatever you're implying..." He trailed off.

Holding up my hands in surrender, I shrugged. "Whatever you say."

"How did you meet Nora?" he asked, almost as if he couldn't hold the question in any longer, navy eyes boring a hole into my forehead since he refused to make eye contact.

I leaned back in my leather seat, spreading my legs wide. "She came to the Red Clover looking for a story. Gang violence, unsolved murders, all the secrets of the underworld. Tenacious little thing."

Ellis huffed in annoyance, his eyes flicking to my crotch and away again. "I'll be having a word with Alec. When he sent me to Neverland to look after two employees, he left out that part."

A humorless laugh escaped my lips. "Likely for Sienna's sake. He's more of a stalker than I am."

Ellis sighed, rubbing his inner thigh. "Did you look into this ex of hers?"

A pit of fury opened up in my stomach at the mention of him. "Jameson Moore. Family of corrupt politicians. Her own family is much the same, and the marriage was likely securing allies from across party lines. He's a prick, that one. Plenty of coverups for his cruel behavior towards women from a young age."

Ellis's fist curled with anger, the other moving to his thigh again and shaking as if he couldn't help it. "I'll fucking kill him."

In this, at least, my estranged brother and I were in agreement. "Not if I get there first."

Nora

The flight to Chicago went by relatively quickly. I'd downloaded ten books, a few fantasies, a bit of smut, a handful of thrillers, and my very first why choose romance. Sienna also enjoyed reading romance, preferring more wild tales of sentient doors and something called omegaverse. I wasn't quite as inundated as she was in the world of fantasy smut. You'd think my anxiety would be too much to manage reading, but falling into a world entirely separate from my own was as relaxing as a spa day for me.

The current book followed a badass female getting her revenge on. Like, hardcore stabbing every bad guy who stepped in her path. I never read blurbs, just went off vibes. And her blue hair and dagger caught my eye. Reading her story was boosting my own confidence to handle mine. The terrible things these Kings did to her was unlike anything I'd experienced, and still she stood tall and fought back. And so would I.

Could I take a life? That wasn't a question I'd ever asked myself. And until recently, I'd only seen murder in movies, or at crime scenes after the fact. Declan seemed unphased, almost passive, when he pulled the gun and shot Mason. Did the lives he ended haunt him? He seemed haunted by something, but that wasn't a secret I'd uncovered yet.

Just before I boarded my flight, I used a public computer café to see if anything important landed in my work email inbox. There was a shrieking–because I could feel her screams through the screen–email from Sienna. She wouldn't forgive me for this, but who even knew if I'd be returning. There was a second email from Marge. Ignoring Sienna's, I pulled up the thread.

Hi dear. Found some interesting documents regarding O'Rourke. Not sure what they'll mean to you, but here you are. Come by for tea soon.
Marge

I'd only opened one attachment to see a birth certificate, but the names weren't ones I knew. Further investigation would be needed, so I filed it away for now.

There was an email from my boss. This one I opened nervously. My first shot at a headline article about the recent gang violence, and if he hated it, I might just throw myself out of the plane.

Miss King,
Exceptional job. This is great work. Welcome to the world of true crime journalism. We'll run this next print.
Alec

Pride warmed my limbs, and for a moment, everything fell away. I'd done it. My first crime news story. This might roll some heads, but Londoners deserved to know what criminals ruled their city. As I was signing out with renewed faith in my plan, a news article caught my eye and I gasped at the subtext beneath the headline. Low level journalist, Mason Avery, leaps from building in apparent suicide.

How on earth Declan had managed that setup was escaping me at the moment. I pushed it from my mind and didn't dwell on the fact that I wasn't even sad he was dead. Instead, I cozied up for seven hours of quiet time and managed to read two books of this series, cheering on the assassin, Seraphina Valdis, in her quest for vengeance. And also finding out just how much dick this girl can handle. Five princes at once was wild. But two? Maybe that was something I could get on board with.

A car waited for me at the airport with a driver I recognized who worked for my parents, but right now, I trusted no one. Ducking in the opposite direction, I snagged a cab and headed for my parents' house, periodically checking to see if we were being followed. Not that it mattered. My parents, like Jameson, would likely know I was back in town the moment I got off the plane. They loved him. My mother was a social climber, and my stepfather was a creep. They hated each other, and the marriage was one of convenience. Like my own engagement to Jameson, there was no marrying for love, only money and power.

I didn't remember my biological father all that much, considering I was so young when he died, but in the few memories I did have, he seemed to really care about me. He was too kind for this world and died too soon. My mother said he had a heart attack while driving, died in the accident. His death was the first informal investigation I ever began, and the one that convinced me the world I grew up in was full of liars.

Because my mother was fully engrossed in the life, I knew she would never tell me what really happened, so I quietly looked into the accident. When I got my hands on the autopsy report, it was obvious he was murdered. He had ligature marks on his neck, but the most horrifying detail was that his tongue was ripped out. Someone didn't want my father spilling secrets.

It was impossible to find someone who would look into his death when everyone in this damn city was corrupt. Not bringing justice to my father would be one of my biggest failures.

As soon as my cab pulled into the gated drive, the guard recognized me and let us through. My mother stepped out on the front porch, arms at her sides, showing very little emotion. Her golden hair was styled into a sophisticated coiffe, and she wore a fitted burgundy dress that cinched her waist and showed off her surgically perfected body. Almost every inch of her was plastic. The only natural part of her was the color of her hair. Sure, she had highlights, but the golden-blonde locks were all hers, and mine. My eyes, though, came from my father. She never looked me directly in the eyes, not since his death, and I wondered if that was out of guilt or heartache. Probably guilt.

"Welcome home, Primrose." Cecilia Kingsley Roosevelt smiled serenely, opening her arms in greeting.

As if that woman knew what a proper hug was. I ignored her, stepping around her and stomping into the house, but alas, she followed.

"Cecilia," I snapped, whirling on her. "Let's not pretend you care that I'm back for any reason other than to secure another political alliance."

Abandoning my father's case even after I told her about my findings was the first nail in the coffin that held our mother-daughter relationship. The second, and final, nail was her reaction the first time I showed her a bruise on my stomach, courtesy of Jameson.

"Oh, honey." Cecilia spoke softly, patting my cheek. "Bruises heal. Broken alliances don't. Keep those marks to yourself, understand?"

My mother followed me into the house, unruffled by my comment. You didn't get as far as she had in life surrounded by sharks if a single comment broke your facade. I supposed that was a lesson I did take to heart. But unlike her, I still had one of those. Whirling around on her, I narrowed my eyes and snarled. "Where is Lyra?"

The question did make her eyes dart away, and that tiny reaction pleased my ego. But then her mask returned and she smiled, brushing an invisible spec of dirt from the fabric of her dress. "She's at the venue managing the decor team. I'm assuming you will be attending this evening? It would be so good for everyone to see you."

She meant it would be so good for her image. "Did you even care that I left? Did you even look for me?" Why I was asking when I already knew the answers irritated me. Even now, some tiny piece of the little girl I once was, craved a mother's affection.

Cecilia patted my shoulder. "I knew you'd return. You're not the kind to abandon family."

She wheeled away from me then, fleeing the room gracefully before I could process her response.

Abandon family. Did she mean herself? Certainly we both knew our relationship was anything but loving. The words sunk into my flesh, and my stomach churned. She meant Lyra. My mother, I was convinced, gave Jameson the idea to use Lyra.

I never had a sister. Any hope I had when I was young of becoming an older sister was smashed after my mother had a procedure to prevent pregnancy. The only reason I knew about it was my nosiness. One night I found her on the patio. Several valiums and rum drinks later, she confessed how much she hated children, shouting into the night sky, then laughed about the means she took to prevent any future accidents.

My stepfather made her pay for that. He wanted a son. She let him have a mistress. My younger brother's name was Felix Theodore Roosevelt. We never became close. His life was curated from day one, and his dictator father would never let me, a dirty defector, around the future president.

They couldn't keep me away entirely, though. I sent Felix letters for a while. He never wrote back, but when I could, I would sneak information to him about me, about the world, and just hoped that one day he would be able to think for himself.

Felix was rarely in the public eye without his father. And he wore his mask of charming indifference even better than my mother. Sometimes I thought there was something more, some tiny bit of defiance in his bright-blue eyes, but that was likely just my wishful thinking.

He was doomed to follow the path of the corrupt. And maybe it was too late to save him, but I would burn this family to the ground before I gave up on Lyra.

Nora

When I finally made it to my old room to shower and find a dress for the charity ball, I was greeted by two large gift boxes on my bed. The first was white with a red ribbon, and had a card from Jameson.

Looking forward to our reunion. Your gilded cage awaits.

He didn't sign it, but there was no need. The dress was ivory, a nod to our pending nuptials. And it was hideous. The flowing skirt and terrible sleeves were not my style at all. It was a designer dress, and just the type of thing our families would approve of. The type of dress a dutiful wife of a powerful man would wear.

Shoving the dress aside, I moved to the other side of the bed to the next one. The box was navy blue with a gold ribbon. A gasp slipped from between my lips when I pulled the velvet gown from the box. The dress was a deep emerald green, with a sweetheart neckline and fitted bodice. The floor-length fabric split at the center, nearly to my damn coochie.

Gold silk gloves and a sparkling hair pin were also tucked inside the box, along with a card.

Did you think you could escape us so easily, little dove?
Meet you on the dance floor.

This card wasn't signed either, but there was only one man who called me by that nickname. And two men who could make my heart race and my thighs clench. He said "us" in the note. Were they together? That was odd. From everything I discovered, the two were estranged. Did they realize I'd spent time with both? Would they make me choose?

A thousand questions rushed through my mind, but there was only one way to get the answers. Without a second glance, I tossed the ivory dress to the floor and laid out the other. I had about an hour to get ready, and with the knowledge that Ellis and Declan might actually be in attendance added a bit of pep to my step.

My mother left for the event without me, but I didn't mind. Having the car to myself was preferable over faking interest in anything she had to say. The Field Museum hosted all kinds of events and was a favorite for charity galas. What they were pretending to raise money for this time, I wasn't quite sure. There were only a handful of charities ethically run by politicians, and the others were all facades. Rich people pretending to care about poor people, the environment, and education. The best way for the rich to stay rich was to stomp their fancy shoes on the lower classes and make them think it's the only way to live.

I grew up in a wealthy family and was privileged to have many things that most had to beg for. That didn't last long. When my mother found out I was giving away thousands of dollars from my trust to non-profit organizations, she cut me off, threatened to put me in a conservatorship. And then Jameson showed up. He was incredibly good at sympathizing. Fooled me, even though I saw through most people like him. Letting him put his hands on me would forever be my biggest regret.

The car pulled up to the red carpet, and attendants rushed to assist. I found a black cape coat in my closet to wear over the dress. Nearly winter, Chicago was already cold as hell. The wind bit at my face, but I relished the feeling. I loathed being hot, and winter was my favorite season.

Just when I was feeling relaxed and prepared for this unhappy reunion, the doors opened and a ball of fury in the form of my cousin nearly tackled me to the ground. Lyra threw her arms around me, and I hugged her back instantly.

"You shouldn't be here." She choked out the words. "Come on."

Before I could speak, Lyra tugged me into a room to the left, away from the main event. The museum had several areas blocked off for closed exhibits, and Lyra pulled me past the no entry sign of one of those rooms. The lights were dim, but I could still see the sallow look of her face, her too-thin arms, and the cloud of pain in her pretty eyes.

Tears threatened to spill from my own, but she grabbed my hands and squeezed, shaking her head. "Do not for one fucking second blame yourself. This is that asshole's fault. You shouldn't have come, but I knew you would."

"I'm so sorry he dragged you into this because of me." I choked back the tears. "How did this even happen?"

She rolled her eyes, some of the feisty girl I loved still in there. "He basically kidnapped me. Threatened my family, not my mother, because he knows she's a witch just like yours. But my papa, I'd die for him."

Rage simmered in my veins, but not shock. Jameson would go to any lengths to get what he wants. "I'm going to destroy him. I swear. He sent me a photo of you."

She sighed. "I figured. Fucking dick. He really doesn't hurt me much, unless I act up. And well, you know how big of a brat I am."

I cupped her face with my hands. "Please be careful. He...I think he killed my friend. Dr. Beck."

Her eyes widened. "I heard about her. He did that?"

I nodded, unable to speak further about her. "I'm going to put an end to it. Once and for all. Even if I have to marry him first."

Lyra made a disgusted face. "Absolutely not. I'll go out there and shoot him right in the head before I let you do that."

"As appealing as that sounds, I don't want you going to prison for life either." I smiled, taking her in. She wore a purple gown with a deep neckline, showing off her perky cleavage and adorable freckles. Lyra's fair skin glowed in the soft light. Her hair was pulled into a low bun, with wisps falling gently around her face. She wore silver earrings and a smattering of glittering rings. Kissing her hand, I pulled her back to the main room and let an attendant take my coat. "Let's do this together."

She nodded, standing tall in her heels. Lyra was long-legged and thin, always having a few inches on me, even when I wore heels. She was only three years younger and felt more like family to me than anyone else.

"You look hot as hell, by the way." She glanced down at my dress. "Who on earth picked this out?"

"I think he's a serial killer, actually." I giggled. "Luckily he seems to like me."

Lyra grinned. "I'll say."

I kept her close as we made our way to the bar and sipped on champagne, blessedly ignored, but still garnering a few curious glances. I was about to say as much, when he sliced through the tiny bit of happiness I'd felt at being reunited with the cousin.

"Well, I don't believe that's the dress I left for you, Primrose." Jameson's voice was low, and his grip on my bicep was bruising. "You know how I hate when you disappoint me."

113

Declan

"I really don't see why I couldn't wear my own fucking leather jacket," I grumbled, readjusting the suit coat and unbuttoning my shirt. Ellis arched a brow, staring pointedly at the offending button. "Don't fucking look at me like that. I wore the damn three-piece suit, but fuck your ties and strangling shirts.

Despite pretending he hated me and ignoring me for most of the time on the plane, Ellis had tailored suits waiting for us at our hotel. My brother was not only wealthy, but well-connected. He looked every bit the aristocrat in his charcoal bespoke suit, designer shoes, and watch. In fact, he looked hot as fuck, but after his unease every time I made some kind of crass comment, I refrained.

Ellis was hiding demons, and not very well. He presented himself as well-mannered, confident, and an equal in most aristocratic rooms, but I knew differently. He held positions on multiple boards and supported many charitable organizations, but Provocateur was his baby, his true love. My big brother spent most of his time there, pretending it wasn't his favorite place to be.

He never participated, though. Of course I hacked his security cameras, but even when I watched for hours, he never entered a play room. Until Nora. And the cameras in that room were beyond hacking, even with my skills. Which meant Ellis and Nora would be telling me about every little thing they did. Perhaps even act it out, although I had a feeling Ellis would refuse.

"Please remember everyone at this event will be a rich asshole, and if we don't want to be kicked out immediately, you need to refrain from calling them rich assholes," Ellis berated me, adjusting his emerald-green tie. Which I knew he ordered after I showed him the dress I had delivered to Nora.

Based on everything we knew about her prick of an ex, he likely had some ghastly dress for her, and that wouldn't do. If she showed up in anything but the one we chose, I'd cut it off of her. Maybe that was insane. But this woman burrowed into my veins like the sweetest drug, and my addiction was everlasting.

"I'll be on my best behavior, boss," I purred, winking at him. Ellis frowned and fidgeted, and it pleased me to get under his skin. If anything, he deserved it. He was my first friend, my first crush, my whole fucking world. And then he left.

I knew what we did was wrong on every level, but I could never bring myself to feel bad about it, as much as our father tried to make me think otherwise. He painted Ellis as a predator, a pathetic, weak boy, selfishly taking my innocence.

In the beginning, it was difficult to keep my father's words out of my head, and I hated Ellis for years. Only after our father turned on me, used me, did I realize he was the true predator. And I would never be sorry for how Ellis made me feel, even if it was ten shades of fucked.

My slightly shorter, muscular big brother sighed. "No, you won't, but try. For Nora."

I rolled my eyes. He was an ass for using her. "Fuck off, Ellis."

He grinned, and that smile made my legs feel weak. I wanted to see him naked.

The event was as pretentious as I expected it to be, with several hundred guests, all wearing their finest clothes and droning on and on about their wealthy little lives. We circled the space, keeping an eye out for Nora or that prick, Jameson Moore. Luckily for us, we didn't have to wait long. Ellis was closer, quickly reaching them near the main bar across the room. The dead man had a grip on Nora's arm, and I could tell by the way she winced it wasn't pleasant. The girl next to her must have been her cousin. She was about to speak when Ellis came up beside Moore and began a conversation, mostly likely about money, the way the asshole's face lit up. The fake charm oozed out of him. Ellis, with his cleverness, ignored Nora completely and began walking away from her, Moore's attention fully distracted.

While she was staring wide-eyed after them, I snuck up behind her. "You look ravishing, love."

Nora nearly jumped out of her skin, her green eyes widening even further. "Holy hells, you scared me."

"Who the fuck are these guys?" Her cousin peered up at Ellis and me, unafraid.

I noticed the shadow of bruises around her neck and instantly liked her for how fierce she was, despite very recently being assaulted, most likely by Moore. "We're her villains. Come to take her away."

Nora shoved my shoulder and smirked. "Lyra, Declan. Declan, Lyra."

Lyra's eyes widened. "This one must be the serial killer."

My own eyebrows shot into my hairline. "Couldn't be me. I'm a pacifist. Have you been telling tales, Nora?" She laughed, and it made my dick half-hard just to hear that sound. "Come, dance with me."

She placed her hand in mine, and a ridiculously giddy feeling swept through me when she did. Nora was easily the most stunning woman in the room, a goddess with her crown of golden hair and a dress that fit her curves to perfection.

"How did you get here? How did you know I was here?" she demanded as soon as we began dancing.

Nora followed my lead across the floor, and I pulled her in close, my lips brushing against her ear when I leaned down. "You're not the only one with a mind for solving problems. And you know how good I am with my fingers. A few keystrokes later, and here we are."

Her cheeks flushed at my comment. "Well, I don't know what you hoped to accomplish, but I came here to save my cousin. She is the only person left in this city that I care about, and he's not going to take her from me."

Her words were clipped and fearful, which immediately pissed me off. No one, especially not a dick like that guy, was allowed to make her feel so afraid. "I'll just kill him. Problems solved."

Nora rolled her eyes, and I itched to smack her ass. "That was Lyra's plan too."

I chuckled, squeezing her lower backside. "I like her."

She narrowed her eyes at me while simultaneously stomping on my foot with her heel. "Yes, well I love her. She is basically my sister. And you're not allowed to like her like her."

The grin on my face was nefarious as fuck. "Are you feeling jealous, little dove?" Twirling her out of my arms and back in, and the feel of her body flush against mine brought my dick fully into the conversation.

She blushed, her pale cheeks turning a tempting shade of pink. "No. Maybe. I'm feeling...territorial."

I smirked down at her, my golden goddess. "The feeling is mutual, love."

A heavy arm landed on my shoulder, jarring me. "May I cut in?" Jameson Moore sneered the words, attempting to stay calm and sounding anything but. "Do you know my wife?"

Nora was ready to snap at him, but I stepped in front of her. The asshole was tall, roughly the same height as Ellis, and therefore shorter than me by a couple inches. Looking down my nose at him was truly a pleasure. His soft brown hair was styled and dull, and he looked like every other vanilla fuck in this place.

"Your wife?" I feigned ignorance. "No, can't say I have had the pleasure. Nora, though, I know quite intimately."

Jameson's face fell a fraction, and that almost got me as hard as hearing Nora moan my name. The man reached out as if he were going to grip my suit, and I snatched his wrist just before he could.

"That would be a terrible idea, you pompous ass. I have no problem killing you right here in front of all these fancy people."

The idiot's face was turning red with fury. He ripped his arm from my grasp and adjusted his dull brown tie before speaking calmly. "Primrose, where in the world did you meet this eurotrash?"

"Primrose is gone, Jameson," Nora spoke, her voice calm and confident. "If you thought murdering Josephine would bring me to heel, you're wrong. Stay away from me. Stay the hell away from Lyra. It's over."

I was so fucking proud of her in that moment. She was a fierce lioness, and I was seconds away from fucking her on this dance floor, just so everyone could see this beautiful creature belonged to me.

"Lovely chatting with you, Moore." Ellis clapped the asshole hard on the back. "I'll be certain to mention your name in a few royal circles. I believe it's important for the true wealth to know who they're dealing with." Ellis held out his arm to Lyra. "Miss, can I escort you out?"

My brother, the graceful fuck, ruined anything Moore might do next with a few strategic moves. It was hot as hell. Wrapping an arm around Nora's waist, I stepped around her ex, pausing to leave him with one final word. "Come near her again, I'll fucking kill you."

Ellis

Nora and her cousin Lyra were snuggled next to each other on a loveseat across from Declan and me. We took the captain seats on the opposite side, and I was only slightly jealous of Lyra's position next to my girl. She was mine. From our first meeting, I wanted her. From my first taste of her delicious cunt, I needed her. And when I watched that fucker put his hands on her, I knew then she was mine, and I would do anything to protect her.

There were only a few problems with this plan, the glaring one being my brother. Declan seemed just as wrapped up in her aura as I was. Would this come to a fight? He was stubborn when we were kids, and that likely hadn't changed in the last decade.

Declan opened a gift bag near his feet and pulled out a box, sliding it across the small table to Nora. "Your new phone."

She stared at it with a frown. "I stopped using phones so Jameson couldn't find me."

Declan nodded. "We know. But he's not coming for you again. You don't need to worry about him."

Nora picked at her nude-colored nails, fidgeting.

Lyra covered Nora's hands with her own. "I agree, Nora." She put an exaggerated emphasis on the name. "P.S. It's weird calling you that."

Our girl smiled shyly. "I always hated Primrose, you know that."

Lyra huffed. "Duh. It's just new. But it suits you. Grandmother would approve, too, I think."

I sat back in my chair, watching their exchange and envying the obvious bond between the two women. Glancing over at Declan, our eyes met briefly, and he looked away first. Once upon a time we had that too.

Nora sighed. "I wish she was here. She's the only family I liked. Besides you." She squeezed her cousin's hand and shifted her gaze to Declan and me. "Grandmother Eleanora Kingsley. She was British, actually, and my father's mother. Which is probably why I liked her. She was my only connection to him after he died."

"What happened to him?" Declan asked before I could.

Her eyes held back tears. "Car accident. Supposedly had a heart attack and crashed, but I think it was covered up."

"Was it investigated?" I leaned forward, wanting to hold her, comfort her.

Nora shook her head. "No. My mother had moved on before the funeral ended. Got a new husband with better connections."

I frowned, hating that. Nora's childhood sounded lonely. "It's never too late to investigate a murder, if that's what you think it is. And I'll help, in any way I can."

Declan pulled a second box out of the bag at his feet, this one a new laptop. "A computer for you, to work from home and not random internet cafés. This is the twenty-first century. And while your very dated knowledge of staying off the grid is adorable, it's time to upgrade."

Nora tossed a throw pillow at Declan 's head, and he didn't even try to block it, unphased.

"Feeling feisty? I can help you work that out. Don't think I won't take you over my knee right here in front of everyone."

Nora's face turned the prettiest shade of pink, and my dick throbbed at his declaration.

Lyra barked out a laugh, breaking the sexual tension. "Well, as hot as that sounds, I really don't want to see it. So save the spankings for later. Can I get a phone, too?"

Declan pulled out a third box with another new phone, apparently having thought of everything without including me in the plans. "Both phones and the laptop are programmed with phone numbers you might need, and the laptop has more security than the FBI."

Lyra arched a brow at him, crossing her arms. "So are you like some kind of computer nerd? Is this what computer nerds look like in England, because, sign me the fuck up."

Nora nearly choked on the sip of wine she was in the process of drinking, the most adorable giggle bubbling out of her. "Computer nerd, mafia assassin. A man of many talents."

Declan smirked, a wicked thing and completely filled with lust. "Would you like to share with the class my other talents, little dove?"

Fuck. That was a sexy as hell pet name. I didn't even have a pet name for her. Was their connection deeper than ours? A voice locked away in the back of my head berated and teased me. Because it wasn't just her. I was jealous of them both. That fucked up part of me still wanted him too.

The plane suddenly felt too small, and my hand involuntarily moved to my thigh, pressing down on the wound still healing.

A shadow dropped over me, and I gazed up into Nora's emerald eyes. "Hey." Her voice was soft, and she curled up in my lap, wrapping her arm around the back of my neck and teasing the hairs at the nape. "Thank you, for coming for me."

My thigh forgotten, I wrapped my arms around her, swiping my thumb over her lips. "I will always come for you." She smiled, nodding, and I gripped her chin before she could speak. "But next time you feel the urge to run off into danger, foxy, call me first."

"Foxy, huh?" she teased, her eyes sparkling playfully. "I like that."

Declan chuckled. "Cute, you've got a pet name for her now."

Relief eased through my body. The word just came out, and it was too late to take it back. Declan's ribbing barely registered. It didn't matter what he thought, as long as the goddess in my arms was happy with it, I would be too. Tugging Nora's face to mine, I kissed her softly. "I mean it, Nora. You've got two rabid bloodhounds with your scent, and we won't give it up."

"That includes visits to the Red Clover," Declan added.

Nora huffed in irritation. "I will not give up my career because of one incident."

"What's the Red Clover?" Lyra cut in, narrowing her eyes on Nora. "And what incident?"

Declan responded first. "Oh, just a dangerous bar filled with bad men planning to do bad things. Nora nearly got herself kidnapped. Luckily he was an idiot."

Lyra pinched the bridge of her nose, as if she was more disturbed by this news than anyone else. "Thank fuck I'm here now. How did you even survive so long without me?"

Nora

The work week was particularly tedious, and finally over. Tonight, Sienna and I were taking Lyra out on the town. She was settling into life in London with finesse. Even though she grew up with wealth just like I did, Lyra didn't mention not having any now. Her parents cut her off, which we both expected. They tried to play nice at first, but as soon as Lyra threatened to go to the police about Jameson, beautiful silence. My inner crime junkie thought there was maybe more for them to hide. Knowing what I did about my own parents, and the secrets Jameson kept, hers were likely just as corrupt. I vowed to look into them on her behalf once my current story was complete.

Lyra appeared from the hallway, hair wrapped up in a towel and sporting a fuzzy white robe. "How's work going?"

I decided to work from home today, with the weather being particularly wet. Autumn in London was the wet season, and while I enjoyed the rainy days, staying cozy on my couch was more appealing than the office. Besides, Sienna wasn't at the office today either, interviewing some celebrity for her column.

Our boss didn't seem the least bit worried about the missing employee turning up dead either. Being that he was friends with Ellis, and Declan was the one who disposed of the creep, Alec Vasiliev likely knew exactly what happened. He'd been particularly curt to everyone in the days after, except for me.

"Work is going," I huffed. "People keep turning up dead, and even with all the attention I'm bringing to the seedy people committing the crimes, it hasn't lessened. Arrests have been made, but nothing sticks."

Lyra pretended to stroke her imaginary beard in consternation. "You need to find the ringleader. Arrest the big bad, and everything falls apart."

She wasn't wrong. But with Declan and his stalker moves, the chance of me hitting up another meeting for insider information was low. An idea weaseled its way into my mind.

"All right, spit it out." Lyra nudged me with her elbow. "You've got that sly grin on your face."

Keys rattled in the door before I could respond, and Sienna walked in. Her clothes were soaked, and she wore her jacket over her head like a veil, shielding her hair. "I need wine, immediately. It's been a day."

Lyra hopped up and went to the kitchen, pulling a bottle of pinot grigio from the fridge and pouring three glasses, then promptly returned to pass them out. "Nora has an idea that will likely get her in big trouble with her scary hot boyfriends."

I nearly choked on my wine. "They're not my boyfriends."

Sienna snorted a laugh into her own glass. "You're right. Boyfriend isn't a strong enough word. Stalker soulmates, maybe?"

Pretending to ignore her comment, I sipped my wine. "So, there's another pub I need to visit, not far from Neverland. How about we use that fancy VIP access of Alec's to go dancing."

"And?" Lyra teased with a grin.

"And that will give us a cover, so if some 'stalker soulmates' are looking into my whereabouts, that's where they will look."

"What happens when your boyfriends show up and find us, but not you?" Sienna rolled her eyes, but smiled, clearly accepting my plan.

I finished my wine and snapped my laptop shut. "They won't. I'll be super quick."

"Lies, lies, and more lies," Sienna sighed as she walked down the hall toward her room. "Give me an hour and I'll be ready."

Tonight I opted for a fitted leather skirt, thigh-high boots, and a silky camisole top, all hidden beneath a long raincoat like a creep. Everyone in the city matched, though, with the continuous rain. Sienna whined about how annoying it was to manage her hair if it got wet and used the world's largest umbrella to stay dry. Our plan was simple, and hopefully Declan wasn't stalking me too closely tonight. Sienna went into Neverland to be seen at our table, ordering three drinks. And if anyone happened to ask, Lyra and I would be right back from the bathroom.

I wanted to go alone to snoop, but Lyra refused. After everything that happened, I understood. Letting her go alone to a known gang hangout wouldn't have been an option if our positions were reversed. We rounded the corner, and I instantly pulled Lyra back before the two men exiting the pub could see us.

"What is it?" she whispered, trying to peer around the corner.

"One of those men is Harold O'Rourke," I whisper-shouted back. "Declan's father and the leader of the 3M Crew. Why would he be here?"

"Oh, dear," Lyra gasped dramatically. "Are the Sharks and the Jets about to rumble?"

Her *West Side Story* quip was not lost on me, and I remembered she was a theater kid. Peeking around the corner, I watched Harold go into another door, just off the main entrance of the pub. The beast of a man he was with stayed outside, blocking the door.

Turning back to Lyra, I pleaded with my eyes. "Can you channel your inner Maria and go flirt with that big-ass bodyguard so I can sneak in there?"

Lyra's painted pink lips turned up into a smirk, and her voice shifted to the character's. "I feel pretty, oh so pretty!" She sang out the words, and I slapped my hand over her mouth.

"This is a terrible plan, I take it back." I sighed.

She pulled my hand away and laughed. "I got this. Just be careful in there. Five minutes tops before he gets suspicious."

Before I could respond, she was gone, sashaying her way over to the burly man by the door without her umbrella coat. Lyra stumbled right as she got to the curb, and the man, moving quicker than I expected for someone built like a damn bear, caught her before she hit the ground.

"Oh, thank you." I could hear the tremble in her voice even from here. "I think I'm lost. My boyfriend kicked me out of his car. And I just, I need, oh, I'm sorry to bother you."

The man stared at her, frowning for a full minute before speaking. And as soon as he did, I knew he was a goner. "Sounds like you dodged an asshole, miss. Let's get you inside to warm up and I'll call you a car."

He practically carried her to the main entrance of the pub. He was easily twice her size, and his hands looked big enough to crush a man's skull. But I heard the lilt in his voice. The beast was happy to play the rescuer. Lyra was a beauty by any standard, and I figured I had more than five minutes now.

As soon as they were inside, I bolted for the other door, opening it gently to peer inside. There were stairs leading down into a dark space, but the voices I could hear were far away. Filling my veins with as much courage as I could muster, I tiptoed down the stairs.

It was a musty basement, and at the far end was another room with the door mostly shut. Staying as quiet as I possibly could, I crept to the door and listened to the men on the other side. At least two voices.

"If another one of my men goes missing, O'Rourke," a man snarled, "I will retaliate."

"I've lost one, too, Russo," Harold growled back.

"Who the fuck is doing this? And how is the *London Times* getting all their intel? Someone is telling secrets." The man spat the words. "When I find out who, he's dead."

"Why not just take out the reporter?" A third man spoke. "King or whatever. Take her and squeeze her until she gives up the source."

Silence, and then the first man spoke. "What is it, O'Rourke? You've got a look about you. What do you know?"

"It's a Reaper." He spoke quietly. "One I've hired, I'm sure of it. I recognize his work on at least three of the bodies."

"Including my man?" The first guy sounded even angrier. "Give him to me."

Harold shuffled around, or sounded like he was walking. "I will. I need him for a few more hits. Listen. If we can get the Irish and Moreno's crews out for blood, we can take control of the city together. Stir the fights until they're weak, then finish them together."

The two other men were silent. "You'd turn on the Irish? I know the story about the Murphy girl. I know your secret, O'Rourke."

A chair fell to the floor, as if someone rushed out of it. "Especially for that. I'll give you my Reaper, you give me allegiance."

My heart raced at what I was hearing. The meeting was wrapping up, and I desperately needed to get out of there. I raced up the stairs and to the door as quietly as I could. Opening it slowly, I peeked out, praying Lyra still captivated the bodyguard. Luck was on my side, because no one was at the door. With a few quick steps, I made it to the entrance of the pub just as the other door opened. I spotted Lyra at the bar with the bear man.

"Lyra," I gasped. "Tom called and said you jumped out of his car. I've been looking all over."

The beastly man swung his sharp gaze over to me, which seemed to take effort, considering how intently he was watching my cousin. "He threw her out," the man snarled.

My eyes widened, and I feigned horror. "How awful. Lyra, maybe I should take you to my place?"

She gave me a small smile, keeping up with her damsel in distress look. "Thanks, Nor."

I helped her out of the chair, and the bodyguard followed us out. As soon as he opened the door for us to exit, I shoved my umbrella open to block our faces from the men standing outside the other door.

"Benjamin," Harold shouted. "What the fuck are you doing?"

The beast of a man looked at Lyra for one long moment before returning to Harold's side without a word. Lyra and I hurried away, practically running to Neverland.

"So," she asked as soon as we were inside. "Did you get any juicy information?"

I grinned at her, my heart still racing. "You bet your ass I did."

27

Declan

It had been two whole weeks since the little trip to Chicago. Nora's ex remained in the city and didn't appear to be making moves to get to her, at least, no obvious ones. Of course I was tracking him, and her, and anyone else connected to her. Managing all my duties to my father was becoming a burden. And he could tell my attention was no longer fully locked in to his needs.

Several times he hinted at my distracted attitude being related to a woman, but I never gave him any information, never let my guard down when he asked pointed questions. Nora was a flame in the dark world that I inhabited, and I'd be damned if I let him snuff her out. Besides, when she wasn't with me, she was with Ellis. I waited for the jealousy to set in, but it never came. Seeing them together didn't fill me with rage the way it did when I caught other men ogling her. If I was being honest, the feeling spreading through my veins each time they kissed...was longing. And if I was being even more honest, the longing was for both of them.

Ellis had been everything to me, once. And some broken piece of my soul still wanted him, even though it was wrong on multiple levels.

But dwelling on all the things I wanted but couldn't have wasn't my modus operandi. Moving on, I checked through all my cameras, noting where everyone was.

My phone rang, and I ignored it. My father had called twice today, unheard of for him. Everyone under my father's rule did what they were told, when they were told the first time. He wasn't technically the leader of only one particular gang or club, he was a mole in all of them. That was his biggest secret. Harold O'Rourke used the fears and secrets of others to move them like pawns in a chess game. The whole underworld of Europe would probably implode if his double-dealings were discovered. And there were only two people in the entire world who knew this. Me and Burkett. Benjamin Burkett moved from Boston to London when he was a teenager, roughly thirty years ago. Not much is known about his childhood, and I've searched extensively. He slipped into my father's world with ease. The man was a damn bear, broad in the chest, built more like Ellis and our father. Ben was bigger than both of them.

Which is why my father kept him close. I was his secret assassin, sent out for specialized kills and making people disappear without evidence. Ben was his muscle. The man could practically crush a skull with his bare hands, and he made sure everyone knew it too.

Despite his loyalty to the world's worst father, I liked Benjamin. There was something about him that told me he still had his own mind, his own code of ethics. And as much as I tried to keep tabs on the guy, he slipped away every once in a while. That only impressed me further.

My phone buzzed again, and this time I answered. "Burkett."

"Now that I know your phone works, get to the warehouse," he growled down the line, and I rolled my eyes. "Don't sass me, kid. Got a name for the Reaper. Russo."

Curious. Russo wasn't just another gangbanger. He was the leader of the Sinistro. Not exactly an easy hit. My interest was officially piqued. "A bold move."

Benjamin grunted. "I stay out of the whys, you know that. Have you seen the recent articles? It's bad for business and Harold needs the situation handled. Guessing it's related."

Of course I'd fucking seen them. The woman I continued to stalk, who haunted my dreams and stirred my nightmares, was who wrote them. And maybe I slipped her a detail or two. Nora had a clever way with words that got my dick hard every time I read her stories. Multiple arrests had been made since her articles went live, which only made my stalker tendencies increase. Despite my warnings, and Ellis cautioning her, Nora was as determined and fierce as ever. She would not back down until the corrupt were behind bars.

"I'll be there." I hung up the phone before he could say anything else and powered down my devices. Then I shot off a text to Ellis, telling him to keep an eye on Nora. He never asked me why when I sent similar messages, almost as if he knew I had business to handle and she could be in danger. My little dove was a danger fucking magnet.

Ellis

You sound worried. Should I be worried?

Declan

Not yet. He is still in the dark.

Ellis

He's not as absentminded as you think.

Declan

And I'm smarter than he thinks.

Ellis

You are. Kinder too. Stay safe, Dec.

In the last two weeks, my brother and I had begun texting regularly, chatting more than we ever had in the last decade. At least through messages, things felt easier, like we could pretend we were just two friends. My blood heated when the phone lit up with his name nearly as much as it did with Nora's. But that was not something to be discussed or analyzed.

Nora

The moment one begins to hope that things are finally looking up is the moment everything falls apart. I was having a lazy weeknight at home while Sienna and Lyra were out shopping. With all the recent excitement, I had a few dozen emails to respond to and another article to write. In the two weeks since I stumbled upon Harold, two more bodies had been found, both with symbolic tattoos confirming they belonged to different gangs, and one I thought I recognized from that meeting. Hard to say when I barely saw the men leaving the club. Declan all but admitted to assisting in the schemes to bring about disruption in London's underworld, but the one called Russo, he didn't claim. And after a bit of exceptional sleuthing, I could also place him in the area of three of the dead men, and I said as much the other night when he snuck into my apartment. The memory of that night still got me all hot and bothered.

"I know you killed some of the men," I panted, my hand fisted in his sandy brown hair. "I know you're part of this, more than you let on."

Declan laughed darkly, raising his head from between my thighs. "Did you just accuse the man with his tongue teasing your needy cunt...of murder?"

I moaned when he curled his fingers inside me, my hips bucking, wanting more. "Yes. Don't stop."

But he did fucking stop. Declan loomed over me, fingers still pumping slowly in and out of my pussy. "Now what kind of girl does that make you, little dove?" He used his other hand to squeeze my cheeks hard enough to pinch, my lips parting. He leaned down and spat into my mouth. "You're a filthy slut for me, aren't you, Nora?"

His words and fingers were driving me insane with want. "Yes."

Declan hummed in satisfaction. "Only me. Say it."

I shook my head, and he snarled. "You. and Ellis. Only you and Ellis." It was a declaration I'd wanted to share since they both showed up in Chicago.

Declan smirked, his thumb rubbing circles over my swollen clit. "All right. Only me and Ellis. Now scream my name when you come, little dove."

My body ached, remembering how rough his hands were and how good it felt. After being in a fear-based relationship, I wasn't sure if I'd ever be able to enjoy sex, let alone rough play. Of course neither one of them had tried to have sex with me yet, but their hands and mouths were doing plenty, and Declan's touches were never gentle. Even then, I felt safer with him than I ever had with another man, except for Ellis. It was strange how quickly that realization came to me. They were both my safe space.

Returning to my work, I was elated to see several emails from the ancestry website. After the email from Marge, I was positive there was more to Harold O'Rourke's background, his stories, and those of his alleged sons. Things just weren't adding up, and women tended to experience untimely deaths whenever he was around, including their mother. Elsa Bainbridge was treated for cancer, but after sweet-talking the right people, I learned she was never actually diagnosed. And further, there was no record of her ever giving birth to a second child. So what exactly was this asshole covering up? That plus how successful Harold's seedy businesses were with his supposed sons living separate lives was too suspicious. Not just suspicious, it felt planned. Calculated.

Before I could click the ancestry emails, another caught my eye. It was from Jameson. Every cell in my body shouted at me to simply delete it, but I couldn't. The stupid journalist brain needed to know what he had to say. Opening the email, his words were brief, and an audio file was attached.

Have you looked at the USB drive I left for you?

Can't imagine the eurotrash would still want you after seeing that. J

I'd completely forgotten about the drive. It was stuffed in a drawer, which was fucked up. I should've thrown it away, but some tiny voice in my head made me keep it. Clicking the audio, I instantly recognized my own drunken voice. No, not drunk, drugged. My speech was slurred.

"Tell the Senator how much you want his cock, Nora," Jameson ordered.

Shuffled sounds as if he were moving me around scratched against my ears. "I want your cock."

"Fifteen minutes," Jameson snapped. "Her mouth only. Understand?"

The only sounds after were grunts and gagging. I slammed my computer shut, bile rising in my throat. Blind with shame and rage, I barely made it to the toilet before retching. There were no memories stirring from the audio, not a single time I could remember being so drunk I'd forget being assaulted like that. But there were mornings, more than one, where I woke with headaches and blurry knowledge of how the nights before had ended.

Tears streamed down my face, and I curled into a ball on the tile floor. How many nights? How many times? Jameson was a monster, even now he was taking from me. Ruining me for anyone else. Voices called my name, but I was too weak to respond.

"Girlfriend, come see what we—" Sienna's words ended abruptly, and then she was shouting. "Lyra!"

Footsteps approached, and then two bodies pulled me up. Lyra's hands were on my face. "Nora? Baby, talk to me. What happened?" But I couldn't get the words out. "Sienna, call the guys."

My body was no longer under my control, and I couldn't even shake my head to tell her no. They'd come, and I'd have to tell them what he made me do.

Declan

Ellis picked me up from the Red Clover on his motorcycle. It would have been comical if we weren't rushing to Nora. I could almost enjoy holding on to him like this, my dick pressing into his backside. He drove like a damn street racer, winding through traffic and ignoring all traffic signs. Again, if I wasn't so fucking anxious, my dick would be hard right now.

Sienna called only minutes before, her voice shaking with fear. She and Lyra came home to find Nora in the fetal position on the bathroom floor, smelling like vomit. They determined she didn't take anything, but something clearly triggered her. My money was on Jameson. I fucking knew that pompous piece of shit wasn't going to leave her alone. And now I'd have to kill him, which was fine with me but may upset her.

I blamed myself. While I was still keeping an eye on Jameson, he wasn't a completely ignorant person, and something must have slipped through the cracks. My father had been riding my ass lately, furious about all the press focusing on cleaning up the city, and with another body discovered only two days ago, feelings between clubs were anything but civil. Surprisingly, I did not dispose of the most recent body. There were several now that were not my work, but someone else's who was equally skilled. Another Reaper. I made it my business to know them all, and there were none who could match my skill to set up a crime scene. And yet, these showed finesse, and a serious knowledge of party lines. The fact that I hadn't been able to unmask this person was driving me crazy. And the fact that I let it distract me enough that Jameson maybe got to Nora pissed me off.

No matter, he would die soon, I'd find the other asshole messing with my city, and we'd all live happily ever after.

Ellis parked the bike quickly, and we chased each other up the stairs to their apartment. Lyra had the door open before we could knock. "Where is she?" he demanded as we both scanned the room.

"She's still in the bathroom. We cleaned her up, but I couldn't get her to move." Lyra's voice shook, but I barely heard the words coming out of her mouth before I charged into the bathroom.

Nora was curled up on the floor, her eyes staring at nothing. Her face was a mess of tear streaks and makeup, and she was still the most beautiful thing I'd ever seen. Bending down slowly, I scooped her into my arms as gently as possible, pressing a kiss to her forehead. "I've got you, Nora."

She whimpered in my arms, a silent sob, and I swore to all the gods whoever put her in this state would meet the full force of my wrath. Ellis was just behind me, and I carried her into the living room, settling on the couch and refusing to let her go. Ellis sat on the wooden coffee table across from me, our knees pressed together, and leaned forward to stroke her arm.

"Nora, love." Ellis spoke softly. "Please tell us what happened. Your friends are worried. Let us help you."

She blinked once, scrunching her fist in my shirt, tugging it down. I could feel the heat of her cheek against my chest. And the tentative shake of her head.

With a more firm tone, I responded first. "Nora, you will tell us what happened. I'll burn the whole damn world down one way or another."

Ellis reached for her hand, and she let him take in, pressing a kiss to her knuckles. "Was it your ex?"

She nodded before finally speaking. "When I left, it was like he knew it was coming. There was a note and USB drive on my nightstand." Her words caught in her throat.

"That piece of shit," Sienna snarled. "What was on it?"

Nora shook her head. "I still haven't watched it. He sent an email, with an audio clip. Said it was from the drive."

It was taking every ounce of my love for this fucking woman in my arms to keep me seated in that moment. "What did you hear?"

Fresh tears fell down her pale face. "Me. And him. And another man. Doing...something I have no memory of. I don't want to say it. He said he'd leak it to my boss. He said you'd leave me and—"

"Nora." Ellis stopped her, his voice steady. "There is nothing on this fucking planet that he could do to make us leave you. Don't even think it."

"Love?" I spoke slowly. "Do you have the drive?"

She nodded. "Sock drawer. I can't watch it."

I kissed her forehead again and stroked her hair. "You don't have to, but I am, all right? I will fix this. But I need to see what he did to know what it is I need to fix. Is that okay?"

She sighed but nodded again.

"Good. Why don't you get cleaned up with your friends and snuggle up in Sienna's room?"

Lyra and Sienna leapt into action, and a smidge of relief filled my chest when Nora walked on her own with them. Her face was still pale, and she was likely still dissociating, but we'd bring her back. Ellis went into her room and came back with the drive. Plugging it into her computer, I quickly scanned the email he sent her and then played the videos. There were seven of them. Seven videos with seven names.

"I don't know if I can keep my shit together watching whatever is about to happen." Ellis's voice shook with rage.

"If she can endure the doing of it, we can watch it," I growled, keeping my voice low. "I want to know exactly what he did, so I can plan my retaliation appropriately."

Hitting play, we sat in silence through all seven videos. They weren't long, each man was given a short amount of time with her. Jameson was giving them a taste and promising more if they did whatever he needed them to do. The men knew they were being taped, that was obvious, but the chance to get their dicks sucked was just too tempting. Nora was clearly drugged. Her movements were all wrong, her eyes glazed, and she could barely speak. After the final video ended, a deadly calm fell over me.

"Whatever you have planned, I will be fucking involved," Ellis snarled, his fists shaking at his sides, one hand digging into his thigh. "He's fucking dead."

"He will beg for death before I give it to him," I whispered, my rage turning ice cold. "Get Alec and let him know he's on watch duty for the three of them. He owns a townhouse in Mayfair. They can stay until we return."

Ellis nodded in agreement. "Sienna will throw a fit."

"She won't, because it's for Nora." I snarled, irritated with the Russian and his damn refusal to accept what was so obvious to everyone else. "Those two need to get over themselves and fuck already."

Ellis huffed in annoyance. "A problem for another day. Let's go hunting."

30

Ellis

As it turned out, planning to murder someone is not all that difficult. Declan, apparently an accomplished murderer, did most of the planning. As we were moving into the sharing secrets stage of our resurfacing friendship, he mentioned the killer stalking our beloved city featured in a few of Nora's recent articles was, in fact, him. But not all of it was his work, and that was vexing him. And if a prolific killer such as my brother was vexed by another killer in the city, well, I was ready to fly us all away on a permanent vacation to my cabin in the Alps.

Murder, as Declan put it, happened everywhere, so it would not matter where we went. Today was such an example, as we were flying off to the US to kill someone. Declan sat across from me in one of the captain's chairs, his legs splayed wide and his eyes glued to his laptop. He was tracking Jameson Moore and his closest associates. The man was a coward and likely surrounded himself with cannon fodder in the form of bodyguards. It should unnerve me how little I cared about that. But anyone who would associate themselves with him was nothing but garbage. Dec already looked most of them up, and their many secrets, which included deplorable acts I won't even name. Thus, their deaths meant nothing to me.

"You've been staring at me for several long minutes, brother," Declan mused, clicking away at his computer.

Ignoring his comment, I stood from my seat and busied myself by preparing a drink.

"I'll take one as well," he called back to me.

I poured two glasses of scotch. Returning to our seats, I held out his glass. Declan locked eyes with me, his finger grazing mine when he accepted the glass. His wolf-like eyes were always a marvel to me. They changed color in the light, and never, ever gave away what he was truly thinking.

"So." I cleared my throat and sipped my drink. "What happens when we arrive, then? Just walk up to his house and start shooting? Do we have machine guns?"

Declan's lips twitched with a smile. "And how many mafia movies have you watched to prepare, Ellie?"

Ellie. Dec hadn't used that nickname since we were children. My stomach churned, flipping on itself, and all I wanted was for him to say it again, even if he was teasing me with it.

Instead of voicing such shameful things, I pressed my free hand into my thigh and ignored the quip entirely. "If we are going to be more subtle, I'd still like him to know who exactly came to end his life and why. I would enjoy seeing the piece of shit piss himself before we end him."

Declan smiled. "That can be arranged. How he dies is up to us, how we leave him for others to find is for her to decide. He tried to ruin her, and we will return the favor."

I nodded, liking the sound of this plan so far. "Is that what you've been doing pecking away on your keyboard?"

He stopped typing and sipped his drink, arching a brow at me. "You sound jealous. Needing some attention, big brother?"

Why, even now, was he so fucking good at niggling beneath my flesh with the slightest comments? I was the older brother and I should be taking charge. "Fuck off, Dec. Just tell me the plan. We're nearly there."

Our plane was landing in Boston. Jameson Moore had hopped a last-minute flight to Boston on a private plane, likely assuming we wouldn't be able to find him if he wasn't flying commercially. But Dec tracked his accomplices. He was meeting the very senator from the tapes. I could barely think of it and the image of Nora, drugged and on her knees reared up in my mind.

Declan seemed to sense my changing mood and finally spoke. "Jameson and the soon-to-be dead senator are attending an opera tonight. Unfortunately, the senator won't make it to the final act. You see, he has a severe allergy that I plan to exploit."

I leaned forward, curious. "What is he allergic to?"

Declan smirked, his eyes glinting with mischief. "Cyanide."

A laugh escaped my lips, and Declan chuckled with me. "Brilliant."

"Yes," he agreed, a smug look about him that only he could make look endearing. "When he is whisked away to the hospital, they will find a pocket of rather damning photographs. Police will find much more on all of his devices. He shall be dead and ruined all in one evening."

"Perfection." I grinned. "Then what of the real target?"

Declan leaned toward me, his voice pitched low. "When Jameson is rushing about in panic, he shall find himself suddenly without guards, and we will escort him instead."

"Can't I just strangle him in a closet, cut off his dick, and stuff it in his mouth?" I grumbled, imagining such a scene with great pleasure.

Declan hummed in response. "The idea does get my dick hard, but I'd like to draw out his pain a little longer."

He was right. Jameson Moore deserved every ounce of pain we could deliver. I wanted him to beg for his life. Grovel and apologize for what he did to Nora, what he tried to do even after. Declan had the right of it. Suffering first, death later.

31

Declan

The rich and powerful too often forgot how vulnerable they were amongst each other. When one of their kind died before their very eyes, upending the safety of their polished cages, chaos ensued. Watching the man who hurt Nora struggle to breathe and die was almost magical, but the truly theatrical bit was seeing his fat body fly over the balcony of his private box into the seats below. Death by a broken neck before the poison could finish him off and photos flying everywhere. Truly, it was a masterpiece.

Jameson ran from the room, well, he stumbled. His own glass was laced with GHB. And as he staggered into my arms, the drug working its way into his system, his eyes widened in true fear. He tried to call out for help, but the poor fool's speech was already slurred. Ellis assured anyone who looked our way that we were getting our friend home after too much to drink.

My brother was the right man for such things. He looked like them, fit into the upper echelons with grace. While we both wore the fancy suits he had tailored for the occasion, Ellis fit into his like it was a second skin. He looked like James fucking Bond, and fuck if I wasn't hard as hell for him.

Nature was a cruel bitch, forcing me to salivate over someone who could never be mine. Maybe in certain fucked-up circles, but never in the light of day. And perhaps I needed therapy for these thoughts, but they couldn't be sending me to hell any quicker than the whole business of being a murderer for hire.

And now, with Jameson tied up and bloodied, Ellis throwing sucker punch after deadly punch, how could I not have such thoughts? His jacket was gone, bowtie tossed aside and sleeves rolled up to offer him more range with his punches. His crisp white shirt was now splattered with blood. Pressing my foot against the wall, I shoved off and stalked toward Ellis.

Clapping him on the shoulder, I stopped him before he could throw another punch. "That should do, Ellie. We need him to be able to speak yet."

My brother whirled to me with a snarl, his face nearly looking deranged with bloodlust.

"Fuck, you look good like this." Pulling out my phone, I snapped a quick photo of him.

Which broke him of his bloodthirsty mood. "Why in the hell did you just take my photo?"

I shrugged. "Because you look hot and I want to document everything. Just in case Nora wants to see it all someday." Ellis rolled his eyes, and I smirked. "Speaking of, time for a video."

Setting up my phone on the stand, I positioned it to face the sad fuck tied to the chair. He was groaning, head down and blood dripping from his face. "Look here, Jameson. It's time for your big moment. You always wanted to be the most important man in the room."

Stalking toward him, I slapped his face hard enough to send his head flying. He whimpered like a little bitch, causing a zip of pleasure to run through me.

"You just told me to stop hitting him and then go and do it yourself." Ellis sighed behind me. He poked the man in the chest. "Look at the camera now, asshole. Tell everyone what a pathetic pissant you are."

I barked out a laugh at his words. "Hell, brother. We need to work on your intimidation." Pulling out a pocket knife, I flicked the blade out and touched the tip just under Jameson's nose, forcing his head up. "Now, tell Nora how sorry you are. That you are, as my brother said, a pissant of a creature. And that you will never bother her again, lest you wish to have your tiny dick and balls shredded with a cheese grater."

Jameson was nearly in tears, the drugs in his system making his speech difficult, but not impossible, to understand. He did grovel and beg. Apologized to Nora over and over. None of it mattered. These were words of a coward, not sincere. And he would die pissing himself.

"Please," he begged. "Please don't kill me. I'll never touch her again. I swear it."

Ellis launched a punch at Jameson's face, sending a tooth flying from his mouth. "No, you will never touch her again. Or any other woman, for that matter."

Jameson began to cry, a horrible, sniveling sound that needed to end. Snatching up the tie I discarded earlier, I stuffed it into his mouth. "No more games, only pain." His eyes widened, but he was tied up and unable to do anything to stop me from plunging the blade directly into his dick. His screams were terrible, and he wailed like an infant, which was almost rude. To the infants.

Ellis grabbed the knife from my hand and sliced it across Jameson's throat. "Fucking hell, I couldn't take another moment of that horrible sound he was making. Do men always die like that, or is he particularly irritating?"

I could barely concentrate on his words. Watching Ellis slice open that fucker's throat was quite possibly the hottest thing I'd ever witnessed, with the exception of seeing Nora's perfect cunt for the first time. Said image filled my head, and my dick swelled, pressing against my tailored pants. Ellis looked down, as if he could see straight through them. He swallowed, and I watched his throat bob with the small movement.

Licking my lips, I stepped closer to him. He moved back, countering me. We continued this dance until his back hit the wall. Ellis was easily more muscular than me, but I was taller. Staring down at him, I gazed into his navy eyes, searching. The lights were dim in the empty warehouse. There was not a soul within miles of this place. And right then, in that moment, I wanted him.

Without speaking, I reached for his belt, slowly undoing the buckle, his zipper. He didn't move, barely breathed, as I continued. When my fingers reached the edge of his briefs, grazing his skin, Ellis shivered, but still, he did not stop me.

Slowly, I dropped to my knees in front of him and began to pull his pants down when he finally moved.

"Wait." The word was strained on his lips.

I stared up at him, an ache in me, a need. "Ellie. Let me. I want this, always have."

Ellis's eyes blazed with desire, and he stared out at me for several long moments before he responded. "Fuck it." Without dropping his pants, he pulled his boxer briefs down just enough for his dick to spring free, bobbing in my face, thick and hard and fucking glorious.

Afraid he might change his mind, I grabbed the shaft and wrapped my lips around the head of his dick, moaning the instant a bead of pre-cum landed on my tongue. The salty taste was addicting, and I wanted more. I leaned further in, taking every inch of him until my mouth was so full I could no longer breathe.

"Fuck. Fuck. Fuck," Ellis groaned, his hand moving into my hair and tugging hard, but not to make me stop. "Dec. Fuck."

His noises only spurred me on. Slurping down spit, I increased my movements, swirling my tongue and hollowing out my cheeks to take him all the way to the hilt. I teased his balls, massaging them with one hand and wrapping the other around his backside to squeeze his toned ass. This man was a fucking god, and having him at my mercy was sending chills down my spine in the best way.

Because he was, at my mercy. I was on my knees, but Ellis was losing his shit. His legs shook, and the sounds coming from his perfect lips were my newest addiction. His body tightened, and satisfaction tugged at my belly.

Ellis's hand in my hair pulled tightly, forcing me onto his cock, controlling the pace of my movements. I relished this new position, seeing the man who was so polished and perfect coming undone for me. Since we were teenagers, I'd dreamt of this. Fucked my hand a thousand times to the idea of it, and it was nothing like the real thing.

"Fuck. Dec," he groaned in agitation. "I'm going to fucking come." He looked down at me, eyes feral, and when our gazes met, he grinned like the devil. "Swallow it all, baby."

I nearly came in my fucking pants at the command, but focused on my task, and in three more strokes of my tongue, Ellis unloaded hot cum down my throat. We groaned in unison, and I lapped up every last drop.

Standing suddenly, I grabbed his throat, forcing him to look at me once more. "I've wanted this for years, Ellis. And you can never make me regret it."

His words were quiet, but I heard them clearly. "I don't want you to."

Declan

It wasn't exactly shocking to see my older brother flee from me the moment we returned to London. He was always fleeing the scene. For two decades, I sharpened my edges, covered my skin in steel armour, and buried anything resembling a feeling to the deepest pits of my ruined soul. And yet, watching him turn away on the street without looking back sliced through every defense as if it were made of silk. I was a teen again, foolishly in love and wanting only one person in all the world to love me back. And for a moment, it was only us. Covered in blood and looking so fucking sinful, Ellis was impossible to resist.

I meant my words, even if I should be locked up for them. And now it was time to tell the only person whose opinion I cared for. Nora King. The siren had lured me in from the beginning with her sea-glass gaze and heart-shaped mouth. Then further captivated me with her wit and bravery. Would she throw me out when I shared my secret? Perhaps, but the time for secrets was ending. The lies wrapped around my life in the shadows had become a noose, and until she came along, I was prepared to hang.

Nora was working late at the office, one of the only employees left in the building, and I was deciding how to surprise her. Grabbing her as she stepped out the door might be a little much. And as thrilling as it was to see a bit of fear in her eyes, tonight I would not hide in the shadows. I needed to see her face when I spilled my secrets.

My car was parked directly in front of the main entrance, so I could see her exit. Checking the security cameras, I noted she was no longer at her desk and her things were gone. What was taking so damn long? Anxiety began to crawl up my spine. When the passenger door opened, I raised my gun and aimed it at the intruder.

Nora's eyes went wide. "Well, this is certainly a new way of greeting a girl."

"Fuck." I tossed the weapon away, snatching her throat. "You scared the shit out of me. Naughty, naughty girl."

She grinned, leaning into my touch. "Thought I might try surprising you for a change."

I squeezed my fingers into her thrumming pulse. "You succeeded. And I won't let it happen again."

Nora's grin became particularly sly. "We shall see about that. So, where are we going?"

Nipping at her mouth, I let her go and proceeded to pull into traffic. "It's a surprise."

She scoffed. "Of course it is. Are you going to tell me how things went in Boston? I know he's dead. Several people are dead, actually. A strange affair at the opera."

She was far too clever for her own good. We didn't tell her where we were going, only that it was to find Jameson. Nora continued to remind me how tenacious she can be. "Yes, what a shame to lose a political figure like that, what was he? A senator? A tragedy."

"He was...on the tape?" Her voice was quiet, and it filled me with rage that she had anything to sound so dejected over.

But I wouldn't lie to her. "Whatever you want to know about the tape, I will share with you. You lived through it, and even if you can't remember, you survived it." I took her hand, squeezing it. "More than that, you flourished."

She smiled softly, her eyes twinkling in the lights of the city as we drove on. "Thank you. I don't think I need to know right now."

We drove on in silence, comfortable silence, until I found a place to park close to the theatre. Nora opened her door and exited the car before I could assist, so I swatted her ass and she yelped.

"What was that for?" The little minx elbowed me in the stomach.

I snatched her arm and threaded it through mine. Even in her stilettos, she was still several inches shorter than me, and I slowed my pace to match hers. "I'm trying to be a gentleman here and you're ruining it with your graceful independence."

"I'm certain there's a compliment buried in that self-pity somewhere." She laughed.

Her smile stopped me in my tracks, and to hear her laugh was easing all the worries I had about sharing my secrets with her. "Tell me, Nora. Does your enjoyment of reading include only romance books, or do you enjoy the original writer of scandalous love?"

We came to a stop at the entrance, and her gaze swung from me to the building before us. Her eyes widened, and her lips parted in surprise. "Oh my god. Is this The Globe? Are you taking me to see fucking Shakespeare right now, Declan?"

I laughed, an easy grin on my face. "So crass. Shakespeare would have loved you." I tugged her forward, and we made our way to the upper gallery. I guided her to a set of benches to the left.

The theatre was beginning to fill up, and Nora stood at the edge of the balcony, taking it all in. Stalking up behind her, I stripped her of her coat and wrapped my arms around her waist. She wore a simple forest-green shift that paired beautifully with her golden hair. Leaning down, I kissed her delicate throat and groaned at the tempting glimpse down her dress.

"Did I tell you how stunning you look this evening, Miss King?" I murmured, nibbling her ear.

"Not until just now." She leaned to the side, giving me further access to her throat. "Why is no one coming up here to sit? The theatre is nearly full, but this whole section is empty."

My nibbles turned to bites, and she moaned so prettily for me. "I bought all these seats so I could have you to myself. Tonight's play is *A Midsummer Night's Dream*. Reality fades, the wicked fae prey on humans. And we shall see how quiet you can be while I fuck your tight little cunt."

Nora

His words scorched my flesh as deeply as the bite marks on my skin. And oh gods, was this stirring my desires in such a delicious way. Declan's hands trailed down my body until they rested on my hips. He walked us back to the first bench, his calves bumping into it as he spun me around to face him. The lights dimmed, and the voices hushed when the play began.

"Now, fair Hippolyta, our nuptial hour."

Declan's gaze bored into mine as his hands deftly untied my dress until it fell open. I wore a black lace teddy beneath and silently thanked Sienna for choosing it when his eyes turned feral.

"The tempter or the tempted, who sins most?" Declan quoted the bard, whispering the words underneath his breath as his knees hit the floor. He snarled, biting the lace, one hand reaching for my breast and kneading my fleshing with bruising fingers.

Every touch lit my body on fire, and my legs were weak for this devil of a man. He reached between my legs, forcing a finger beneath the lace and teasing my flesh.

Declan looked up at me, a demon's smirk on his lips. "You're soaked, little dove. Tell me what you want."

If he refused me now, I might actually die. "I want you to fuck me. I need you to fuck me, Declan."

"You are that shrewd and knavish sprite."

Declan stood suddenly, towering over me in the shadows of the cove we owned in this moment. He unbuttoned his jeans and pulled out his cock in one movement. He was long, slightly curved and pierced. Not that I was an expert on dicks or anything, but his was making my damn mouth water.

"I've never...fucked anyone with a piercing," I confessed, unable to look away as he stroked his dick languidly.

Declan's eyes became ravenous. "I've tasted you. Stretched your pretty pussy with my fingers. Now I need to feel you wrapped around my dick."

His commands were impossible to ignore, and as if in a trance, I stepped closer, bracing my arms on his shoulders as I straddled him. Declan ripped the pretty lace, exposing my flesh, and teased my entrance with the head of his dick, the metal piercing cool against my sensitive clit.

"Sit, little dove," he ordered.

I leaned in and bit down on his bottom lip. "Make me."

His answering growl was all the warning I got before Declan thrust his hips up and shoved mine down, his cock filling me up to the hilt. A cry escaped my lips just as the audience laughed at the scene taking place on the stage below.

My cry melted into a moan as Declan continued to fuck me with abandon. His length curved inside me to hit a spot I didn't even know existed. "Fuck. Dec. Fuck."

He hummed in appreciation, maintaining his steady deep thrusts. "You feel so fucking good, Nora. I knew you would. Tell me who this cunt belongs to, little dove."

Declan amplified his words with one hand reaching down between us to rub his thumb over my swollen clit. His other hand ripped the fitted lace cup and freed my breast so he could twist and torture my aching nipple.

If anyone were to look over just now, they might have seen the shadow of a woman, facing away from the stage, perhaps hugging her man. They wouldn't have known his cock was bringing me closer and closer to the edge of oblivion, or that a scream I surely would not be able to hold in was building in my chest.

"Who. The. Fuck. Do. You. Belong. To." He enunciated each word with a thrust.

"You, Dec," I moaned. "You. Please. Make me come."

He groaned at my words, and my body squeezed him tighter and tighter. "Good fucking girl. Now bite down unless you want them all to hear you."

His wicked hands worked my body expertly, and the orgasm was at a crescendo. Before I could scream, I latched onto his throat, biting down as pleasure flooded my body. Declan groaned, his mouth sucking my abused breast hard enough to leave a mark. Hot cum filled me suddenly, his own orgasm following mine.

Declan held me there, our hands and mouths exploring, as if even now we couldn't get enough of each other. He pressed his forehead to mine as our breaths slowed. "Sorry. I meant to pull out, your pussy felt so fucking good and I lost control."

A giggle escaped my lips. "I'm on birth control. And I'm clean."

"I never doubted that," he whispered. "And I am as well. I would never do anything to harm you, Nora."

I believed him, completely. "I know."

He nodded, as if he needed to hear me say that. "Now can I tell you a secret?"

Curiosity bubbled up in my veins, and the hairs on the back of my neck stood up. "Is it a secret I want to know, especially with your dick still inside me?"

Declan cocked his head and grinned. "Especially because of that. I did something only a true deviant would do. And maybe you'll think I'm disgusting. Depraved. But I couldn't help myself, and I am not sorry."

His words were alarming, but still, it was curiosity that filled me. "Tell me."

Declan leaned in, his lips touching the shell of my ear. "After we killed your ex, I got on my knees and sucked the life out of Ellis's dick."

"If we shadows have offended, think but this, and all is mended."

Absorbing his declaration, I watched as his eyes darted away, a sheepish look coming over his face. He spoke with confidence, but hidden beneath his boldness was a lost soul, someone searching for a connection. I could see it in them both and knew something was there before I went looking for a way to make it right. Because it did feel right, his desire for Ellis, and I wanted him to have his first love back.

Cupping his face in my hands, I brushed my lips over his softly. "This secret won't scare me off. In fact, I may have a solution."

"You're insanely calm for someone just hearing about how I gave my brother head after committing murder." Declan arched a skeptical brow. "What do you have a solution for?"

Maybe I was just as insane as he was, because the part about the murder barely registered in my mind. "I started looking into something. What if...Ellis isn't your real brother?"

Declan opened and closed his mouth twice, rendered speechless for several seconds as the applause escalated around us. "Well, that would certainly deserve my applause. And I'd be going to hell for one less sin."

"I need to get cleaned up, you brute." I rolled my eyes, and the rogue smacked my ass, which only jostled us both and reminded me his dick was still very much nestled inside me. "And I'll share more with you, but only together, with Ellis."

He nodded. "Go see him first. Big brother needs you."

Declan's words filled my heart with hope. It was selfish of me, but I was afraid of what my findings might do for us. Would they choose each other? Their bond was one born from a lifetime of loving each other, and I was something shiny and new. And dispensable. But they deserved the truth, and even if it meant losing them, they would have it.

Ellis

The plane ride back to London should have been awkward as hell, but it wasn't, at least, not for Declan. For me, it had been torturous. He was in high spirits, going on and on about how hot it was to take that fucker out together. That part of the evening was indeed satisfying. Spilling my seed down Declan's throat was, well, there were no words to describe the ecstacy of that moment. At forty years of age, I'd experienced my share of delectable mouths wrapped around my dick. As the owner of a club intent on bringing pleasure to all, I'd received orgasms that made my eyes roll nearly to the back of my head.

But with every one of those experiences, I was never in love with the person. The only person I ever loved was Declan. And then father caught us. We were teenagers, horny, stupid teenagers. And the fact that we were brothers was an afterthought when my dick was in his mouth. All those years ago, and again the other night. The euphoria of that moment was something I would never forget.

And it will never happen again.

The only person who would know about what transpired between us would be Nora. She deserved to know. Because, as insane as it sounded, I was falling in love with her. We'd barely known each other for a handful of weeks, but every moment she was away from me, the air grew too thin, the shadows too dark. Only when she was near could I truly breathe. I wanted her to know every secret I ever kept, every scar. The thought brought me out of the clouds, and my thigh began to ache.

As soon as I was alone in my apartment, after the flight home, I'd cut three deep lines into my leg. The anxiety of what I'd done was too much for me to handle, and I craved the pain that would give me relief. Only to loathe the shame that came after. It was an endless cycle, a maze I was desperate to escape if only I knew how. And perhaps Nora was the key, her light shining through the edges of a locked door I never dared to open.

Straightening the lapels of my suit, I feigned strength and control and made my way down to the club. Nora and I planned to meet here tonight, our first since Declan and I returned to London nearly a week ago. I was ignoring him, and she hadn't mentioned him in the few times we spoke. She was almost coy on the phone, which seemed out of character for her, but then again, perhaps I didn't know her all that well. In only a few months' time, we'd been intimate and I'd killed for her, but did that mean I understood her heart? How could I, when mine was so jaded?

"You look like someone just ran over your dog, boss." Merrick chuckled, sliding a drink my way when I reached the bar.

Sighing, I sipped the drink without comment. He was far too opinionated, even if he was correct. My self-loathing came to a halt when Nora walked through the doors. She wore a beautiful red dress with a velvet corseted top and a silk skirt that brushed the floor. Her hair was curled and draped over her shoulder, drawing my eyes to a simple gold choker adorning throat. My mouth went dry at the sight of her.

Merrick slid a glass of champagne to her when she reached us. "Looking gorgeous as always, Miss King."

She smiled at him, and jealousy gnawed at my heart. "Thank you, Merrick. Seems to be a lively night."

He winked at her, and I wanted to stab him in the eye. "It's Fetish Fest. Almost all our members come out for it. And we open the guest list a bit for new blood."

"Fetish Fest?" Nora arched a brow, turning to me. "What does that entail?"

Before I could respond, Merrick answered her. "In the lounge you'll find the space reimagined with all sorts of toys, costumes, and more. Guests are encouraged to try new things and find new partners. It's a celebration, and a night to discover your truest desires."

Unable to share her attention with Merrick for another second, I stood suddenly and placed my hand on her lower back. "Shall we go see it? I'm quite proud of the event and what it has become. I'd love to know your thoughts."

Nora blushed, and the rouge on her cheeks stirred up butterflies in my stomach. "I'd love to." She smiled at me. "You look handsome, no, hot as shit, if I'm being honest. Navy really is your color."

Her compliment soothed my nerves some, and we moved through the throngs of guests, chatting more casually. With my second drink nearly gone, it was time to speak with her more privately.

"Shall we go upstairs?" I offered, coming up behind her as she examined a table of various collars.

"I've never really understood collars," she mused. "It's an ownership thing, right?"

I brushed my hand over a furry collar with sparkling jewels. "That is a part of it, but not nearly all. It is a commitment between two people, generally a dominant and a submissive, a bond not unlike what a wedding band represents. The two people choose each other, and trust each other."

Her emerald eyes bored into mine as I spoke, and it was as if all my secrets were laid bare, my chest flayed open and everything within exposed for her to see.

"Well." Nora's fingers reached up to touch the delicate choker necklace she wore. "That's...intriguing. Can't say I find the idea of marriage enjoyable after the last relationship, but this feels more intense. Maybe we could play at it? Just for tonight?"

In all my years in the community, I'd never collared a partner. The idea of doing so with Nora had my dick listening more intently to the conversation. I gestured to the table. "Choose one."

She smirked, returning to the collars and plucking out a navy leather band. She held it out to me. "It will match your suit. And your eyes."

Understanding trickled through me. "You want me to wear it?"

Nora nodded, eyes twinkling. "Would you be my submissive for the night?" Her voice was pitched low, and my own gaze was glued to her mouth, painted rouge to match her dress.

"As you wish, my lady." I bowed my head and held out my arm to guide her to the same room we played in before. Once inside, the noise of the event died away. "We will need a safe word."

"That's fair." She smiled. "How about butterfly?"

My lips quirked up at her choice. "Do you like butterflies, Nora?"

She laughed. "I did when I was little. My birth father had an insect hobby."

Her eyes dimmed slightly at the mention of him, and I filed that away to chat more about soon. "Butterfly it is, then." Dropping to my knees before her, I held out the collar. "Will you do the honors, Madame King?"

Nora chuckled, her fingers brushing mine when she took the leather piece from my hands. She circled me, bringing it around my throat and threading the clasp at the back of my neck below my hairline. It felt strange, but not entirely uncomfortable.

"Now then, my good boy," she purred. "Take off your clothes."

Nora

When Ellis began to undress, I thought my own clothes might burst into flames. My skin was hot all over, and my brain was short-circuiting at the sight of this hot daddy energy man on his knees for me. And I was correct about the collar, he looked hot as hell with that on. Even though it was only for tonight, for the scene, I decided to lean into my role as the dominant, try something new, be someone else.

His eyes were trained on me as I circled him, and such attentiveness reminded me I was still the prey and he the predator. But for now, this predator was leashed. His shirt was off, giving me a delicious view of his chiseled, broad chest, and he remained on his knees.

"Stand up, and remove your pants," I ordered, but Ellis hesitated. Something in his eyes told me there was a line being crossed here. "Ellis? Was that okay?"

He sighed, standing with a slight grunt and walking toward me. "Do you mind, if I keep them on for now?"

There was a secret here, and while I wished he would tell me, his eyes told me now wasn't the time. "Very well. Then undress me."

Ellis swiftly changed from serious to wicked at my command. His rough hands pulled through the laces of my corset with skilled efficiency. In seconds, I was nude, having forgone lingerie tonight.

"Fuck," Ellis cursed, dropping to his knees. "You are the most exquisite creature. Please, my queen, tell me what you need."

Seeing him on his knees before me reminded me of my time with Declan, and I couldn't say I hated to see these two men worshiping at my feet. But no, now I wanted something else. "Lay on the chaise like a good boy. And I'm going to ride your face until you make me scream."

His navy eyes widened in near shock, but he recovered fast. "Yes, goddess." He moved the chaise slightly, so it was angled directly in front of the full-length mirror. Ellis lay down on the velvet chair, his head closer to the end with the armrest and his legs dangling off the edge. He was far too large for it, but this position would work for now. "Your throne awaits."

A ridiculous giggle escaped my lips, and I held my head high as I sauntered towards him. Using the armrest to hold most of my weight, I straddled his face, hovering slightly above him.

"Nora, love," Ellis growled beneath me. "Are you going to make me beg for it? Please sit the fuck down and let me drown in your delicious cunt."

He didn't wait for me to respond, but grabbed my thighs and pulled my legs down, his tongue finding my clit instantly. He groaned, and my hips rocked of their own accord. I leaned my head back, eyes closed, and relished the feel of his wicked tongue.

Ellis pinched my thigh, and I yelped, looking down and ready to berate him, but his eyes were feral, stealing my words away. "Eyes on the mirror, Nora. You like to watch, don't you? Watch your pretty face while you come all over mine."

"Filthy man." My words melted into a moan when his mouth resumed its exploration. I did as he said, staring into the deep green eyes of the woman in the mirror. She was someone else entirely, someone strong, confident, and so sure of what she wanted in that moment. Her body moved with fluid grace, hips rolling in time with the strokes of Ellis's tongue. One of his hands squeezed my thigh and the other reached up to tease my nipples. I moaned again and again, the sounds becoming more urgent when he sucked my clit between his wicked teeth.

My lips parted, and my skin flushed red. "I'm close. Fuck. Don't stop."

Ellis growled his approval, the sound vibrating through me. The hand on my thigh edged between my legs, and he slipped two fingers inside me, curling them just so as he sucked hard on my swollen clit. I screamed, the sound choked and feral. The girl in the mirror looked unhinged, crazed with lust and sexy as fuck. It was the first time I truly saw myself and loved who was looking back.

"Ellis." I tried to sound stern, but his name came out more like a plea. "I need you to fuck me now, I want to watch."

He lifted me effortlessly from his face, just enough to scoot out and turn around. Ellis was behind me instantly, his hands roaming my naked flesh greedily. When he slipped a hand in his pocket and pulled out a condom, I shook my head. "Don't need that. Birth control. But...I, um. I had sex with Declan. It's only been him. Just once, since you both got back."

The words blubbered out of my mouth, and I cursed myself for sounding so idiotic.

Ellis didn't seem to notice. He tugged at my chin, pulling me in for a searing kiss. "I trust you. And I trust him."

His declaration was shocking, but he gave me no time to think on it, devouring my mouth with his once more. There was desperation in his touches, as if he needed me to feel him, to know all of him in that instant. Ellis pulled away first and shifted my head to face the mirror again.

"Look at you," he murmured. "You're glistening like starlight." His hand reached up and fingers threaded in my hair, tugging hard. "Now watch as I fuck you like you deserve, my love."

I was supposed to be the one in charge, but the desperate tone of his voice and the head of his cock pressing against my backside was too tempting to ignore. "Then fuck me like you own me, Ellis. Make me yours."

He wasted no more time, tugging my legs wider on the chaise and leaning over me like a beast, still wearing the collar. Ellis teased between my legs with the tip, rubbing the shaft back and forth to coat his member with my arousal. "Don't look away," he snarled just before pressing the head of his cock to my entrance and sinking inside me.

Several unintelligible sounds escaped my lips, and I nearly closed my eyes in bliss, but he twisted my nipple, forcing my gaze back to the mirror. Ellis's face complemented my own, untamed and free, living only for the moment we now shared. His length was thick and stretched me in the most exquisite ways.

Ellis groaned, a deep and throaty sound. "Nora. You feel too fucking good, love. I'm not going to last."

"Me either," I whined. "Make me come, Ellis."

His thrusts were deep and punishing, a steady pace that was driving me insane with pleasure. Reaching around, Ellis circled my clit with his fingers, slicking them with my juices. Our bodies molded together, and every touch he delivered set my soul on fire. When our eyes locked on each other in the mirror, I was done. The orgasm exploded through me, and I shouted his name, squeezing tightly around him.

"Fuck, good fucking god," Ellis moaned, thrusting harder until he thickened and unleashed inside me. His pace slowed, and he circled my waist with his muscular arms. "If I were to die right now, I would be content."

"Even though Declan isn't here?" I grinned at him in the mirror. "If he was, maybe he'd be on his knees, mouth open—"

Ellis squeezed me tightly and groaned. "He told you. I should have known he would." His head dropped to my shoulder, hiding his face. "How are you not disgusted by what we've done?"

Wiggling my ass against him to get his attention, I stared straight into his navy eyes when I spoke. "Because I don't think what you did was disgusting. And if you give me just a little more time, I'll prove it to you."

Nora

After another week of sweet-talking my way into every hospital in Ireland, as well as unearthing any and all newspaper articles from approximately thirty-five years ago, the hunch I had about Declan's birth parents finally came together. And it was not exactly good news. Well, depending on how the two men handled it. Hopefully not shooting the messenger. There were a couple questions I needed answered as well, like if this thing between all of us could realistically work.

Never in my wildest dreams would I have envisioned my life this way. I was falling in love with two men. It wasn't a matter of choice, because there was no choice to be made. The only way forward was together, but until I had proof, I wasn't sure that was possible.

Ellis and Declan had a tentative truce with each other, particularly when it came to me. They both took me on dates, both treated me to some of the most mind-blowing orgasms with toys, tongues, and wicked fingers. And finally, both men lavished upon me the most exquisite sex I'd ever experienced. You'd think such big, bad men would be more concerned with their own pleasure. Maybe that was rude to think, but can you blame a girl after the wreckage of a relationship I had before them? Both Declan and Ellis could not be more different than the ex. They were attentive in their own ways, spending more time learning the sounds I made, the way my body responded to their touches. How could I not love them?

The only thing Declan and Ellis did attempt to do was tempt me into a new line of work. It was subtle, and not out of malice but fear for my safety. I wouldn't end the career I'd only just fallen in love with because it was dangerous.

Jameson had been the one person I did fear, and he was dead. His death was in the news, but it was all the terrible, underhanded dealings he was involved in that splashed across the media. His family was ruined, and even my own mother and stepfather were not spared from the scandal. It would take them decades to recover, and any kind of social climbing they had in mind, well, those bridges were burned. Several other important members of society had also experienced bizarre deaths.

I knew it was all related to the USB drive and whatever Ellis and Declan saw on it. You'd think, because every bit of evidence mattered to me, every bit of knowledge was important, that I would want to know what happened, and yet, I never asked. If I had, they would have told me, but I didn't. That trauma was over, dead and gone, and I refused to let my future happiness be affected by it.

Sienna did force me into a couple therapy sessions, and I had to admit, therapy works. The therapist was exceptionally good at her job and helped me reach the place I now existed in, which was mainly in the arms of Declan and Ellis.

My nerves were getting the better of me, though. Ellis, I'd noticed, was never fully undressed when we were intimate. And with Declan, we seemed to be in positions where eye contact was minimal, if at all there. Both men were keeping me at a distance in some small way. And even armed with the long-hidden information I now had and they most definitely deserved to know, this plagued me. I needed to know their true feelings first. Maybe that was selfish, but I needed this all the same.

Tonight I planned a date for the three of us at Ellis's apartment above his club. I thought maybe being so close to a place where I watched him come to life would help my cause.

Lyra, Sienna, and I went shopping for the perfect outfit, lingerie, and of course, new shoes. Lyra and Sienna became fast friends, which didn't shock me at all. Both women were strong, loud, and braver about their wants than I'd ever been. So tonight, I'd be channeling my inner Lyra and Sienna power.

Stepping through the doors of Provocateur, I headed for the bar. Merrick greeted me with a winning smile and a glass of champagne. It may be cliche, but it truly was my favorite drink. The bubbles fizzed all the way down to my belly in the most delicious way.

"You're looking particularly stunning tonight, Miss King." The hot bartender winked at me, grabbing a few ingredients with finesse and mixing another cocktail. "Hot date?"

I smiled at him. "You could say that."

"Anyone I know?" Ellis quipped from behind me. "He wasn't lying. You're ravishing."

My insides melted at his compliment, and I stood from my bar chair, taking his offered arm. "As do you."

Ellis was without his normal suit coat, wearing black trousers and a crisp white shirt with the sleeves rolled up. The top two buttons were undone, giving me just a teasing glance of his chest hair. This man would be naked before the end of the night, so help me.

We walked through the club, Ellis greeting many of the guests by their first names. As much as he hid himself away, seeing the easy smile and ease with which he made others feel calm in a stimulating environment brought a rush of emotions to the surface. He was so many things for so many people, and I wanted to be a safe place for him.

"Is Declan here yet?" I asked as we stepped into the elevator leading to his apartment on the second floor.

"Of course. He hacked his way in the back entrance with my keycode." Ellis chuckled, turning our bodies until I was pinned between his muscular body and the back wall of the lift. With one hand, he gripped my chin and forced my head to the side while the other gripped my hip. His lips grazed my neck, nibbling my flesh. "Should I be jealous that you're thinking of him while here with me?"

Goosebumps prickled my skin, and I moaned when sucked on my neck like a damn vampire. "If it makes you feel better, I think about you when he's between my thighs."

Ellis groaned my name like he was confessing a sin. "You're a fucking temptress, foxy."

The new pet name Ellis came up with was adorable, but when he said it like that, his voice deep and wanton, I was prepared to drop to my knees and take him right here and now. The elevator dinged and the doors opened before I could move.

"Well, well, this is certainly a show I wouldn't mind watching," Declan drawled from inside the apartment as he leaned against a concrete pillar. The space was industrial style, with brick walls, high ceilings, and an open-concept floor plan with two bedrooms.

Ellis nipped at my neck one last time before pulling away, wrapping his arm around my waist possessively and walking toward his brother. "Evening, Declan. See you found your way into my place."

Declan looked every bit the deadly assassin in all black, from his boots to his leather jacket. His hazel eyes tracked my steps like a predator. He held out his hand to me, and I placed mine into his, then he tugged hard enough to force me to stumble into his arms.

"Hello, gorgeous," he purred, pressing his lips to mine in a searing kiss. Declan pulled away first, guiding me to the plush couch across from the wall of windows. "Champagne? Then maybe you can tell us what this little rendezvous is all about?"

The London skyline gazed back at me, city lights twinkling in the night sky. I sipped the glass of champagne he offered, needing a bit of liquid courage before my speech. Ellis settled into the leather armchair to my right, and Declan took the seat next to me on the sofa. It was time these men learned the truth about their parents. Their very separate parents. And the betrayals of Harold O'Rourke.

"I'd like to propose a dynamic," I said, my words only shaking slightly with anxiety. "One that includes all three of us."

Ellis

Nora's words settled over me, and I tried to keep my face neutral.

Declan's was anything but, a feral grin and wicked eyes settling on her. "Aren't you full of surprises? What exactly do you have in mind, Nora?"

To her credit, she didn't flinch at all, which meant this was something she'd thought through. "I want you, Declan, every dark corner of your soul, I want for myself."

"It's yours." His response was immediate, like a reflex. He'd chosen her long ago, I could see it in his face.

My heartbeat raced when her doe eyes locked with mine. "I want you, too, Ellis, equally. All the things you hide from everyone else, I promise to keep safe, if you'll let me."

Words failed me in that moment, and my hesitation instantly changed the mood for the worse. Her eyes brimmed with tears, and I could already feel her pulling away. I dropped to the floor on my knees before her and took her hands in mine. "Nora, love. Look at me." She did, and fuck she was beautiful even with tears beginning to stream down her cheeks. I brushed them away. "I am also yours, always..." Fear gnawed at my insides.

"What are you afraid of, Ellis?" she whispered. "Please tell me."

My eyes darted to Declan, his own face unguarded. His eyes blazed with lust, and I knew my feelings were not one-sided. My thigh burned with shame just from thinking about him in that way.

I shook my head, terrified. But if I continued to keep this all in, I knew it would destroy me. In fact, it was destroying me, one cut at a time.

Leaning back on my heels, I dropped my head in shame. "Years ago, when Dec and I were children, we were inseparable. Closer still as the years went on. And then it was different. They say you never forget your first love."

The words poured out of me, cascading into the silence, echoing off the walls and encircling us. It was strange how quickly they flew from my lips, after all these years. "When our father walked in on us, he tossed me out. Threatened to call the cops and have me locked up for what I'd done." Nora squeezed my hand, opening her mouth to speak, but I wasn't done with my confession. Standing, I began unbuckling my belt and dropped my slacks to the floor. The navy-blue boxer briefs did not hide the scars.

Nora gasped, her eyes wide. "Ellis. What happened?"

My eyes burned, and I balled my fists at my side to keep from reaching for my thigh. "I was alone after that, and ashamed. The one person I cared about the most, I hurt." I couldn't look at Declan, so I kept my eyes on Nora. "I was disgusted with myself. And this was an outlet. A way to bleed out my affliction. I craved the pain and it became an addiction."

"Fuck!" Declan jumped to his feet, eyes blazing with fury. "You didn't hurt me, Ellis. I loved you. I was in love with you, and what we did, I wanted that. I wanted you and I didn't care how fucked up that was."

Squeezing my eyes shut, I dropped back into my chair, pants still pooled at my feet. I started to pull them back up, but Nora was there, on her knees before me, caressing my thighs. "Don't hide. You have nothing to be ashamed of, and what your father did to you was so fucking wrong."

Her words meant everything to me, but they just weren't true. "He was right to send me away. I should be punished."

Declan stopped his pacing, fingers splayed at his sides. "Is that why you're sending him money? He threatened to go to the cops if you didn't?"

I nodded, because what was the point of secrets now? "Yes."

My brother screamed profanities, calling our father every horrible word he could think of. Nora continued to massage my thigh, pressing her lips gently to my scars. My dick hardened, blood rushing to the member the further up my thigh her lips went.

"No more money for that asshole." She spat the words. "He's a liar. You didn't do anything wrong, Ellis...because Declan isn't even your real brother."

Declan

From a young age, I knew I was fucked up, but it was quite possibly time for me to seek outside help for this particular moment. When Ellis dropped his pants and showed us his scars, I got instantly hard. Not because he had perfect, muscular legs. Not because he had a bulge hiding in his briefs I was itching to see. No, because of the scars. All these years, he was hurting, just like me. He was inflicting pain to his body, for me. And that knowledge got me so fucking hard for him. If that wasn't worthy of grippy socks and a padded cell, I didn't know what was.

I was so focused on Ellis, Nora's words took a full minute to register in my mind. "What did you just say?"

Ellis frowned at the woman between his legs. "Nora. I don't know where you got this information, but Declan is my brother. I was at the hospital when he was born."

Nora shook her head. "You were at the hospital Declan was born at, but it wasn't your mother who birthed him." She swung her gaze to mine, emerald eyes shining with truth. "Your mother's name was Aoife Murphy. I don't know who your father is, but it's not Harold."

Ellis grabbed her hand. "How do you know this?"

Nora kissed Ellis's palm and let him go, walking to me. She wrapped her arms around my waist and squeezed tightly, but I was too stunned to hug her back. "Harold's DNA is in the system from past arrests. I took yours, and they don't match. Then I plugged yours into an ancestry database and found the Murphy family. Aoife Murphy died giving birth, at the same hospital where Ellis met his new baby brother."

It was difficult to absorb her words, because they were insane, but Nora was not a liar. And she would never invent something so bizarre. "Why the fuck would Harold O'Rourke make us believe we were brothers?"

Ellis stood up suddenly, still half undressed, but not seeming to care. "Our mother—my mother—said you were hers. She claimed you. They both did."

Harold was not my father. The reality of this was sinking in. "He ruined us. He ruined you." The words were barely above a whisper. Fury shot through my veins like a drug. "He made us both think what we did was incest."

Nora's arms tightened around me. "It wasn't, it never was. Whatever his reasons were, I don't know, but I do know he's an asshole."

Ellis stood directly behind Nora, brushing her arms as if out of habit, which, I noticed, was better than cutting open his flesh. "Is he...are they my biological parents?"

She nodded, turning her head to the side to look at him, my brother in everything but blood. "Yes. I checked yours too."

Ellis suddenly wrapped his arms around us, one hand going to the back of my neck as he pulled me in, our foreheads pressing together and Nora sandwiched in the middle. "I'm so fucking sorry, Dec. I never should have let him push me out."

The fury coursing through me exploded into desire. "I don't blame you. And I don't want to talk about it anymore tonight. I knew what we had then was real, and now that we're here, I need to fucking feel you."

Nora slipped out of the sandwich, attempting to tiptoe away.

"And where the hell do you think you're going, little dove?" My words were a deadly purr.

Her cheeks flushed. "I thought I'd just go, let you two have some time."

"Absolutely not." Ellis barked the words.

I grabbed her wrist and tugged her back, wrapping my other hand around her throat. "You're still mine, Nora. And you've brought the one man I care for more than anything back to me. I need you both."

Her eyes dilated at my words, and I could practically smell the arousal between her thighs. Her lips parted, and I smashed mine into hers. She moaned, melting into my grip, and I squeezed her throat territorially. Ellis gripped the edge of my jeans and began undoing the zipper and buttons.

"He's right, foxy." Ellis's voice was rough with emotion. "We owe everything to you, and we will never let you go. That dynamic you began to propose? Count us in, love."

Nora

The logical side of my brain said I should stop what was about to happen here. Scolded me for letting them carry me into the bedroom and slowly peel my clothing off. Emotions were running high, Ellis and Declan barely had time to process the news I'd shared. They should spend time together, working things out, maybe even talking to the man who lied to them for so many years.

"Nora," Ellis growled, forcing my attention back to him. "I can see your pretty head swirling with a million thoughts. Send them away. Declan and I are exactly where we need to be. With you."

Was he a mind-reader now? Instead of responding, I began unbuttoning his shirt. His body was sculpted by the gods. It was mesmerizing. His shirt fell to the floor, and I ran my nails up his chest, teasing the smattering of chest hair, mostly black with a few pieces of silver, just like the lush hair on his head. I was the luckiest girl in the world to have this man staring at me the way he was now, as if I were the most important person in his orbit.

Declan stalked up to us from behind, walking the three of us forward until Ellis's legs hit the edge of the bed. "Take his dick out, little dove," he demanded. "He's dying to know what your sweet cunt feels like."

My mouth watered, and I licked my lips, following his command. Slipping my fingers inside the elastic band, I tugged the briefs down his legs, kneeling in front of him and staring almost directly at his thick cock bobbing in my face. Butterflies flooded my lower belly, and I swore I was about to combust already. Without thinking, I reached for it, wrapping my hand around the thick shaft. A long sexy as fuck vein throbbed at my touch. My tongue slid out, and I was just about to taste the drop of pre-cum tempting me when Declan's hand fisted in my hair, stopping me.

But it was Ellis who spoke first. "We don't want you to do anything that will upset you."

For a moment, I didn't understand what he meant, and then a flash of a memory crossed my mind, and anxiety crept up my throat. Because of the tapes they watched, and the audio I heard. I didn't need to watch, but I knew what I heard. It meant everything to me that these two men cared so damn much.

Declan's grip in my hair was hard, but not painful, and he tilted my head back to look up at him. "I want you, in every possible position. I want to see you fuck Ellis, and I want to feel your tight ass grip my dick so hard I see heaven. But only if you want those things too."

A needy moan broke free, and my body ached for these men. "I want everything. From both of you. And right now, I want to taste Ellis. Please."

Declan hummed his approval. "That word is a sin coming from your lips." Using the grip he had in my hair, Declan easily pushed my face toward Ellis, angling me just so. "Open wide, love."

My lips parted immediately, and Ellis stroked his shaft twice before guiding the head of his dick to my waiting mouth. I widened my lips further to take him in and breathed through my nose when the tip touched the back of my throat.

Ellis groaned, sliding in and out of my mouth slowly. "You feel so fucking good, Nora. Look at you. Fucking perfection."

His praise spurred me on, and I reached for him, caressing his thigh where his scars were with one hand and wrapping the other around his thick length. His breath hitched when I sucked harder. Declan controlled the pace, speeding up slightly. The fact that he was here, watching, was feeding my voyeur kink. Lust curled in my chest and pulsed with greedy desire the longer he looked on.

"You belong to him, little dove," Declan growled, his voice like gravel, rough and dripping with desire. "And you belong to me. You will only ever get on your knees for us, no one else."

I moaned a yes, my body lighting up with pleasure and relishing every second of this exchange.

Ellis pulled away suddenly, cursing under his breath. "Too fucking good. I need that pretty pussy before I come."

"On the bed, brother," Declan commanded, the word brother leaving his lips with a laugh. "I want to hear her scream for you."

Ellis sat down on the bed and lay back, stroking himself while I crawled on top of him. His navy eyes were beautiful, even in the dim lights.

"I've been waiting ages for this."

He smirked up at me. "Been dreaming of my dick, baby?"

I blushed but didn't shy from his words. "And Declan's. I want both of you at once." These monstrous men really knew how to make a girl feel wanted. And they were all mine. Straddling Ellis's muscular thighs, I positioned myself in earnest, the head of his dick just barely caressing my entrance.

"She's soaked for us, brother," Ellis groaned and lifted his hips just the smallest amount to tease me.

Declan chuckled from behind me and reached around to tease my already sensitive nipples. "Of course she is, horny little thing, so desperate for us." Without warning, he grabbed my hips and forced me down onto Ellis.

His dick was fucking huge, and the stretch was painful for half a second. But then pleasure oozed down my legs, all the way to my toes, and I shuddered. Ellis was making the most feral sounds, his hips gyrating beneath me while I rolled my own. We found a rhythm easily, our bodies already so in tune with each other.

"Fuck, Nora," Ellis practically snarled. "I fucking love—"

His words were completely drowned out by a series of very loud pops, like fireworks. They were echoing around us outside the windows, and somehow below all at once. All three of us froze. Those weren't fireworks, they were gunshots.

Declan

The loud booms were, unfortunately, very familiar. Screams, cries of pain, and gunfire. The fear that lurched up my throat wasn't for myself, it was for them. Fear for Ellis and Nora, and fucking rage that I just got cockblocked by a gunfight. Striding out of Ellis's bedroom, I snatched up my clothes, shoving my legs into my jeans and rushing to find out what the fuck was going on. A terrible feeling crawled up my spine, and I knew this wasn't an accident. We wouldn't be going downstairs to a random robbery of Provocateur.

Pulling out my phone, I called Burkett, but he didn't answer. I tried two of my father's men, but their voicemails only added to my unease.

"What the fuck is going on?" Ellis was at my side, also fully dressed in jeans and a T-shirt. If we weren't about to run into battle, I'd be teasing him about the casual attire.

Nora scooted under his arm, and he held her close. "Those weren't fireworks, right? I don't recall any holidays in England with fireworks in November."

Cupping my hands around her face, I kissed her hard, memorizing the feel of her in my arms. "Please, Nora. Lock yourself in Ellis's room and do not open it until we come back."

She frowned, ready to argue, but Ellis joined me, shoving my hand aside to grip her chin and crush his lips to hers. When he pulled away, her lips were swollen and her eyes wide, looking delicious as fuck. "Please, love. I need to go check on my staff. And I can't help them while I'm worrying about you."

Nora sighed but nodded. "Fine. I'll stay. Please be careful and come back to me. Should I call the police?"

I shrugged. "You can try. They're either already on their way or have been paid to stay back. We're about to find out." Turning her around and swatting her ass, which looked so fuckable in Ellis's sweatpants, I sent her to the bedroom. "Behave. And be safe."

Ellis stalked into his kitchen and opened a cabinet with a keypad lock. He pulled out two guns. My eyebrows nearly reached my hairline, and he simply shrugged. "What? I'm always prepared."

"Do you even know how to use a gun, brother?" I smirked, taking one of the semi-automatic pistols and checking to see that they were loaded.

Ellis rolled his eyes at me, pulling out extra magazines. "Yes. I've practiced with professionals. I do own a club that isn't exactly mainstream. Now let's go fuck up whoever decided to come for me and my shit."

He looked devilish, his eyes filled with fury and his jaw ticking in irritation. My dick was half-hard again and causing too much tightness in my damn jeans. I adjusted, and his eyes dipped to my crotch. "I'm fucking hard for you, Ellie. Deal with it."

Ellis smirked. "I plan to."

Those simple words nearly had me ripping his clothes off instead of handling whatever the fuck was going on downstairs. Ellis moved head, going to the stairs instead of the elevator. The sound of gunshots had waned, and more cries of pain could be heard the closer we came to the club. The back stairs lead into the club from the hallway furthest from the main lounge and bar. Guns raised, we walked silently down the hall, checking each room. Guests and staff were mostly dead. Five bodies so far. The sound of a shot rang out near the front, and we ran for the lounge as quietly as possible. A man dressed in all black stepped into the hall suddenly, gun raised at Ellis, but I was quicker.

A single shot rang out, and the man dropped, the bullet going through his skull.

Ellis looked back at me in the dim lighting, eyes glinting. "Think you just saved my life."

I shrugged, pretending that didn't affect me as much as it did. "Probably won't be the last time. Next one, don't hesitate."

Stepping in front of him, I edged into the open room. Almost immediately, gunshots exploded. Ellis and I dropped to the floor, crawling behind an over-turned table.

"Drop your weapons and come out!" a man shouted at us.

"Fuck you!" I snarled back at him, shooting off a couple rounds in the direction of his voice. A thud made me smile. Got one, at least.

"Damnit, man. You shot me," another said, and this one sounded familiar.

Ellis spoke first. "Merrick? What's going on?"

Merrick, the bartender, if I remembered correctly, laughed. "You're a fool, Ellis. Did you think Harold O'Rourke was just going to let you and Declan desert him?"

The dead man's words chilled me to the core. "Where is Harold?"

But Ellis was fuming. "You work for my father, you piece of shit? You are fired, Merrick!"

I scoffed. "Pretty sure he doesn't give a shit about being fired right now, Ellis."

"I never worked for you, you prick," Merrick sneered. "Now he's got your girl too."

That comment was enough. My blood boiled and rage fueled me into action, with Ellis at my side. We rushed out from the table, shooting at every man still standing. A bullet caught Merrick in the leg, and he screamed like a little bitch when he went down. It ended almost as quickly as it began, everyone dead except for Merrick. Ellis got to him first, kicking his gun away and pulling the man up by the throat. My big brother was a beast, and it took little effort to haul the dying man up and slam him into the wall.

"What the fuck did you say?" Ellis snarled into his face. "Speak or I cut your dick off with a dull blade."

Merrick groaned, but he caved immediately. "Just a distraction. As soon as I saw you I gave them the go ahead."

My vision blurred as his words settled over me. My skin tingled with fear. Ellis aimed his gun at Merrick's dick and pulled the trigger. The man dropped instantly, horrible sounds coming out of his mouth. He'd bleed out soon enough. We ran for the stairs, not speaking, barely breathing. I reached the top first and shot the lock off, not waiting for Ellis to use the keypad.

"Nora!" I shouted for her, but the apartment was silent. It was also a mess. Stools around the island were tipped over, a bloody kitchen knife on the floor. "She got one of them, at least."

"Declan," Ellis's voice was strained, and his eyes were filled with fear. "We have to get her back."

Taking two quick steps, I grabbed his shoulders and pressed my forehead to his. "We will. I'll kill him. And anyone else who gets in our way."

Ellis nodded.

"Her place first. Sienna and Lyra could also be targets, and Nora would murder us both if we left them unprotected. We may need help."

Ellis's voice was steadier when he spoke next. "Alec. He has the connections. And I'll pay whatever he wants to make him use those alliances to get Nora back."

Nora

My brain ached with the force of one hundred migraines. I couldn't detect any life-threatening injuries as feeling slowly returned to my limbs and my rattled senses settled. Memories of the night before, if it was in fact only the next day, slowly creeped in. I'd dressed quickly in a pair of Ellis's sweatpants and a hoodie, having no time or interest in getting my dress back on when his clothes were easier to access. Then I'd snatched a blade from the knife block in his kitchen before locking myself in his bedroom.

Fear and anxiety flooded my system as I waited for them to return, and only when I heard sounds inside the apartment did I realize my phone was out in the living room. Cursing my fight or flight brain for ruining any chance of calling for help, I tucked myself into his closet and waited.

The wait didn't last long. Several sets of footsteps stomped down the hall, and someone kicked open the door when the lock wouldn't budge. Hiding in a closet wasn't exactly sneaky, and it was the first place they checked. But I was ready for them. I slashed my knife across someone's arm and stabbed the other man in the gut. He fell to the floor, bleeding and cursing. With my blade gone, I tried to pummel the other two, but my efforts were useless.

A man backhanded me across the cheek, and pain shocked my system so quickly I fell to the floor in a daze. "Fucking bitch."

"She got me good, man," the man on the floor groaned.

Another man cursed. "Thompson, get him out of here. We'll manage."

One of the men left with the injured man under his arm, and two remained. I tried to crawl away, to do anything. When one of them grabbed my ankle, I kicked out with my other foot, my heel connecting with his nose. He shouted at me just as the other man whipped out a small black object. I'd never been tased before, and when the volts hit my chest, all the air in my lungs whooshed out of me.

"God damn, she's a feisty one." The man with the taser chuckled. "No wonder they both want her. Harold's going to enjoy having her as a pet."

The man whose nose I broke groaned. "Can we go now? On the off chance Declan survives, I don't want to be here when he comes looking for her."

"They'll kill you," I groaned, my voice scratchy and my mouth dry. "Walking dead men."

Taser man hauled me up over his shoulder, my body limp and unable to do anything at this point. My head bobbed against his back. He patted my ass and laughed. "They're both likely dead already. And you'll be wishing for it soon enough."

The man who tased me was incorrect. I didn't wish for my death, but I sure as shit wished for his. Without moving too much, I slowly opened my eyes to take stock of my surroundings. Seeing a dingy warehouse with a table of torture devices would have been better than this. The room I was in appeared to be a bedroom. The walls were plain, off-white paint and zero decorations. A window with light-filtering curtains kept the room relatively dim. The bed I was tied to was just as boring, ivory colored blankets and a simple iron bed frame. I tugged my wrists, which were uncomfortably tied to the metal frame above my head. Thankfully, I was still wearing Ellis's clothes. Not so thankfully, there was a camera setup on a stand pointing directly at the bed.

Suppressing my desire to vomit, I remained calm, taking slow breaths and forcing my mind to stay fully present. I would get out of this situation, and even if terrible things happened before I did, they would not break me.

The door opened, and I schooled my expression just as Harold's eyes dragged up my body to my face. It was so obvious Declan wasn't his son; they looked nothing alike. He had a similar broad build to Ellis, but his eyes were dark brown, not the mesmerizing navy I'd come to love. His silver hair was styled to look unkempt, and his face was scruffy with a five o'clock shadow. Whatever emotions he was feeling now, they were carefully concealed behind a mask of indifference.

"Good afternoon, Nora," he spoke calmly. "Or should I call you Primrose?"

He was trying to rattle me by knowing my name, but the asshole would have to try harder than that. "Wow, you have the skills of a basic investigator. You'll have to try harder than that."

Harold smirked. "He said you'd be a handful. After my guys returned bloodied up, I was rather impressed."

I shrugged. "Guess your sons are just rubbing off on me. They'll be coming for me, you know that, right?"

He sighed, settling into the armchair across from the bed and near to the camera. "I'm sure they will, if they're still alive. I'd hoped the robbery would take them out, but I've had a habit of underestimating them."

"So you took me to get to them?" I arched a brow. "Not a solid plan, unless you want to die."

Harold leaned forward. "Actually, Jameson Moore gave you up to me." My body stilled, and he smirked again. "I know he's dead now. But before his death,

I received quite a bit of money. And after his death, I received a letter promising more, if I kidnapped you."

That bile I'd been holding down surged up my throat, but I asked the question, even if I could already guess the answer. "And what did he want you to do after you took me?"

Harold O'Rourke sat back in his chair, crossing his left leg over his right knee. He wore dark jeans and a plain grey henley shirt under a leather jacket. Dark-brown eyes bored into my skull for nearly a minute before he spoke.

"Moore paid me half a million dollars to remove Declan and Ellis." His voice was low, annunciating every word. "Then another half million, if I continued the tapes he made of you. I assume you know the ones I speak of?"

Yep, I was going to vomit. I did know, but not as well as he assumed. "Continued?"

He scratched his chin in thought. "Jameson Moore wants revenge, and even dead, there are quite a few friends in high places that want the secrets he kept to stay buried. I'm to make my own video with you, then deliver you and the video to them."

Well, this was a terrible twist, and yet, Harold didn't seem particularly keen on the plan. "So, why haven't you?"

Harold stood from the chair and walked to the edge of the bed, staring down at me with a thoughtful brow. "You know about my sons. About Declan. But you don't know everything."

"I know Declan isn't your son, and that Ellis's mother never had cancer," I stated, my curiosity fully piqued at the turn of this conversation.

"I don't take kindly to blackmail and have no interest in creating a film to be used against me later." Harold leaned forward and untied my hands. "Perhaps I didn't handle things quite right with my sons, and it's time they knew the truth about both of their mothers."

Scooting away from him to sit up and rub my aching wrists, I was fully invested in this new information. "Why am I here?"

Harold O'Rourke sighed. "To convince my sons not to kill me."

Ellis

Breaking the news of Nora's kidnapping to her best friend and her cousin went exactly as we expected. Terribly. Sienna fumed the entire car ride over to Alec's townhouse. Lyra screamed profanities, occasionally punching me in the back of the head, as Declan was driving. I accepted the hits, considering they felt more like tiny taps from an enraged rabbit, and because she was right to be furious. We failed Nora, and who knew what the fuck was happening to her now. Of course Declan and I tried contacting our father. Scratch that, my father. It was so strange, and also made the most sense. Harold O'Rourke was a master manipulator, and separating us worked to his advantage. He didn't answer our calls, and there was no movement on any of the cameras he had access to. So for now, we waited for our backup to arrive.

There was a twelve-hour delay to begin our plan of rescuing her due to the fact that Alec was in Russia visiting his family. A part of our plan that was necessary. The Vasiliev family was incredibly well-connected, and not just with royalty, but the black market. Alec left the "family business" for a career of his own, something we bonded over years ago. Asking him to request assistance from his family wasn't exactly a small thing, but I was desperate.

When we arrived, men dressed in simple black suits surrounded the car. They patted each of us down thoroughly and checked the car. Two of the men drove away with the vehicle, and the other two escorted us inside. This wasn't the first time I'd visited his family flat, but it was the first time I'd seen so many people inside it. Not people, bratva. The faintest feeling of guilt ate at the back of my mind for asking him to step back into this life, but then Nora's beautiful face appeared and the feeling faded. The time for apologies would come later, when Nora was safe, and I would owe Alec a lifelong debt.

The bodyguards brought us to his informal living room on the first floor, near the rear of the home. The Victorian townhouse was six stories, with the master suite spread out across the entire second floor and the upper levels mainly bedrooms. Alec sat in a dark-brown leather armchair near the fireplace. The room was rich in color, with cozy couches and dark wood accents. He stood as soon as we arrived, a drink in one hand and his other resting inside his pants pocket, looking casual and powerful all at once. Which he was.

"Welcome." Alec dipped his head in greeting.

"Let's skip the pleasantries," Sienna snapped. "Nora is missing and apparently we need you to find her."

Alec sighed but didn't respond to her bluntness. "Please, sit. Marlena will bring refreshments, whatever you'd like."

A woman entered the room wearing a simple gray dress, accompanied by a man in a gray suit with a tray of water glasses, which he placed in front of each of us. Lyra sipped her water then pivoted to Declan. "Will you check the cameras again?"

Declan already had his laptop open, his fingers flying across the keys. "Nothing yet. She hasn't been seen in any of the warehouses, club houses, or flats owned by 3M Crew. There are very few places I have access to, and I've checked them all."

"Well, keep checking," Lyra snapped, her cheeks pink with agitation. "Where the fuck is she? What...what is he going to do to her?"

Declan didn't answer that question, which was more unnerving than if he had. He likely had a better idea of our—my father's particular predilections.

"Wouldn't he have called by now if he wanted something?" Sienna asked no one in particular.

Alec responded first. "Not necessarily. Keeping you all in the dark for a few hours makes you more desperate, more likely to do what he wants when he does contact you."

"I will find him before that happens," Declan grumbled beneath his breath, still focused on his computer. "Ben's phone just turned back on. I'm tracking it now."

I noted Lyra's face flushing a deeper red at the mention of Harold's second in command. "Would he...is he helping Harold do this to Nora?"

Declan shrugged. "I don't know yet. Ben is a private type. And he never seemed particularly sadistic. If he is involved, I'll put a bullet between his eyes."

Lyra frowned, staying silent.

"Speaking of the beast. I've found him."

"Where?" I asked, relief at something finally happening running through my veins. "Let's go get him."

Declan's eyebrows rose up into his shaggy hair line. "No need. He's here."

As soon as the words left Declan's mouth, another man in full tactical gear stepped through the open double doorway into the room and stopped, addressing Alec. "Sir. There is a Benjamin Burkett here, and he wishes to speak to your guests."

Alec arched a brow at me, his eyes moving to Declan before he responded. "Let him through, guarded."

Declan huffed a laugh. "The man is a beast. You'd need at least a dozen men to subdue him if he decided to attack."

Alec smirked. He wasn't a small man himself. Nearly as broad in the chest as I was, and as tall as Declan. Alec Vasiliev cut an imposing figure, and I was certain he knew how to handle himself in any manner of fighting. "At least he'd make an interesting opponent. Could use a challenge."

Sienna scoffed, her bright-blue eyes narrowing. "Says the business man in his fancy suits. When have you ever been in a real fight?"

She crossed her arms and sat up straighter on the loveseat when Alec stalked toward her. With one hand on the back of her neck, Alec leaned down and whispered something in her ear. To her credit, Sienna kept her face neutral, but it was clear to everyone in the room the tension between those two was coming to a head.

Footsteps sounded on the stairs. A group of six men surrounded the red-headed grizzly bear, as if escorting an enemy into the room. His dark-brown eyes assessed every square inch of the room, lingering on Lyra before landing on Declan.

"Hey, kid." His deep voice was calm and unaffected.

Declan was on him in seconds, a blade he'd hidden somewhere now pressed into the man's jugular. "Where the fuck is Harold?"

Benjamin didn't even flinch, didn't try to protect himself. "I don't know, but I will help you find him."

Declan

Benjamin was impervious to my threats, which was not surprising, but entirely fucking irritating. The knife I pressed to his throat was pointless, because we both knew I wasn't going to kill him, at least not right now. Slipping the blade closed, I stuffed it back into my jacket. One of Alec's little groupies narrowed his eyes, likely wondering how he missed it when they patted me down.

"Don't get comfortable," I growled at Ben. "Just because I haven't killed you yet, doesn't mean I won't."

Before he could respond, a tiny ball of fury launched at Ben, she slapped him across the face, the sound echoing in the silence. Lyra's hand probably hurt more than his face, but I gave her props for trying.

"If Nora is hurt in any fucking way, I will cut your balls off and feed them to you," she seethed, shoving her finger into his chest.

To my surprise, Ben smiled down at the girl, rubbing his cheek where she smacked him. "Solid form, kitten. Be sure to use your claws next time."

If we thought the room was silent before, the blood pumping through my veins now echoed like a drumbeat.

Ellis broke the awkward tension first. "Do you two know each other?"

Lyra's face was redder than her auburn hair. "Not at all. I don't associate with sewage." With her chin held high, she stomped away from him and took a seat on the couch.

Ben, not taking any of her very unsubtle hints, proceeded to follow her, taking up so much of the couch it was impossible for their bodies not to touch. He rested one arm on the back of the couch behind Lyra's head and the other on his knee.

"How did you know to come here, Benjamin?" Alec cut into the awkwardness, his tone dangerously low.

Benjamin chuckled. "At the risk of being attacked again, well, I followed them from Lyra's." He dipped his head in my direction. "I've been keeping an eye on Lyra. And when I heard about the ambush going down at Provocateur, I went looking for her."

"You knew Harold was coming to my club to take Nora?" Ellis growled, his navy eyes furious. He looked hot as hell like that, and part of me was itching to see Ellis in a down and dirty brawl.

Lyra twisted in her seat, ready to hit him again, but he snatched her wrists between one of his bear-sized hands and held her arms down in her lap. She fumed, and I was certain the girl was preparing to bite him, so he spoke quickly.

"No." He shook his head, his eyes locked on Lyra's. "I didn't. Harold's been keeping me out of his dealings lately. And I have never been in the business of harming women and children. I swear it, Lyra." She glared back at him, her anger softening only slightly, and he continued. "Was at the Red Clover when several crew left in a hurry. Jace spilled the beans, the idiot."

"I didn't see you when we made our way downstairs to kill the assholes shooting at us." I arched a brow at him, tentatively believing his story.

"By the time I arrived, it was over, and I saw you two taking off. Followed ya." He shrugged. "Put a tracker on your car and waited for your next move."

"Clever for a brute." I smirked. "I've checked all of Harold's regular spots. Nora hasn't been seen at any of them."

Ben sighed, releasing Lyra's wrists and returning to his relaxed position. "No one is talking, including Harold. He's shut me out, too, kid."

This was interesting. Why would Harold suddenly ice out his most trusted crew member? The riff between my fake dad and his best friend was an interesting twist, but one that helped us. There was one place I never thought about, one that existed before he became the leader of the 3M Crew, even before he knew Benjamin.

I could feel Ellis's eyes on me before my own gaze swiveled to meet his. Harold was taking us all down memory lane. He wasn't showing up on any of my cameras, because he was holding Nora in the one house I refused to go back to, the one where he ran Ellis out. "We're headed to Peckham."

Sienna leaned forward from her position on the loveseat. "What's in Peckham?"

Ellis was still staring back at me, his face unreadable. "Our childhood home."

His hand moved to his leg, pinching his thigh through his pants. Standing abruptly, it took three long strides to reach him. I knelt between his thighs, threading my fingers with his. Ellis's eyes darted around the room, his breaths growing more rapid by the minute, but I couldn't give a fuck what anyone saw now. With my other hand, I grabbed his chin and forced him to look at me. Before she was taken from us, Nora gave us a gift that could never be repaid. Freedom. The freedom to be ourselves, to feel what we had always felt, even when we were told it was wrong.

"That place was a prison for me, once," I whispered, although the room was silent as a church in that moment. "No more. I won't let it be hers. Or yours."

Benjamin cleared his throat. "What's going on here, kid?"

Ellis sighed, closing his eyes for a moment until his body relaxed, and squeezed my hand. "Harold O'Rourke is not Declan's father. Nor was Elsa Bainbridge his biological mother."

"Well, thank fuck for that." Lyra sighed dramatically, and everyone stared at her. "What? I thought we were getting on board with incest here. You couldn't cut the sexual tension with a chainsaw. Damn."

Sienna laughed, and Ben smiled at Lyra, his lover boy eyes not subtle at all. Even Alec smirked, a knowing glint in his own viper's gaze. Relief was palpable, lifting a weight I hadn't realized I'd carried for so long. Every day I'd missed him, wanted him, needed him. Not because he was my big brother. Because he was always meant to be mine.

"Well, now that everyone knows Nora's boyfriends are boyfriends, can we go kick your not father's ass and bring her home?" Sienna stood, hands on her hips and curls falling in her face.

I squeezed Ellis's hand again. "Fuck yes we can."

Nora

Despite Harold's speeches about a peaceful resolution, I was still locked up in this room like a princess in a tower. He did remove the camera, and left me untied to roam about the room, so that was something. The walls were plain, but the paint was rough beneath my fingers, as if someone painted over old wallpaper. The floors were natural wood, stained and scratched from years of use. The furniture was newer. Everything about the room pulsed with a history hidden beneath its coverings. I opened the closet, only to find empty space with a handful of banker boxes. Naturally, I opened them. How could anyone leave a journalist unsupervised and think she wouldn't snoop?

The boxes held an assortment of papers, receipts, photographs ,and an old photo album. The album was obviously of Declan and Ellis. Even as children, I could spot them instantly. The photos weren't what you'd expect from a family album. No family photos at holidays, no school pictures. They were more like documentations, and no one was smiling. It was strange as hell. I knew my men had irregular childhoods, but this hurt to see. And their mothers were nowhere to be found.

Setting the album aside, I pulled out the random photos and found one of Harold with Aoife. I recognized her from my own sleuthing. She was beautiful, with Declan's sandy brown hair and hazel eyes. She was snuggled against Harold, and they were both smiling. They had to be teens here, which meant Harold's family was connected to hers long before he met Elsa. As far as I could find, Elsa Bainbridge grew up in South Carolina, a member of a wealthy Southern family with solid political connections. Ellis was actually born in the United States, then moved with his mother and Harold to England. The O'Rourke's were from Northern Ireland, which made sense for him to befriend Aoife Murphy, a daughter from a prominent syndicate family. So maybe Harold wanted Aoife, but was forced to marry Elsa? But how did Aoife end up pregnant with Declan and then given over to Harold?

A knock on the door to my room startled me enough to send photos flying. One of the men working for Harold stomped into the room and laid a dress bag and small tote on the bed.

"You will be joining Harold for dinner this evening." He left the room before I could reply.

Curiosity forced me to my feet, and I moved to the bed, unzipping the bag. Inside was a shimmering golden cocktail dress. Dress was honestly a bit of a stretch, considering how little fabric there was. The tote held a set of toiletries, including makeup items and a pair of strapping gold stilettos. Considering I had no other options, I quickly showered in the bathroom and used the items to prep for this dinner. Perhaps Harold thought if I was looking refreshed and fed, his sons wouldn't murder him for taking me. That was unlikely.

It bothered me they hadn't stormed the proffered castle yet, but that must've meant we were somewhere Declan didn't have cameras, and was the last place either of them would look.

It took roughly an hour from wet hair to finishing touches, and I was just strapping my feet into the heels when another knock came at the door before it was unlocked. The same man from earlier stood in the doorway. He looked me over, his eyes lingering on my bare legs before slowly rising to meet my own steely gaze.

"Time to go." He smirked, and it wasn't pleasant. More like he knew a secret, and I wasn't sure it was one I'd enjoy discovering.

Harold was waiting in the dining room. This space was painted a deep red but had the same feeling of fresh paint covering old memories. Everything about this house was like a giant bandage that I was itching to rip off.

Harold kept his eyes on my face, unlike his sleazy man. "Good evening, Nora. Please, join me for a meal."

I was hungry, considering I couldn't remember my last one, and I wasn't entirely sure what day it was. "How long have I been here?"

He pulled out a chair for me, and I sat down. "Only a day. I'm sure my boys will find us soon enough."

"Why not just tell them?" I asked, curiously.

Harold sighed, pulling out the chair at the head of the table to my right. "They would never believe me. I thought perhaps I could share my story with you first."

"And then what, use me as a human shield?" His plan wasn't great.

Harold chuckled, a deep and almost pleasant sound. He poured us each a glass of wine. "Something like that." He held up his glass. "To our tentative alliance?"

I picked up my glass and clinked it with his. "To your sons."

Two men, including the leering one, brought us plates of food. I sipped the red wine and nibbled some at the steak and vegetables. It was surprisingly delicious, but some part of me was still feeling anxious, so food was difficult to ingest. Harold spoke of his life while we ate. He recanted his tales of childhood, and his love for Aoife, how they were a modern-day Romeo and Juliet.

His men continued to refill my wine glass, until I wasn't sure how much I'd drank, and a slight dizzying feeling traveled up my spine. I snatched a bread roll and sipped a glass of water instead of the wine to steady my brain.

"Aoife should have been mine. And when she came to me for help to escape the abusive man who knocked her up, of course I dropped everything." Harold sighed, his voice filled with anguish. "But Elsa had shown her true colors by then. She was vile. Jealous. She followed me to the hospital where I took Aoife to have her baby. The doctor said Aoife died of a blood clot, but I knew it was Elsa."

My heart ached for his childhood love. "That's horrible." I reached out my hand to squeeze his.

Harold's eyes locked on mine, and his rough fingers brushed over my palm softly. "Thank you, for hearing my tale. It's been too long since I confided in anyone."

His voice sounded deeper, luring me in, and my body responded, leaning across the table, still holding his hand. Harold was handsome, and his life was filled with tragedy.

He separated his sons. He said Elsa died of cancer. The thought thudded into my head, dispersing the fog taking over my brain, and I frowned. "Why did you say she had cancer?"

Harold pulled my hand toward his face, leaning on our joined fingers. "Elsa had gone mad after Declan was born. I tried to tell her he wasn't mine, tried to protect them. She hurt those boys when her mind broke. But I couldn't let them know. One mother was murdered, the other insane, I just wanted to protect them."

I nodded, understanding, and the happy fog settled over me. My body relaxed, and when he brushed his fingers down the length of my arm and back, pleasure zipped through me at his touch.

He broke them apart. He lied to them. The thought forced its way through my mind, and I pulled away from him, suddenly confused why we were so close.

"But you separated them. You blackmailed Ellis." Suddenly my head weighed a thousand pounds, and heat slithered over my skin. What the hell was this?

Harold stood from his chair and pulled mine out, dropping to his knees in front of me. He stared up at me, desperation in his eyes. "I panicked. It wasn't right, and I only want to make it up to them." Harold gripped my calves, massaging my legs. "Please help me, Nora? I can't help what I am."

I was falling under a spell, my body shuddering from the close contact, even with the tiny voice in my head screaming for help. What was happening? He drugged me.

A siren blared in my head at the thought, and I remembered Sienna recanting a night she had years ago when she tried ecstasy. These weren't my feelings. Harold's hands on me went from bliss to bile in seconds. I shoved him away and stumbled out of my chair.

"You drugged me," I slurred, my mouth feeling like it was full of cotton.

Harold's soft frown twisted into a sinister smile. "Thought I might actually convince you to fuck me for a moment there."

My heart raced at his words as he stalked closer. I stumbled back, unsteady with the drugs flooding my system. "Get away from me."

But he didn't. Harold was on me in seconds, pressing his body into mine against the wall. I tried to hit him, but my motions were slowed, and he slammed my hands above my head easily. He leaned in, his mouth roving over my flesh, and I wanted to scream, but I couldn't. A strangled moan left my lips instead.

"I can see why my sons are so enamored with you." Harold chuckled. He used one hand to hold my wrists in place while the other groped at my body. "You'll be my pretty little bird, locked away so my sons behave. As long as I have you, they'll do as they're told."

"They won't," I snapped, the drugs making my voice sound weak. "They'll kill you."

Harold pulled my body against his. "Human shield, remember?" His teeth bit at my breast through the flimsy dress and the rage burning off of him now was new. The calm facade was gone. "This is my fucking empire. My fucking city. And they're my fucking sons to do with as I see fit. And some slut from America won't be taking any of it from me."

His hand cupped between my legs painfully on his final words and the part of me still raging against the drugs screamed in protest. "If you rape me, they'll know," I panted, my body at war with my thoughts. "Kill you."

"We'll just see about that." Harold's other hand slipped under my dress from behind and squeezed my ass. "I applaud your dead fiancé for what he tried to do with you. It takes more finesse to train a female. Aoife was my first. Elsa my second. You're stronger, which will make it all the more fun to break you."

"Fuck you. I won't break." The words felt stronger, but my body still melted under his touch.

Harold laughed, his fingers teasing between my legs over my panties. "You will. They all do."

A man ran into the room, tripping over his feet when he saw us. "Sir. There's," he stuttered over his words, a look of terror on his face. "There's men every-where. Dressed like Reapers."

Declan

The plan was relatively straightforward now that we had the Russians at our disposal. I knew their help would cost Alec, and might be a price he didn't want to pay, but I didn't care. Not now. Not when Nora had been in Harold's devious hands for over twenty-four hours. There were twenty of us in total. Alec and ten men, including Benjamin, stayed at his townhouse. The man refused to fight my father, but I think it was more about leaving Lyra. It was obvious he was infatuated with Nora's cousin. How in the hell they met was a curiosity I'd sate another day.

It took five blacked-out SUVs to haul us out to my childhood home. Ellis's, too, but mine even longer. Ellis hadn't returned since the night he left, and as soon as I was fully ready to be on my own, I never looked back. The house held too many ghosts. The mother who was never really mine, the father who tortured me until I became his trained killer. Of course he'd take Nora there.

"I'm scared, Dec," Ellis whispered in the silence. "Not for myself. For Nora."

Unease clouded my head, and I shook it away. No. I couldn't let myself think of what he may be doing to her. The lengths Harold O'Rourke went to just to make me his personal hunger and Ellis his banker were enough to tell me he'd do whatever he needed to stay in control. She would be alive, that much I knew. Harold wanted our obedience, and if he killed her, we'd raze the city and crucify him at the center of the blaze. "She's strong. Whatever he's done, we will get her through it."

Ellis sighed, but didn't speak again, leaving me to stew in my own negative thoughts. I couldn't tell him I was just as scared as he was, not when I needed to be strong, impenetrable. If there was one thing Harold did to me that would work in my favor now, it was the ability to turn it all off. To shut down emotions and handle business, the killing kind of business. He molded me into a weapon, and now that deadly force he created would turn against him.

"I can't believe you wear this shit all the time," Ellis grumbled in the seat next to mine, fidgeting in the tactical gear.

He looked hot as hell in it, and I said as much. Ellis rolled his eyes, but a hint of red bloomed over his cheeks and I knew he enjoyed my assessment. Every man wore the same clothing, with matching vests, weapons, and masks. We would descend on the house dressed as a group of Reapers. The 3M Crew wouldn't know how to find us among the group, and as bullets rained down and weapons were drawn, Ellis and I would sneak into the house to find Nora.

The area wasn't exactly rural, so police would likely descend as soon as neighbors heard gunshots. Ours were all fitted with silencers, but Harold would have a handful of men with average semiautomatic pistols, all of them noisy.

"Why this mask, anyway?" Ellis asked, his hands brushing over the skeleton mask.

I shrugged. "I liked playing COD. The first time I killed for Harold, I wore the mask. I guess it helped. Like it wasn't really me, just a character I was playing."

Ellis's navy eyes borrowed into mine, anger lighting them up. "I hate him."

The revelation wasn't exactly something I planned to share, but Ellis didn't give me pity, or fear, he only shared in my anger for the man who raised us. "Me too."

We parked only a block away along the nearest park. It was late evening and nearly winter, making it easier to march down the street without notice. We split into groups to descend on the house from all sides. Ellis and I were entering from the garden. The green space behind the house was small and unkept. The garden wall had a wrought iron gate, which was guarded, but he didn't expect us. He was quickly dispatched.

There were four more inside the gate, and all were dead before they could scream.

We made it to the back door of the house when several men within began to bark out orders, sounding the alarm. I rounded on Ellis, smiling behind my mask and clapping him on the back. He couldn't see me, but I was sure our feelings were mirrored in this moment. "Let's go get our girl."

Ellis

Despite my general knowledge of and proximity to bar fights, combat was not exactly my forte. But Declan...he excelled at it. I knew how to shoot a gun, Harold put them into our hands when we were kids, and I would still go to the range from time to time, but my skill was nowhere near as precise as Declan's. He moved with the grace of a jungle cat, and his aim was impeccable. My dick stirred as I watched him work, which was probably a sign I needed therapy. Getting a hard-on watching your once brother turned lover murder people was definitely on the psychopath scale. Although technically he was never my brother by blood, he would always be my family. We only had each other then, and after all these years apart, that hasn't changed.

For two decades I pretended my life had a purpose, that I was fulfilled. While my club did bring me happiness, especially bringing people together to celebrate their kinks, I didn't realize how alone I truly was until Declan came back into my life. Declan, and the girl we were here to rescue.

Our cover was officially blown now that we'd entered the house. It was strange, being back here after so many years. Considering my last day at this place was the day Harold caught Declan and I, it wasn't exactly giving me happy feelings. My anxiety rose up from my belly and threatened to squeeze my chest until I could no longer breathe. Reaching for my thigh without thinking, I pinched at my flesh through the pants, needing the pain.

Declan tugged my wrist away from my leg and slammed me into the wall. "No, Ellis. No more hiding from your big feelings on your own."

His words cut through the fog threatening to overtake me, and irritation flashed over me instead. "Because you've mastered all those big feelings of your own, Dec?"

He leaned in, pressing his forehead to mine, our masks smashed into each other's. "Go on, then. Let it out."

I shoved him away, spinning us around until he was the one pressed against the wall. This was stupid, reckless, even, when gunshots rang out around us, men screaming as they died. Whether it was this place, or all the death surrounding us, I wasn't sure, but the time for masks was over. I ripped off my own and then his. Declan's hazel eyes glinted dangerously in the dim lights of the kitchen.

Before he could speak, I smashed my lips to his. Declan growled, his tongue fighting mine for dominance, but I was in control right now. I wrapped my hand around his throat, squeezing tight enough to bruise. Dec didn't shy away, he leaned into it, taking the pain I was offering and the kiss.

I pulled away first. "I'm sorry I left you that day, Dec. I'm sorry I wasn't strong enough to take on Harold. I'm so fucking sorry."

Declan stared back at me, the pain in his eyes mirroring my own. Part of me itched to run from him even then, to hide behind the edge of a razor blade against my skin. He was right, though. The time for hiding was over.

Dec reached out and brushed his thumb over my bottom lip. "I'm sorry, too. I found you, years later, but I was too scared to reach out to you. I should have."

One of our men walked into the kitchen then, interrupting us. "We have Harold."

A sigh escaped my lips, my gaze still locked with Declan's. "Let's end this."

Declan nodded, and we followed the guard upstairs to the bedrooms. The house was destroyed, blood and bodies in every room. This would be a bitch to clean up, but Alec would help us with that. We made our way to the master bedroom where Harold waited, surrounded by our men with guns drawn. They were smart to keep weapons directed his way, if there was anything I'd learned from this monster, it was to always have a plan, a way out. Scanning the room, I realized immediately that Nora wasn't here. And there was his plan.

Before I could move, Declan launched himself at Harold, pummeling his face with punch after punch. He pulled Harold to his feet and slammed our father into the wall. "Where the fuck is she?"

Harold spat blood onto the floor, his face already starting to swell, and smirked. "Didn't I teach you better than that, son? Already letting your emotions get the best of you."

"I'm not your fucking son," Declan snarled.

Harold looked entirely unfazed. "I raised you. I made you into the man you are now. You're mine."

Dec cursed, ready to launch another punch at the old man, but I caught his arm. "Easy, brother. We need him to tell us where Nora is, then you can kill him."

Harold's gaze darted to mine. "The diplomat. Or is it the doormat?"

Once, his words would have cut through my bravado, but no longer. Declan was right, no more hiding. Stepping up beside my brother, I faced down our father. "I let you run me out once, even believed all the terrible things you said about me, but not anymore. It's over, Harold. You no longer hold any control over us. Now, give us Nora and we'll consider letting you live."

Harold remained unbothered. He licked the blood from his lip and smirked. "No. You're going to let me go, then I'll tell you where she is."

"Not a fucking chance," Dec spoke through gritted teeth. "Tell me now, or I start slicing off fingers."

"She's a beauty, that one," Harold continued, as if Declan hadn't spoken a word. "Feisty, too, even after I dosed her. Had to tie her down just to keep those kitty claws in check."

Rage surged through my veins at his words, and now it was my turn to beat the man to death. In a flash, I pulled a blade from my hip and pressed it to his throat. Harold's haughty gaze faltered for a moment, the navy eyes we shared wobbling between me and Declan. The sharp edge of my knife dug into his skin, a trickle of blood oozing out. A weird energy buzzed through my body at the sight of it.

"You don't scare me anymore, old man," I whispered, my voice laced with a dangerous edge. "We will find her, with or without your cooperation. And I swear, I will fucking slice your throat open without a second thought if she's been harmed."

"Fuck me, Ellis." Declan chuckled. "That was hot as fuck."

Harold narrowed his eyes but had enough sense to look nervous. "You're disgusting, the lot of you. I gave you everything. Made you into the men you are today. And not only did you let that little whore turn you into—"

My vision blurred with red fury at his words. Without thinking, I sliced the knife across his jugular. Blood pissed from his neck. It took Harold several seconds to realize he was dying. His eyes bugged out of his head when he dropped to his knees. Pressing his hands to the wound wasn't doing a damn thing. The wound was too deep.

"Holy fuck, Ellie." Declan laughed, wrapping his arm around my shoulders and standing beside me. "Thought I was going to be the one to lose my shit."

My breaths slowly evened out as I waited for the anxious feelings to come, for the guilt to settle over my shoulders, but all I felt was relief watching Harold

O'Rourke bleed out at my feet. "Tell me I didn't just ruin our chances of finding, Nora."

"No. He wasn't going to tell us." Declan smirked. "But I think she's here."

His words struck me with renewed hope. "Here? In this house?" I followed Declan out of the room.

He stalked out of the bedroom and into the hall, pausing long enough to look up. I followed his gaze to the small door leading to the attic. There was a padlock that looked fairly new. Declan left me to stare up at it, returning moments later with a pair of bolt cutters.

"Just happen to have those handy?" I crossed my arms, watching him.

Declan grinned and extended his arms up, tool in hand, to break the lock. He was taller than me by several inches and had no issue reaching the ceiling. The metal snapped instantly. "He said something about tying her down. A few times, when I started to fight back, he'd tie me up and leave me in the attic for hours, sometimes days."

Hearing his confession only fueled my rage, and I was ready to go back to the bedroom and murder that fucker all over again. One of our men brought a step ladder over, and Dec disappeared into the attic. I was ready to follow him up when he called down to me, his words sending a chill down my spine. "I'm bringing her down. Need to get to the hospital right the fuck now."

Nora

Harold had one of his slimy followers stuff me into the attic. He was supposed to keep an eye on the door, but creepy men just can't seem to resist a helpless woman. Turns out I wasn't as helpless as he thought.

The dress Harold put me in was torn up from being shoved into the attic, and the creeper's eyes were glued to my exposed legs, the fabric ripped nearly to the apex of my thighs. The ecstasy and GHB cocktail Harold dosed me with was wreaking havoc on my senses, and I stumbled away from the man until my back hit the brick wall, my hands still tied together at the wrists. The space was dusty and smelled of mold, and there was very little light. Only two lightbulbs swayed from their cords attached to the roof.

"You sure are a pretty thing, aren't ya?" His voice was gruff with obvious desire, and the glint in his eyes said he would not be taking no for an answer.

"Never tried that stuff, but Harold loves to dose the ladies with it. Gets them a bit eager."

The man stalked toward me, and I had just enough control over my mind to come up with a plan. I ran my hands up and down my body, moaning as if I were feeling what he clearly wanted me to feel. "Untie me? I need to touch myself."

He grunted, stumbling over the wooden floor in his keenness to get closer to me. "That's a good girl. Let's see what you can do." He slipped a knife from its holster on his thigh and cut through the binds then returned it to the sheath.

I dropped to my knees and wrenched the stupid dress down, letting my breasts spill out. The idiot moaned, tugging at his crotch, and I reached for it. "I want to suck your dick."

The man chuckled. "Ya sound like a damn whore, I like that. Choke on it, slut."

He fumbled over himself, quickly undoing his pants and pulling out his very average, likely disease-riddled dick. There wasn't a chance in hell I was putting that in my mouth. My body was succumbing to the drugs, so I had to move fast. As soon as he drew close enough, I opened my mouth and grabbed his legs with both hands, sliding them up until I found the knife I'd seen on him earlier. His dick was centimeters from my mouth, and my strength was fading.

"Open wide, bitch," he snarled at me.

I smiled up at him. "You first." Ripping the knife from its sheath, I stabbed his crotch. I sliced and jabbed at least five times before he backhanded me across the face. The drugs were helpful at that moment, my body already going limp and falling over when he hit me. The pain exploded across my cheek, and my face immediately went numb.

His screams were garbled, as if he had water in his mouth, or maybe it was blood. I couldn't understand anything he was saying, but then I could feel him. He'd managed to crawl toward me, and his hands wrapped around my throat, choking me.

"Fucking bitch," he screamed at me, too focused on strangling me to realize I still gripped the knife. Once again, he was too late. By sheer force of will, I jabbed the blade into his throat, the only flesh I could reach, and it was enough.

The pervert's hands instantly released me to cover the blood pissing out of the wound. Blood splattered over me, soaking through my dress and my hair. He stumbled back, falling to the floor beside me. His breathing changed, and I knew he was dying. I needed to get out of here, but there was nothing left in me. My throat burned, my face hurt, and the drugs in my system were calling me away. Dark spots bloomed across my vision. Screams and gunshots rang out just as I slipped into the darkness.

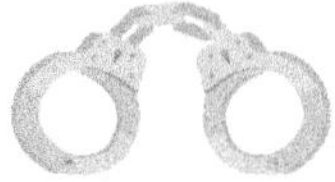

My body ached in all the worst ways, my brain suffering the worst of it. At least, until I tried to move. Muscles twitched as my senses returned, but I refused to move. If I was still locked up in the damn attic, I didn't want to know. The memories before it all went black slowly trickled into my mind.

"Open your eyes, love," Ellis whispered from somewhere nearby. "Come back to us."

His words sent a wave of relief through my body. Ellis said *"us,"* which meant both of my men were still alive, and hopefully everyone else I cared for was safe too.

I opened my mouth, but no sounds came out. My throat burned drier than the dessert and apparently words were too much.

A rough hand brushed over my arm, and I heard Declan's soothing voice. "Don't talk yet, your throat is likely still sore. It's only been two days."

Two whole days had passed since I faded away in that attic. I liked my lips and slowly opened my eyes, warmth rushing through my veins at the sight of

Declan and Ellis on the other side of my bed. Tears pricked at my eyes, and I scrunched them shut.

Ellis squeezed my left hand. "Are you in pain?"

I shook my head the slightest bit, not sure if it would hurt from the movement, but so far it was more like a dull ache. "No. Relieved." The two words croaked out of me, and Declan instantly moved to place a straw to my lips. I sucked in the water slowly, two small sips. "What happened?"

Just as I uttered the question, a nurse entered the room. I assumed we were in a hospital, but as I looked around, that was certainly not true. This was an elegant bedroom, with a massive canopy overhead and rich, warm colors on the walls, high ceilings, and ornately decorated windows.

"Move aside, boys," the nurse barked at them, shoving Ellis out of the way. She smiled down at me. The woman had a slight accent, similar to Alec's, so she was likely Russian. She had soft, brown skin and kind, green eyes, lighter than my own. Her dark hair was piled on top of her head in a messy bun.

"Glad to see you're finally awake." She smiled down at me. She pressed her stethoscope to my chest, checking my vitals. "These two were going insane."

I smiled back at her but didn't respond, and she continued. "Try not to talk too much, your throat can use another day of rest. Lucky for you, the asshole who tried to strangle you wasn't very strong, so the bruises aren't too bad and there's no permanent damage done."

That was a relief. "Stabbed him in the dick," I murmured, the memory of it making me grin. "He cried."

The nurse laughed. "Good."

Declan growled, pacing at the foot of my bed. "If he wasn't dead, I'd fucking kill him all over again."

Ellis squeezed my thigh over the blankets and offered a smirk. "He's very dead, but scared the shit out of us. You were lying next to him, covered in blood and looking near death. Fortunately, the blood was his."

The nurse gently continued her ministrations, slipping a needle into my IV. "Another day of rest and you should be okay to get out of bed." She leaned in close, capturing my gaze with her own concerned eyes. "We cleaned you up, but haven't done a rape kit. Would you like me to do so now?"

The silence in the room was deafening, but I shook my head. "No need. Didn't get that far."

I realized my body was fully clothed under the blankets, and I was grateful for the cozy cotton against my skin.

"Fuck. I thought..." Declan ran his hands through his shaggy hair, and his golden eyes bored into mine. "You were barely clothed..." He stumbled over his words. "I'm so fucking sorry, Nora. We should have found you sooner."

I wanted to comfort him, but couldn't find the words. My body was still heavy, and my eyelids fluttered.

The nurse sighed. "She needs to rest. And no getting out of that bed. I'll come back in the morning."

She left, and Declan and Ellis returned to either side of the bed. It was a massive king-size mattress, and they each perched gently on the edges.

"You should sleep," Ellis whispered, his fingers brushing over my cheek. "We'll be here when you wake up."

When he started to move, I grabbed his hand in a panic. "Stay. Please."

Without uttering a word, Ellis slipped out of his suit coat and Declan his leather jacket. They each removed their shoes then gently climbed into bed, lying on either side of me. I was cocooned beneath the covers with the two men I needed most. The tears burned against my eyes again, and I hiccuped the most pathetic sob.

"What is it, Nora?" Declan's voice was still soft, very unlike his usual self. "What do you need?"

Ellis wiped away a tear trailing down my cheek and sucked the finger into his mouth. It shouldn't have been hot, but it *so* was, and that made me smile. "Don't do that. Turning me on."

Ellis grinned, pressing a gentle kiss to my forehead. "There will be plenty of time for that later." He chuckled, his navy eyes glowing as the setting sun colored the room a hazy orange. "A lifetime of orgasms is in your future. Because we are never letting you go. I love you, Nora King."

His words only brought more tears, but the ache in my heart was anything but painful. Purest joy spilled out of me at his words. "I love you, too, Ellis. And you, Declan."

Declan bit down on his bottom lip as if he were holding his words back.

Ellis reached over me and tugged the offending lips apart. "No more hiding, remember?"

The two men shared a look that I was curious to know more about, but the medicine was fully pulling me back to sleep.

Declan grabbed Ellis's hand and kissed his palm before turning his wolf-like eyes on me. "I love Ellis, so fucking much," he whispered the words. "And if it's possible, I love you even more, Nora. I'm all in."

Nora

I dreamt of them all night. When sleep first took me, I was afraid my dreams would be nightmares, that I would feel Harold's hands on my body or that filthy guard's fingers squeezing my throat. But no, it was only them. Throughout the night, I could feel their warmth wrapped around me, the weight of their bodies pressed against mine giving me peace. The memory of our night together before I was taken filled my thoughts, and I woke with a raging libido. A whimper escaped my lips, and I clenched my thighs.

"Little dove, do not make sounds like that," Declan murmured, his lips against the shell of my ear. "I won't be able to stop myself."

His words only urged me on, and I pouted my lips, turning to face him. "Maybe I don't want you to stop." The words came out a little scratchy, but my throat already felt better, and my head was finally clear.

Declan smirked, and the curve of his lips was positively sinful. His fingers moved into my hair, massaging my scalp and eliciting another moan from my own lips.

"Please, Dec. I need you."

He groaned, tugging my hair back slightly so he could reach my throat. Declan trailed gentle kisses over my jawline. "You're wicked."

Before he could continue, the bedroom door opened and Ellis entered with a tray of food. The scent of bacon and coffee prompted a growl from my stomach. Declan released his hold on my hair, and I sat up slowly, testing my body for any sharp pains from the movements, but so far, I was feeling almost rather normal.

Ellis arched a brow at us, setting the tray of food on a table near the window. "And what's going on in here? You should be resting." He picked up a cup of coffee and took a slow sip, watching me.

He looked hot as hell in navy sweatpants and a simple white T-shirt that hugged his muscular arms to perfection. I resumed my pouting. "I've been resting. And I woke up horny."

He nearly choked on his coffee, an adorable grin gracing his lips. "Saucy girl."

I shoved the covers down and crawled to the edge of the bed, noting my attire. Someone obviously dressed me and washed my hair of all the blood at some point. I was wearing silky shorts and a soft-as-clouds button-down sleep shirt. But the clothing wasn't what I wanted against my flesh. Coffee forgotten, Ellis stalked to the edge of the bed and wrapped his arms gently around my waist, as if his touch might hurt. Before he could stop me, I wrapped my arms around his neck and pulled him in for a kiss. His tongue met mine with languid strokes, keeping our kiss soft.

Pulling away first, I bit at his bottom lip. "I'm not that breakable."

Suddenly a body pressed against me from behind. Declan's hands were in my hair again, tenderly forcing my head to the side to expose my bruised neck. "We know exactly how much of a badass you are, Nora. But parts of you are still healing. If Nurse Simmons hears you screaming, she'll string us up by our dicks."

I laughed, and both men's smiles nearly melted my panties off. "Then don't let me scream. Please. I dreamt of our almost orgy all night, and I need you both."

Ellis groaned. "You could tempt a priest from the church, my love." His hands moved from my waist to the buttons of my sleep shirt. With slow, deliberate movements, he began to undress me. "Rules. There will be no choking, no dicks going down your throat."

Declan chuckled, pulling the shirt from my shoulders as soon as the buttons were undone. "She has two other holes that need filling, brother."

Pleasure zinged through my body and straight to my damn clit at his words. "Yes, please. I've never...done that. Two at once."

Ellis tipped my chin up to stare into his endless dark-blue eyes. "And there will only be us, no one else. You understand, love? I will never let you go. And I won't share either of you with anyone else."

I nodded. "Same goes for you two."

"As if I'd let anyone near either of you." Declan's smile turned feral. "I'm having a hard enough time not killing the nurse every time she touches you." He ripped down my shorts and panties, exposing my body completely, and goosebumps peppered my skin.

"No killing my nurse. But speaking of touching... If I can't suck dick, I think Dec should suck yours, Ellis." Ellis's face flushed, and I arched a brow curiously. "Are you turning red because you're nervous?"

He smirked, slowly pulling his shirt up over his head and tossing it aside. Ellis was sculpted by the gods. His muscles had muscles, and I wanted to run my tongue over every single inch of him. "Not nervous because I don't want to, but because I do. Declan's mouth feels nearly as good as yours wrapped around my dick."

Declan scoffed, tearing off his own shirt. "Is that a challenge?" He rolled off the bed and slipped out of his gray sweatpants, his dick bobbing, hard and tempting with that piercing. In seconds he was back on the bed, pressing his body against mine. "When your pretty throat is all healed, we'll have ourselves a suck-off."

I laughed, the sound turning to a moan when Ellis's mouth latched onto one of my nipples. His teeth and tongue teased my flesh. Declan fisted his dick behind me and slid his hard shaft between my legs, coating his length in my arousal.

"Such a good fucking girl, little dove. Soaked for us already," Declan purred, teasing me with the tip of his cock.

A moan escaped my lips, but there was no pain in the sound, my body was humming with pleasure, and all I wanted to feel was my men. As if he could read my thoughts, Declan lay back on the bed and spun me around to straddle his waist. His head rested at the edge of the bed where Ellis stood, watching with hungry eyes. Pressing my hands to his chest, I lowered my body to meet his, his length filling me instantly. When my hips pressed into his, the slight curve of his cock hit that perfect spot inside me, drawing out another soft moan from my lips. I rolled my hips slowly, taking him in and reveling in the feel of this monstrous man beneath me.

Ellis stepped to the edge of the bed, his sweatpants gone and his glorious, thick length now fisted in his hand. He leaned down and crushed his lips to mine, more thoroughly than before. Ellis groaned into our kiss and pulled apart, looking down at Declan. "Fuck, Dec."

My pussy clenched around Declan's dick when I spied his lips teasing Ellis's balls, sucking them into his mouth. Desire rippled through me, and I leaned in, needing to taste, but Ellis stopped me.

"Nora," he growled. "Rules."

I looked up at him, giving my very best pleading eyes. "Just the tip? I want a taste before Declan gets all of you."

Ellis smirked. "He's just getting my dick wet, love. It's your pretty ass I'm going to fill with my come."

Declan groaned. "Fucking hell, she liked the sound of that. Her pussy is so fucking tight."

With Ellis distracted, I leaned down again and sucked the head of his dick softly, tasting the pre-cum leaking out of him. He moaned for me, and sweet satisfaction washed over me. Ellis wrapped his hands in my hair and gently pulled me off before I could go any further.

"Naughty, naughty girl," he admonished. "Now ride Declan's dick while he sucks mine."

Declan

Nora's perfect cunt wrapped around my dick was better than any heaven I could ever dream up on my own. Add Ellis's dick in my mouth, and the fantasy I'd been concocting in my head since he had me on my knees was officially complete. His shaft was thick and veined, just like every inch of muscle on his body. My own damn dick throbbed with every groan I provoked from his lips. He tasted like salty goodness, and I moaned again when the head of his dick pressed to the back of my throat.

"Fuck, Dec," Ellis growled. "You take me so well. You look so fucking hot like this."

"Yes," Nora moaned, her pussy squeezing me tighter with each thrust of my hips. "Fuck, I'm going to come watching you two."

Ellis leaned forward, driving his dick down my throat. "Come for us, love. I need to see your blissed-out face."

He jerked his hips forward again and again until tears pricked at my eyes and I gagged. Ellis wasn't gentle with me, even as he spoke sweet words to our girl. He fucked my mouth like he owned it, and fuck if that didn't make me love him even more.

Nora's body shuddered, and I could tell she was biting her lip to keep from crying out when the orgasm rippled through her body. She clenched down around my dick, and I groaned, my mouth still full of Ellis.

He pulled out seconds later, cursing. "Fucking hell. Time to switch it up, my loves. I need to fucking come."

My jaw was practically coming unhinged after he abused my throat, and I sucked in several greedy breaths. "Get over here then, Ellie. Let's fill our girl."

Nora's moan shifted into a soft laugh. "Why is that nickname cute and hot all at once?" She squeezed her legs against my hips and pressed her naked chest to mine, smiling and gently rolling her hips to keep my dick aching for more friction.

I leaned forward and kissed her so she could taste Ellis too. Nora whimpered into our kiss, pulling away to find Ellis standing behind her. He yanked my ankles hard, tugging us both closer to the edge of the bed.

"Right there, my loves." Ellis's voice was rough with desire, and he licked his lips hungrily. "Nora, you look stunning, your pretty pussy all stretched with Declan's dick."

Ellis reached down, and I groaned when his finger slipped inside Nora alongside my dick. I began to move, slow long strokes, and the sounds coming out of our girl's mouth were intoxicating. Ellis slipped his finger out, and her moans became whimpers when his fingers moved to her ass.

"So fucking wet," Ellis praised her. She gasped, and I could feel his dick sliding against her thin wall as he slowly filled her. "Good fucking girl, Nora. You should see how gorgeous your ass looks filled with my cock."

I groaned at his words. "Snap a photo. I need to fucking see this."

Ellis pumped slowly, chuckling. "Next time. Right now I just want to feel you both."

Nora started cursing, her words slurred together, when Ellis and I began to move in tandem, finding the perfect rhythm to bring her body to ruin. The sounds escaping her lips increased, and I slapped my hand over her mouth. Her eyes snapped open, dripping with lust.

"Can't have you screaming, little dove," I purred, smirking at the goddess in my arms. Sweat glistened on her face, and the heady mix of her soft mewls and Ellis's grunts was sending me over the edge. "I'm so fucking close."

Tears pricked at Nora's green eyes, and she whined, my hand still covering her mouth.

"Me too, brother," Ellis snarled, his movements growing more desperate. "So fucking tight, Nora. Come with us, baby."

Ellis's deep voice was unhinged and his face overcome with a ferocious hunger. His words spurred me on, and I tilted my hips up slightly to be sure to hit that perfect spot inside our girl that I knew she'd come undone for. Nora's back arched, her perfect tits shoved in my face while we fucked her into oblivion. With my hand still covering her mouth, just tight enough to keep her from screaming, but not enough to cause her pain, I thrusted deeper, keeping our joint pace steady. I could feel Ellis's dick swell in unison with my own, and Nora's muffled screams erupted just as her pussy bared down on my dick. I shouted for her, and for him, their names like a prayer on my lips as I filled her with my cum. Ellis slowed his pace until he gently pulled out of her, and I wrapped my arms around her waist, holding Nora close.

Ellis hummed in satisfaction. "Watching my seed trickle out of your ass and over Declan's dick is getting me fucking hard all over again."

Nora laughed, her body limp against mine. "Give me like an hour and we can do that again."

I snorted a laugh, and she grinned at me. "As much as I want to fuck you again, Nurse Simmons might actually kill us."

Ellis grunted in agreement and gently pulled Nora off of me. He cradled her in his arms, kissing her sweetly. "A nice hot shower, a bit of food, and then a nap."

Her head lolled against his chest as I followed them into the en suite. "Okay, just a little nap."

The bruise on her cheek was more obvious in the bright bathroom lights, and rage flooded my veins. The fucker was dead, but there were still plenty of men alive who helped Harold kidnap our girl. The 3M Crew was without a leader, and others would try to take the city. I'd be damned if I let an outsider come in and turn an already dangerous situation into an all-out war.

Ellis and I discussed it some while Nora slept, and the plan was relatively straightforward. Neither of us wanted to be leaders of the Crew, and Alec needed a way to stay in London, so this just might be it.

Nora

After a week locked in a bedroom, I was finally free. Not that this cage was particularly cumbersome. After our first foray into group play, it was as if we couldn't get enough of each other. When they weren't forcing me to eat or sleep, Declan and Ellis were gifting me with endless orgasms. They showered me with affection and spent more time worshipping my body than I'd spent being held captive, which was likely the point. They thought I didn't notice their attentions were centered on me, and not fully on each other. We'd declared ourselves, our feelings, but there was still one last barrier. One more intimate moment Declan and Ellis so obviously craved, but had yet to succumb to. After the week we shared together, I knew it wasn't just because they felt guilty about what Harold did, or attempted to do. The truth was out there, Declan and Ellis were not related in any way, and while they would always be brothers, now they could be something more.

With the blessing of Nurse Simmons, I was finally allowed to leave my room and venture into the world, and my first request was girl time. Lyra and Sienna visited me only once before Declan and Ellis shunned everyone from our room. I missed my girls, and although we had the world's largest bodyguard trailing us, it was still nice to get out.

Speaking of said bodyguard, I gave Lyra a very pointed look from across our table. We were sitting in a cozy booth at a bougie restaurant Sienna chose while Benjamin Burkett pretended not to watch us from his seat at the bar.

"Don't look at me like that." Lyra rolled her eyes. "I didn't do anything."

Sienna chortled into her cocktail. Her dark curls were piled up atop of her head with golden pins to match her hoop earrings. "Sure you didn't. Someone has a serious daddy kink."

My younger cousin flushed bright red and chucked the cherry from her drink at Sienna, who ducked it easily. "You are a little shitstarter!"

Sienna cackled, and I grinned at them both. "So, you and Benjamin, huh? He's like in his fifties, isn't he?"

Lyra rolled her eyes. "We are not a thing." I continued to stare at her in disbelief until she continued. "Fine. We are not a thing...yet."

Sienna tapped her red painted fingernail against her chin in faux thought. "Not a thing, hmm. So that brief moment of passion in the pantry doesn't count."

Lyra stuck her tongue out, her neck now just as flushed as her cheeks. "We weren't doing much." Her eyes darted to mine, and she winked. "He just wanted a taste and I was feeling lonely."

My gaze swiveled to the bear of a man at the bar. He looked completely at ease, and so out of place. His massive frame wasn't meant for a bar stool, and even with his mildly amiable smile, everyone kept their distance. He should have been a walking alarm bell, but watching Lyra now, I could see she was interested. And the way his eyes glazed over whenever they shifted in her direction, well, that was not a man who only wanted a taste.

I leaned across the table and squeezed her hand. Lyra's auburn hair brushed over her bare shoulders. Her lavender dress had a sweetheart neckline, showing off her delicate shoulders and elegant neck. Yoga really was working for her. "Ly, if you're happy, lean into it. Life is too short not to be happy." My gaze swung over to Sienna. "That goes for you, too."

Sienna feigned ignorance. "Moi? I always go after what I want."

Lyra giggled. "Maybe let the softer side lead for a bit, girlfriend. He'll come around."

We all knew who Lyra was speaking of. I rested my back against the tufted booth and lifted my drink. "I approve of both of your choices. It's not like I haven't done full background checks on both. And I've got two very scary boyfriends who will murder at my request. To new loves."

Sienna and Lyra raised their glasses to mine, and we spoke in unison. "Cheers."

The other reason for our little ladies day out was to give Declan and Ellis time to go over their plans for the crew. A gang like that doesn't just dissolve overnight, and true to his words, Declan eradicated anyone directly involved in my kidnapping. Those who were too loyal to Harold for him to trust were sent away. I was fairly confident this was more like when your parents told you your beloved family pet went to go live on a farm but really they were buried in the yard. I was still wrestling with the fact that it didn't bother me. Perhaps I was too numb after being brought up in a family of liars. Declan and Ellis never kept secrets from me, if I asked for answers, they provided them instantly.

Benjamin drove us back to Alec's house, where the super secret mafia meeting was taking place before the party. Alec was hosting the bratva who came to our aid, and the party was more of a mingling of mafias. The 3M Crew were being absorbed into the bratva, and Alec was taking his place at the head of the table. I did feel a bit guilty about that part, but he seemed to be handling it well. Still, I needed to find time to speak with him.

Once inside the townhouse, we made our way to the third floor where our rooms were located to get ready for the party. The boys, we were told, were still locked away in their meeting. The champagne at lunch filled me with giddy excitement for tonight. Lyra, Sienna, and I all purchased new outfits, each chosen to drive our respective conquests absolutely mad. My neck was still bruised, but the dramatic colors had faded, and the dress I chose would leave them on display. I wasn't ashamed of the bruises I saw as I stared at the girl in the mirror, her eyes bright, shoulders straight. She was a survivor. A warrior who fought for everything she had and refused to lose.

Let them see what I endured, let the people know that I would not cower to lesser men. And maybe, get my boys a little riled up for what I had planned.

Ellis

Sipping my scotch, I tried, and failed, to not to think about Nora. I knew she was back at the townhouse, not only because the trio of women were giggling loud enough to echo through the halls, but because Declan put a tracker in her purse. It wasn't a secret. He snatched it off her shoulder before they'd left and dropped it in, while she watched, then planted a searing kiss on her lips. Benjamin was with them, but we weren't taking any chances. Only a week ago our father kidnapped her with the assistance of too many men that were now our enemies. Allowing her out of the house without us was stressful enough.

Of course she was allowed to go wherever she pleased, but for now, someone we trusted implicitly needed to be with her. Alec and Benjamin agreed with this judgment. Alec already had a tail on Sienna, so that wasn't new. For being such a clever woman, she truly seemed to be unaware of Alec's obsession. The fool was trying too hard to make her think he wasn't interested. That wouldn't last much longer, and Declan and I had a bet going. My money was on tonight, and I planned to tip Nora off about the bet, offering her a reward if I won.

"Well." Alec cleared his throat and held up his glass. "I suppose it's done then. Za zdorovye."

He clinked his glass of vodka to mine and Declan's, offering his toast in Russian, a smirk on his lips and his jade-colored eyes sparkled with secrets.

The man was not one to share emotion, but over the years we'd come to know each other, and in the last few weeks, a quiet friendship between him and Declan had developed as well. While neither Declan nor I were interested in taking over the 3M Crew, dubbing him the new "king" was still difficult. He would be challenged, and no doubt would need to prove himself to the leaders of the underworld. Declan had more pull than I did, and Benjamin offered his services as well.

Benjamin I was less familiar with, and I certainly didn't trust him as completely as Declan. Sure, enough to have him watch over Nora and the others today. He proved his loyalty when he showed up and helped us rescue Nora. But complete trust was earned and would take time. He was clearly infatuated with Lyra, Nora's cousin, and we were all curious to see how that would unfold.

"Alec." I locked eyes with him across his wide oak desk. "Whatever you need, we will help you. I know returning to this life wasn't entirely your choice. I am indebted to you."

He sipped his drink, watching me. "You are, and I won't forget it."

Declan rolled his eyes. "All right then, asshole."

Alec's gaze flicked to Declan's, but his grin was more mischief than malice. "If there's an ass in the room, it's you. Don't forget who runs this city now, boy."

Dec grinned, his sandy brown hair falling across his eyes. I had the sudden urge to brush it out of his face. "Eh, you might be head boy to the world, but I'll be watching in the shadows. If you think I'm giving you all of my secrets, Russian, you're mistaken."

I sighed audibly and stood up before Alec could offer a rebuttal. "Would you both like to take your dicks out and measure now or later?"

Alec chuckled, standing as well. "As if I'd show you my dick. I'd have the kid on his knees salivating in seconds."

The jealousy that roared through my veins at his words was enough to make me see red. My glass shattered in my hand from the strength of my grip, and for a second, I wanted to murder my longtime friend.

Declan stepped in front of me, blocking my view of Alec. He grabbed my face and forced me to look at him instead. "That was hot as fuck, Ellie. But you don't need to murder your friend over it. The only dick I want is yours."

The rage darkening my vision receded as I absorbed his words. I pressed my forehead to his. "Sorry. That was dramatic."

Alec laughed out loud, a rarity for him, and we both spun around at the sound. He came around the desk and clapped me on the back. "Very dramatic, and quite enjoyable. How easy it is to rile you up, old friend." He stalked out of the room and left us alone.

The sexual tension was thick enough to taste, and now all I could think about was getting him naked. Declan's hazel eyes burned with desire rivaling my own. "Let's go find our girl. My dick is hard, and my balls need to be emptied."

I laughed at his crassness, and loved him for it. "Lead the way, brother."

I spotted Nora instantly. The townhouse was already filling with people by the time we joined. Alec forced us to change clothes before attending. It was apparently a black and white affair, and everyone was given a mask to match their attire. Declan, of course, chose to wear all black, from his leather boots to his jet-black shirt. His light-brown hair was swept back in a stylish, unfussy way that he likely put zero effort into, much to the envy of hairstylists everywhere.

His black mask was slim and covered his eyes and the bridge of his nose, making it impossible not to stare at his mouth. The man was a god—not the typical heavenly being, the kind who brought shadows and sin, impossible to resist.

"The white suits you, Ellie," Declan teased. "So pure, so innocent."

I shoved into his shoulder. "We'll see how pure I am when I'm fucking your ass later."

Declan's lips parted, and he swallowed audibly. His reaction pleased me. I was in the mood to dominate and tonight, I'd have him and Nora bending to my will.

"Be a good boy and fetch us drinks. There's a man trying to speak with our girl, and I must intervene."

Before he could respond, I prowled to the opposite end of the room toward Nora. While I chose to wear a white suit accented with a black shirt, handkerchief, and mask, Nora wore a bright-white gown and lace white mask to match. Her blonde hair was curled and laid over one shoulder, a sparkling pin on one side, the style reminding me of Gatsby. Her dress was also in the Roaring Twenties style, made of white silk and silver beading, with long gloves to match. She was a vision, and the number of men unable to look away from her was bringing my possessive side out. I couldn't fault them for admiring her when she was the most exquisite creature in the room, but I could still pluck their eyes out for leering a little too long.

The man speaking to her was facing away from me, and her eye caught mine moments before I planned to shove the man out of my way. She laughed at something he said, stepping to the side so he had to turn and see the angry bull about to run him down.

At least he had the good sense to look nervous. He bowed to Nora and fled before I could catch him.

"Don't you look dashing with your *Phantom of the Opera* mask," Nora purred, her red lips lifted into a smirk as she ran her hands up my chest. "That was Alec's cousin, he'll be staying in London while Alec settles into his new role. Be nice."

I growled, wrapping my hands around her waist. "I'll be cordial, but that's the best I can do. If he stares too long, though, I won't be held responsible for my actions."

Nora giggled, cocking her head to the side, emerald eyes twinkling. "Is that why you're crowding me with your beastly frame into the corner? Too many men looking my way?"

"Can't blame them." Declan smirked, joining us and passing Nora a glass of champagne. "There's not a woman in here who could hold a candle to you, little dove."

Nora blushed. "Well, you look like the devil freshly escaped from hell and eager to cause trouble. My favorite kind of trouble."

Declan's smirk turned sinister, and he reached for her throat, his thumb brushing over her pulse. "You're the temptress here, little dove."

Nora's eyes flicked to someone behind us, and she grinned. "Not the only temptress tonight." Declan and I swiveled around to see who she was smiling at, and I chuckled, knowing I was absolutely going to win the bet. "Well, damn."

She pinched my forearm. "I'm only allowing that because she's my friend and I helped her get dolled up. Did good, didn't I?"

Declan cursed. "May as well end the bet now. Alec is going to shit himself."

He was right. When Sienna walked into the room, every single person there took notice. She didn't follow the dress code, but wore an elegant, floor-length red velvet gown. Her dark curls cascaded down her back, and the sweetheart neckline paired with long sparkling earrings were grabbing the attention of men and women alike. My eyes darted around the room for Alec, and I grinned the moment he walked into the room from the far wall and stopped dead in his tracks.

Nora giggled at my side, and the sound filled me with joy. Her happiness was everything to me.

The man who had been speaking with Nora reached Sienna first, bowing his head and kissing her hand. Another man joined him, bringing her a champagne flute. Declan snickered, and it was entirely too entertaining watching the most powerful leader of the Bratva turn red with envy. Several people jumped out of his way when he cut across the room to get to Sienna, now surrounded by suitors. She ignored him until Alec practically snarled to force them all away.

Declan huffed, glancing down at Nora and winking. "If that was you, they'd all be dead and the party would be ruined."

She smiled up at him with those delicious red-stained lips. "Perhaps we should find a quieter room then? Somewhere just for us."

I offered her my arm, and Declan did the same. The three of us walking out together caused several murmurs, and I enjoyed the attention. Let them see us, proud and happy. We were finally safe, finally ready to dive into whatever came next together.

Declan and I seemed to be thinking on the same wavelength, because we directed our steps to the stairs and up to Alec's office. The party was mainly on the ground floor and first floor, spilling out into the garden. And with Alec fully occupied, no one would disturb us here.

The moment I closed the door, sealing us in, I planned to take charge and speak my desire to take the next step, but before I could, Nora spoke.

"Now that we're alone, I really want to watch you two fuck."

Nora

Ellis and Declan gawked at me, both absorbing my words. I thought it would be Declan who recovered first, but tonight was clearly going to be full of surprises. Ellis moved slowly, like a lion rising up from the long grass. He unbuttoned his suit and tossed the jacket aside. Noise from the party drifted in, but the dull thud of music and voices faded when his navy eyes locked on mine. This man, someone I met by chance in a club, was now the owner of half of my soul.

When he reached for me, I reciprocated, twining my fingers behind his neck as his hands scrunched into the fabric of my dress until he could feel my bare thighs. I gasped when he gripped beneath my ass and carried me to the desk. Alec's desk, but unfortunately I was too far gone in this moment to care.

Ellis sat me down and loomed over me like a king surveying his prize. "Say it again, Nora." His voice was deep and slow, and commanding.

My mouth was dry, and I licked my lips before responding. "I want you to fuck Declan. I know you want it, and I want it too."

"And what about what Declan wants?" the other owner of my heart mused, leaning against the wall and watching us, his golden eyes glinting in the light of the setting sun. "Do my desires factor into this group play?"

Ellis dropped my gaze, his attention pivoting to Declan. "Get over here, Dec." His voice was stern, and my insides melted at this confident man before us.

Declan smirked, his eyes filled with mirth, but he obeyed. He tossed his suit jacket to the floor, looking sexy as fuck in his black attire. He was taller than Ellis, but right now, that didn't matter. It was obvious who was in charge. "And what do you want with me, Ellie?"

Dec's use of the pet name was so fucking hot when his voice was all gruff like that. I felt like I was intruding on a private moment, until Ellis began tracing his thumb gently over my thigh, as if he knew I needed his attention too.

"First I want you on your knees, sucking my dick while I taste our girl." Ellis spoke slowly, deliberately. "Then when you've wetted my dick properly, I'm going to fill your tight ass, while you fuck this goddess who miraculously chose us both."

"Fuck," Declan cursed, adjusting himself. "I like this side of you, brother." He shoved between Ellis and myself, cupping my face with his hands and brushing his lips to mine, his tongue licking at the edge of my mouth, teasing. I whimpered, and he smiled against my lips. "Just needed a taste before my mouth is full of cock."

I nearly giggled, but the mood was far too serious, too erotic, for a giggle. Instead I watched as Declan spun around slowly and began to undress. Reaching for him, I pulled his shirt off, dragging my nails down his back as he removed his pants. His tattoos were hot as fuck, all black ink and accentuating his muscular figure. He angled his head to the side to look at me with a deviant smirk and wink before looking back to Ellis. "You want me to suck it? Fucking make me."

Ellis didn't hesitate. He was in the mood to dominate, and both of his hands instantly reached out, one in Declan's hair and the other squeezing his cheeks, forcing Declan's mouth open. Ellis spat onto his tongue and shoved Declan to his knees. "Take it out, Dec."

The scene playing out before me was hotter than any guy on guy porn I'd ever watched. Declan obeyed, his fingers moving swiftly to remove Ellis's belt and unzip his pants. His dick bobbed in Declan's face, thick and veined, and my mouth watered.

Ellis caught my eye and smirked. "Hungry, love?"

I nodded, biting my lip.

"You'll have your turn." In the next second he groaned, Declan not waiting for further instruction before he sucked the head of Ellis's dick into his mouth.

The way these men pleasured each other, the way they moved as if completely in-tune with the other's needs, was the most arousing thing I'd ever witnessed.

While Declan was still on his knees, Ellis stepped closer and leaned over him to reach me. Declan gagged, his mouth now full of dick, as Ellis yanked my ass to the edge of the desk and shoved the fabric of my dress out of his way. He chuckled. "Nothing beneath your dress? Dirty girl."

I spread my legs apart, giving him a better view. "Only for you two."

Ellis growled his approval as he bent forward and brought his mouth to my bare pussy. He moaned, his tongue flicking out to tease me. "Sinful," he purred. "I will never get enough of you, foxy."

Before I could respond, Ellis dove forward, his mouth devouring me. His tongue lapped at my arousal, and my hips bucked in response to the pleasure he offered. The steady thud of music urged us on, and the room was thick with lust, a mix of whimpers, groans, and wet mouths. Ellis's fingers dug into my thighs, keeping my body still as his teeth grazed my swollen clit. A feral moan escaped my lips, and the two men groaned in response.

Ellis looked up at me from between my thighs, his navy eyes dark with feral hunger. "Come on my face, foxy. Show me who owns this pretty cunt."

With one hand braced against the desk and the other in his hair, I leaned my head back and rolled my hips in time with the swirls of his tongue. Every nerve in my body sizzled with pleasure, and after a few more strokes of his tongue, I was nearly there. When he sucked my clit into his mouth, I screamed, heat pooling between my legs and a heady feeling rushing through my body.

Ellis groaned, lapping at my arousal and rolling his hips to fuck Declan's mouth in steady movements. Declan slurped and groaned when Ellis pulled back from both of us. He looked like a fucking king, his hair disheveled, shirt undone. He slowly began to undress, until his glorious muscles were on display for his both. Declan stood, turning away from him to face me instead. His face no longer a mask of indifference, but flayed open, every emotion there for us to see. He smiled at me, pulling me in for a sensual kiss, the taste of Ellis filling my mouth. Declan peeled my dress from my body until I was fully naked before them. He fisted his pierced dick, stroking roughly before bringing the head of his cock to the apex of my thighs and teasing me.

"Legs up, little dove," he ordered, shoving my thighs wide until my legs were bent. He loomed over me, one hand braced against the desk and the other guiding his dick to my entrance. Without waiting another moment, he slowly filled me, and I moaned, my head lolling back. He laced his fingers into my hair and forced my head back up until we locked eyes. "Eyes on me. Then you can tell Ellis how much I'm enjoying his dick when he makes us both scream his name."

Ellis didn't even respond to Declan's ribbing, but snatched up a small bottle from his pants pocket and popped it open, coating his dick with the clear lube. He stood behind Declan, his hands roaming over Dec's ass casually, as if he had all the time in the world.

Declan continued to fuck me with slow, steady thrusts, nearly driving me insane with the need for more. "Dec. More. Please." I couldn't hold it in; the begging flew from my lips.

"Only when our Dom says so, little dove. Ellis is in charge tonight." Declan sucked in a breath, and I couldn't see, but had a feeling his ass was getting filled. "Fuck. Fuck. Fuck." He cursed again and again, his movements halting.

"Fucking hell, Dec. You feel so fucking good," Ellis grunted behind him, one hand in Declan's hair and the other on his hip. "Fuck, your ass looks sexy filled with my dick."

Declan groaned, the sound almost a mewl, and his cock throbbed inside me. "Fuck. I've been dreaming of this for years, Ellie. No one else. Only you."

Ellis snarled, thrusting his hips at a steady pace. "Only. Me." He punctuated each word with a thrust. "Now fuck our girl good, Dec."

His pace increased at the same moment as Declan's, their bodies thrusting in tandem. Every jerk of Declan's hips was compounded by Ellis's thrusts, forcing Dec's cock deeper inside me, his piercing hitting that perfect, euphoric spot again and again.

Declan's hand tightened in my hair, and he leaned down to tease my peaked nipples with his teeth. The erotic sounds our bodies made were drowned out by the grunts and moans of pleasure all three of us couldn't stop from escaping our lips. There was no covering up what we were doing, and anyone on the other side of that door would be able to hear us.

A small part of my mind that was still coherent wondered if there was a camera in this room. "Dec. Cameras," I said, barely able to manage the words.

"Yes," he groaned, biting my breast and sucking hard. "We are being filmed. But don't worry, little dove."

New heights of pleasure flooded my veins at his words. Someone could be watching us right now, and that thought sent a tidal wave of ecstasy through my body. "Fuck. I'm close."

Declan chuckled. "She's so fucking tight. Our girl loves being watched."

"Let them watch," Ellis snarled, driving in harder. "Let them see who fucking owns you both. You're mine. This ass is all fucking mine."

The deepening thrusts forced Declan into action, filling me more deeply than I thought my body could handle. A scream built in my throat, and my vision blurred. I shouted their names, unable to do anything but take the pleasure zipping through my body. Ellis and Declan's groans filled the room, their pace unchanging, forcing my body into a second wave of pleasure. Then Declan's groan crescendoed into a guttural scream of my name and Ellis's. His dick swelled until he came, filling my overly sensitive pussy with his seed. Ellis followed him, shouting our names and jerking almost erratically as he unloaded inside Declan.

Their joint movements slowed, our bodies still fully connected as we heaved breaths in the silence. Declan's forehead dropped to my chest, and I stroked his hair.

"I love you," I murmured. "I love you both so much."

Ellis kissed Declan's back along his spine, looking up at me over his once brother. "We love you, Nora. More than you will ever know. But I will continue to remind you, every day."

"Every fucking day," Declan echoed his words, his breaths still uneven. "Now give me about an hour and we'll do this all over again."

Nora

My new office was a considerable upgrade from the cubicle I occupied before. Alec announced my new position as Chief Editor of the *London Times* only two weeks after the little welcome party he hosted for everyone. With his new role as leader of the 3M Crew and the Bratva, he didn't exactly have a lot of free time to run things at the office. Sienna was also given a new office of her own, down the hall from mine. She was now Creative Director, overseeing all the more fun, fluff pieces. We branched out to include an entertainment magazine, and that was her baby. I managed everyone else and still took on my own crime pieces occasionally.

True crime was still my passion, and while I'd blown the lid on the murders around the city related to gang violence, crime never slept. There were still a handful of unsolved murders that caught my curiosity. I'd noted them a few months ago. Not as often or as bloody as the gang-related murders, but there was something unique about them. And I still suspected they could be the work of a female serial killer.

Ellis had his hands full with Provocateur, and Declan was often there with him, managing his security team and handling cybertechnology. When he wasn't there, he was pestering me in my office. Not that I minded at all, but it was wildly difficult to get work done when he was bending me over my desk. There was an entire wall of windows, but the glass was reflective, so no one could actually see us when he had my naked body pressed against it. I could see the world, though, and fuck if that didn't make it all the more thrilling.

Both of my men celebrated my desires and fed my kinks. We explored new heights of pleasure together, testing boundaries, and always, always respecting each other's limits. It was the hottest, most insane relationship dynamic I'd ever experienced. And the safest. With my own love life finally coming together, pun absolutely intended, it was my mission to see Sienna and Lyra's love lives succeed as well.

Since the party with Sienna's stunning red dress reveal, Alec had finally staked a bit of a claim. Not outright, of course, but there wasn't a single man in London who would look directly at her. Ellis and Dec told me to let it be, but that wasn't my style. Those two were destined for each other; I knew it in my bones. Sienna said he was keeping secrets, walls still built around his heart that she couldn't get through. Lucky for her, her best friend was a journalist with a need for answers, and I was confident we'd uncover all the skeletons in his closet before long.

My phone pinged, and I picked it up to find a message in the group chat with Sienna and Lyra from my cousin.

Lyra

Girls night tonight. Need to escape the bodyguard and have some real fun. Don't tell your boy toys.

Sienna

I'm in.

I smiled at their messages and responded the same. Only a second had passed before another message came through in the group text with Declan and Ellis.

Declan

> Enjoy your girls night, little dove.

Of course he already knew about it. I rolled my eyes, typing quickly in response.

Nora

> Nosy asshole. No boys allowed.

Ellis

> Don't worry, love. I'll keep Dec busy.

Declan

> As if I can't suck your dick and monitor Nora at the same time. You insult me.

Nora

> Send pics. Or I'll have to find ways to send some of my own.

Declan

> Please do. Just know if there are any men in them, they'll be dead by morning.

I laughed, packing up my things to go down the hall to Sienna's office and prepare to meet Lyra. My cousin was also settling into life in London. All the drama with our families wasn't fully resolved, but I wasn't worried. Our past was simply that. No more threats from my cruel mother, no more creepy family friends, no more fear. We were finally free, and I intended to revel in that freedom with the people I loved most.

The End

Epilogue

Declan

This feeling of anxiety was entirely new. When Nora was taken from us by Harold, that fear was new too. Ever since she showed up in my life, emotions I didn't know I was capable of surged to the surface. Rage and anger I understood, love and fear relating to people I did not fully comprehend. But every day I spent with Nora and Ellis, the cracks in my soul I'd left empty were filled with these new emotions. Once, I thought Harold had taken them all away from me permanently. Ellis and Nora showed me this wasn't true.

Today was another one of those new feeling days, and I couldn't say it was entirely welcome. I fidgeted in my seat on the plane, uncrossing and recrossing my legs.

"Maybe I should get you one of those fidget toys," Ellis teased without looking up from his newspaper. "Those things for kids."

"I know what a fucking fidget toy is, Ellis," I snapped, crossing my legs again and cracking my knuckles. "Perhaps I just use your face as a punching bag instead? Violence relaxes me."

Nora tsked, not even pausing in her typing, laptop resting over her thighs. "No violence in the small airplane, please. You can wrestle when we get there. I can get Jell-O, we can make a whole thing of it." She was curled up in the loveseat and looking entirely too lonely.

Shoving out of my chair, I snarled like a predator and snatched the computer out of her hands.

She gasped, reaching for it. "Hey! I didn't save that yet."

I snapped the laptop shut and tossed it into my vacant chair. "Do you think I can't recover unsaved material on a computer? You wound me." I plopped down next to Nora on the loveseat and pulled her into my lap. Her legs stretched out over the seat, and her ass fit perfectly over my semi-hard dick.

Nora wrapped her hands around my neck, shifting at the waist to face me. "Feeling restless, Dec?" she asked, her fingers massaging the base of my scalp at the nape.

Her green eyes held mine, seeing deeper into my soul than anyone ever had. Of course she could see the thoughts racing through me now.

"Maybe. I need a distraction."

She wiggled her ass in my lap, and I groaned. "I'll be any kind of distraction you want, but first tell me what has you feeling anxious, besides the obvious."

Ellis folded his newspaper and tossed it on the small table, leaning forward to listen to whatever answer I would give. My normal response to divulging feelings was to retreat. I wasn't nearly as eloquent as Ellis, and leagues behind Nora. They were more in tune with what haunted them. We were on our way to Dublin to meet members of my mother's family. The visit would be difficult enough, considering how fucked Harold left things for us. The O'Rourke's were an estranged family of the Irish mob. If Harold hadn't been such an asshole, maybe in another life he and Aiofe Murphy could have been an item, but her brother, who was the leader of the mob at the time, promised her to someone else. Someone who was just as terrible as Harold, my birth father. Finn Kavanagh had slowly taken control of the Emerald Isles, and the Murphys were losing allies. To save his status, Aiofe's brother, my uncle, promised her to Finn.

She fled the abusive asshole when her belly was swollen with me, right into the arms of another monster, Harold O'Rourke.

Nora had discovered most of this information with her insane sleuthing skills, and even made contact with the Murphys, who invited us to visit them. There was still tension between the Kavanaghs and the Murphys, but Harold had built the O'Rourkes up to overtake them both. He was quite talented when it came to playing powerful men against each other, and since his demise, we were slowly unraveling every layer of his duplicity.

I pressed my forehead to Nora's and sighed. "All my life, I thought Harold was my father. And I hated him. Turns out my real father was just as awful. My mother, she never had a chance. What if her family—my family—hates me? Both my biological father and the man who raised me were monsters. Suppose they think I'm one too? Suppose they're right?"

Nora pulled back and cupped my face with her soft hands. "You are not a monster. You can be a super scary, murdery guy, but you're not a monster. I couldn't love you the way I do if you were anything like Harold."

"Agreed," Ellis added, watching us.

She continued, forcing me to listen. "You have her eyes, you know? I bet you have some of her soul too. She did what she had to, to save you. And if you never came into Harold's life, maybe we never would have met."

Ellis stood up and joined us on the loveseat, lifting Nora's legs to sit and massaging her nylon-covered calves with his hands. Nora was dressed in a short plaid skirt and cropped sweater, her knee-high boots discarded on the floor.

"While I could kill him for what he did to your mother, and mine, I don't know what I would have become without you in my life." Ellis's words were soft, vulnerable. "I will never be sorry for what we endured, because it brought the three of us together."

Their closeness and reassurances eased the anxiety in my chest. Wrapping my arms around her waist, I kissed Nora with all the love burning inside me, forcing her to feel the depths of my devotion to her and Ellis in our kiss.

Her soft moans spurred me on, and I slipped my hands beneath her sweater to unclasp her bra. She pulled back, cheeks heated and a smirk on her lips. "We will be landing soon, you know."

Ellis reached over and forced her arms up to remove the sweater entirely, and she let us. "We have forty-five minutes until we land. Plenty of time to fill the cabin with your screams, foxy."

I chuckled, tweaking her pert nipples and eliciting another moan from her lips. "Yes, brother. More than enough time to fill her tight holes. Would you like that, little dove?"

Nora reached between our bodies to squeeze my now very hard dick, rubbing the heel of her hand between my legs until I started to ache for her. "If wanting to be ravaged by two monster dicks makes me a slut, then I'll be your good little slut for at least the next forty-five minutes."

I ripped her hand away and sucked her fingers into my mouth, biting down enough to make her yelp. "Not just any two monster dicks, Nora. Ours. Say it."

She grinned, her eyes flitting between mine and Ellis's. "Or what?"

A grin that could make even the devil run and hide spread across my face. "Oh, little dove. You've done it now."

Nora screamed, jumping up from our laps and attempting to flee, but I caught her around the waist and pulled her back, locking her arms behind her as Ellis stood in front of her, slapping her bare tits and making her mewl for us. He pulled his dick out, and my mouth watered.

"Someone needs to be reminded who she belongs to," Ellis smirked, fisting his shaft and tapping the head of his dick against her red lips.

"Make me," Nora urged. "Mark me as yours so I never forget."

Her words sank into my bones, and my body lit up with arousal. A small part of my brain understood what she was doing. Nora knew exactly how to distract me, how to pull feelings I buried deep down to the surface, and how to soothe the anxiety away when I couldn't do it on my own. Calling her the glue that held us together wasn't enough. She was the spark that ignited our flames, the key to our happiness, and I was never letting her go. Ellis's eyes locked with mine over her head, filled with so much love and need, and I knew my own were brimming with the same. As long as I had them, I could conquer the world.

"All right then, little dove," I purred, capturing her wrists in one hand and wrapping the other around her delicate throat. "Be a good girl and open your pretty mouth for Ellis while I stuff your sweet ass."

There was no doubt the pilot could hear the feral sounds coming from all three of us when the first waves of pleasure spilled over, and I knew our girl fucking loved it, almost as much as I loved her.

Acknowledgements

WOW. This was a story that popped into my head and wouldn't go away, even as I wrapped up the *Daemons & Lumens Series*. These characters were so chatty, and so needy, just like my lovely street team. **wink, wink**

Thank you to my ARC readers and team members for cheering me on, supporting my books, and loving all the worlds in my head that end up on paper. Your support means EVERYTHING to me.

Thank yooouuuu to Nikki and Holly at Naughty Nook PR for keeping me organized and not kicking my ass out whenever I decide to do some last-minute shit (which is always). And to my fellow indies for your knowledge, crazy group chats, and positive vibes. Being a member of the indie community is so much fun because of you!

Thank you to my amazing editor, who always asks questions and continues to make me a better writer! I LIVE for your praise!

And a BIG thank you to all the readers out there who are either just finding my books or who followed me here from my first novel, I love you all so much. Good goddess, I could not do this without you all! Stick around for so many more stories to come!!

SNEAK PEEK from Book Two in the Twisted Desires Series...

Sienna

The office was relatively quiet today, and I was planning to duck out early. Nora was on another trip somewhere around the world with her boyfriends, and it was a holiday weekend, so everyone was leaving the office by noon today. And Lyra was going out with "friends." It was her undisclosed code word for "secret boy toy."

Nora and I were both very open about our own relationship statuses, but she was still in the closet with hers. Couldn't entirely blame the girl, considering the man she was all giddy over used to be an enemy. But if Nora and her men vetted him, I accepted that and gave her the green light too. Her hesitation, I thought, had more to do with her past. She went through a bit of trauma, and after that, it wasn't surprising she wanted to move slow.

Such thoughts brought my mind back to the man I wanted most, but couldn't have. Alec Vasiliev, my boss. It wasn't even because he was my boss, which really, he no longer had that privilege. After everything went down with Nora, Alec was forced to face his own past and take up the mantle of Bratva leader. This was a wild revelation, and yet it made sense. Something about his nature screamed *I would be really good as a gang leader.*

I thought that was his hang up for keeping me out, but clearly I was wrong. Even after I told him that didn't scare me, he shut me out. Well, mostly. He was infuriating in the sense that he made it clear we would not be dating, but somehow any other men I attempted to go on dates with just disappeared. If I took a shot for the number of men that ghosted me recently, I'd be sloshed.

So here I was, friendless and dateless for the extended weekend. Not for long, though. I had a plan to bring the Bratva leader out to play. After two years of working for the man, I knew enough about him to be able to provoke his ire. Nora gave me a bit of a confidence booster too.

"Sienna." She'd stopped me mid-whining. "Do you really think that man is anything less than obsessed with you? Make him face up to it. Give him an ultimatum. He can't keep stewing in whatever it is forever, it's not fair to either of you. Confront whatever it is and move on."

She was right of course, but the outcome of such a confrontation was daunting. "What if he...turns me down?"

Nora sighed audibly over the phone. "Then he doesn't deserve you. Don't forget, you are Sienna fucking Wilkers, clever, capable, and one bad bitch."

Her words settled some of my anxiety and were exactly what I needed to hear. "You're right. Thanks, my friend. Drinks on me when you get back from your trip."

Grabbing my garment bag hanging on the back of my door, I slipped into my en suite and out of my office clothes. Tonight called for a bodysuit, very sexy Catwoman vibes. It was a deep navy blue and made of that super-soft stretchy nylon blend fabric. The gold zipper went from below my navel to just under my cleavage. The neckline was a deep V-cut, with no sleeves to show off my toned arms. I paired the bodysuit with chunky gold heels and glittering gold jewelry.

My hair was naturally curly, not quite ringlets, but curly enough to be a pain in the ass. Nora was helping me embrace it, as she was completely jealous her slightly wavy blonde locks couldn't hold a curl like mine. She hid my straightener, which was allegedly for my own good. I let my hair loose tonight, with a simple gold hairpin on the left side. Transition complete, I called a cab to take me to Provocateur.

The club was not exactly my scene, but only in the sense that it was new to me. I wasn't exactly a vanilla girl when it came to sex, but exploring my kinks was also not something I really delved into with partners. Nora was obviously a regular now, and I tagged along occasionally, but never participated in any of the private rooms for scenes. Of course, Alec happened to be there the one time I thought about it, but tonight I would be taking the plunge into exploring new kinky fun.

To throw him off, I put dinner with my brother on my calendar. I was an only child, an orphan, actually. My parents died when I was young, and I grew up in foster care. And my foster brother wasn't exactly friendly, but we stayed casually in touch. Alec's calendar said he was out of town for business anyway, so no interruptions from that asshat.

Provocateur was bubbling with excited energy, and packed with people. The main lounge was transformed into a disco for the seventies theme night, and the vibes were immaculate. Taking a stool near the end of the bar, I ordered a Grasshopper, one of the theme drinks for the night. The music was too good to ignore, and after finishing my drink in a hurry, and with a little buzz, I joined the crowd on the dance floor.

My hips swayed to the music, and shouted out the lyrics to "Gimme! Gimme! Gimme!" By ABBA with the other ladies around me. A warm body pressed up against me from behind, strong hands gripped my waist, and I didn't pull away.

This was my night to have fun. I leaned down, shaking my ass in the stranger's direction and feeling the music.

"Damn, girl," the man began, but was suddenly cut off and pulled away. "What the hell man?" he shouted, just as I spun around.

Alec was a solid brick wall of muscle and towered over the other man like an angry gorilla. "Leave, or I will have you removed from the planet entirely."

My traitorous libido zipped into high gear at his possessive threat, and my logical mind raged that he could turn me on so easily. I shoved his arm, but he didn't budge. "Hey, asshole. I was dancing with him."

Alec's furious face stayed locked on the other man, until said man began sweating and darted out of the crowd. Only then did he turn his attention to me, but I wasn't having it, not tonight. Storming away from the dance floor, I made a beeline for the velvet curtain and the playrooms behind it. Of course he would follow me, but if I could just lock myself in a room before he did, maybe he'd give up. Not quite paying attention to anything, I grabbed a door handle and rushed inside, shutting it behind me. The room was empty, and the theme in here was definitely pain. The walls were covered in black velvet drapery, the lighting dim, painting everything with a cool blue glow. At the center of the room was what looked like a medical table, with a set of tools and toys next to it. I brushed my fingers over the toys, some I knew, and others piqued my curiosity.

The door opened and shut with a thud, and I sighed, knowing exactly who was here now. "Alec, what the fuck are you doing?"

"Watch it, Sienna," Alec growled, his hands resting casually in his pockets. His bright-green eyes sparked with irritation. "You're asking for trouble."

I picked up a leather riding crop and slapped it against my palm. "Oh really? What kind of trouble am I asking for?"

Alec didn't respond, his lips tightly sealed and devoid of emotion.

I stalked closer to him. "I'm done with this shit, Alec. Either make a move, or let me go."

"Are you threatening me?" He arched a brow, remaining still even as I tapped the crop to his chest.

"I'm telling you I won't have you lurking in the shadows forever like this, ruining my fun," I snapped, pulling every ounce of courage I had left to the surface. "Let me in, or let me go."

We stared at each other in silence for what felt like hours. When he twisted away from me, my mouth went dry and an endless pit of sadness threatened to open within me. He was saying no. Alec walked to the door, his hand resting on the door handle, and he paused. I held my breath, waiting.

Alec spun around, his face a mask of uncertainty. His chest rose and fell in quick movements, and he licked his lips, eyes darkening just before he spoke the two words I needed to hear. "Fuck it."

www.ingramcontent.com/pod-product-compliance
Lightning Source LLC
Chambersburg PA
CBHW051950150726
47999CB00004B/1330